Hunters

OF THE

Lost City

Also by Kali Wallace

City of Islands

Hunters

OF THE

Lost City

BY
Kali Wallace

QUIRK BOOKS
PHILADELPHIA

Text copyright © 2022 by Kali Wallace
Cover illustration © 2022 by Matt Saunders

Library of Congress Cataloging-in-Publication Data
Names: Wallace, Kali, author.
Title: Hunters of the lost city / Kali Wallace.
Description: Philadelphia : Quirk Books, [2022] | Audience: Ages 10+.
Summary: Twelve-year-old Octavia, who grew up believing her town was the only one left after a magical war, meets a girl from outside her town and tries to uncover the truth about her world.
Identifiers: LCCN 2021038798 (print) | LCCN 2021038799 (ebook)
ISBN 9781683692898 (hardcover) | ISBN 9781683692904 (ebook)
Subjects: CYAC: Fantasy.
Classification: LCC PZ7.1.W353 Hu 2022 (print) | LCC PZ7.1.W353 (ebook)
DDC 813.6 [Fic]—dc23
LC record available at https://lccn.loc.gov/2021038798
LC ebook record available at https://lccn.loc.gov/2021038799

ISBN: 978-1-68369-289-8

Printed in the United States of America

Typeset in Chronicle Text & Bookeyed Suzanne

Designed by Ryan Hayes
Production management by John J. McGurk

Quirk Books
215 Church Street
Philadelphia, PA 19106
quirkbooks.com

10 9 8 7 6 5 4 3 2 1

*For every girl who wants
to change the world*

———⟫———

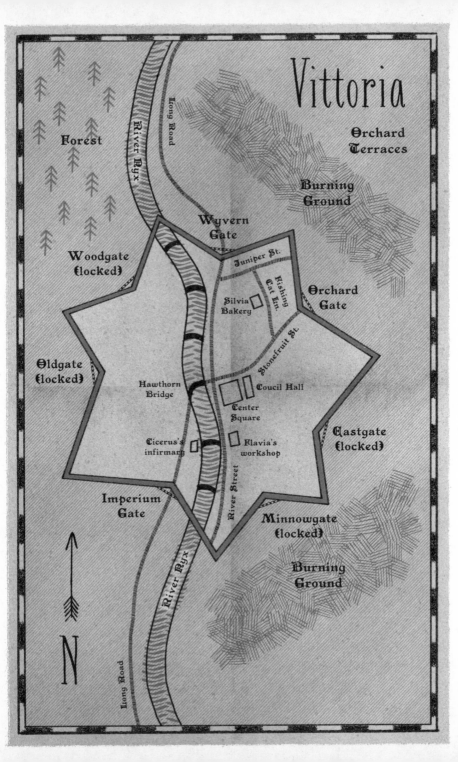

1

The Bells of Vittoria

————≫≫————

Every morning, as the first light of the sun shone over the mountains, bells rang from the seven watchtowers of Vittoria.

Octavia kicked her thick blankets down, jumped out of bed, and threw open the shutters. The morning was cold, and her breath misted as she leaned on the windowsill. The scents of fresh bread and warm pastries rose from her family's bakery below.

The first bell to chime was atop the tallest tower, which overlooked Wyvern Gate on the northern side of town. It rang as soon as the sunlight touched the summits of the highest peaks surrounding the valley.

Movement on the narrow street caught Octavia's eye. Four stories down, a pair of town guards in black uniforms rushed down Fishing Cat Lane toward Juniper Street. She felt an uncomfortable twinge of worry in her chest. It wasn't normal for the guards to be rushing about this early, before the gates were even open. Something must have happened during the night.

She didn't hear any shouts or sounds of alarm. She hoped it was nothing serious.

The guards were gone from Fishing Cat Lane by the time the second bell began to ring. Five more followed in quick succession, and soon all seven bells were ringing together, all around the seven-pointed star of Vittoria's high wall. Their song chased up and down the River Nyx and Long Road, echoed from the rocky mountainsides and the forested hills, and filled the terraced fields and orchards of the Lonely Vale.

For the townspeople of Vittoria, the morning bells meant the day was about to begin. The bells meant it was time to wake, time to rise, time to work. During the daytime it was safe to venture beyond the wall, and it would be safe until darkness fell again. Vittoria was the last town in the world, home to the only survivors of a terrible war, surrounded by a vast and dangerous wilderness.

The worst of the dangers were the monsters, and for those monsters the morning bells meant something else entirely. They were a warning, a signal to the creatures that lurked in the forest that daylight was coming. It was time for them to flee into the darkest thickets and caves, where they would cower until night came again. The creatures were called Ferox, a name given to them by the sorcerer who had created them as weapons of war, designed to attack with ruthless speed and vicious power under the cover of night. That sorcerer was gone now, and the war long over, but the Ferox remained.

The endless rhythm of day and night, safety and danger, light and darkness, defined life in Vittoria. Octavia could feel the bright promise of the morning bells in her bones, just as she would, later, feel the ominous warning of the evening bells. The bells that rang at twilight had a deeper, heavier sound.

Octavia listened until the bells fell quiet. The morning was cold, but the sky was clear and cloudless, streaked pink to the east, with the last stars twinkling in the west.

Clear skies meant good light, good visibility, easier tracking.

Today would be a perfect day for hunting.

The small Ferox that wandered close to Vittoria during the day were not truly dangerous, but they were good practice. And practice was what Octavia needed.

Octavia dressed quickly in her trousers and shirt and too-big leather boots. Across their shared attic bedroom, her brother Albus mumbled unintelligibly and rolled over in his bed. Two cats, a fat ginger and a scrappy gray, slept on his feet. Albus would sleep as long as he could get away with, even if it meant being late to his apprenticeship at the knifemaker's forge. Octavia pulled the shutters closed, grabbed her bag from its hook, and kicked the side of Albus's bed.

"Wake up, stupid," Octavia said. "You're going to be late again."

Albus answered with another grumble. The ginger cat glared disapprovingly.

"It'll be your own fault when Master Aife replaces you." Octavia kicked the bed again. "And she will."

Aife the knifemaker did not tolerate laziness, but Albus didn't seem to care. He had been caring less and less all year. Mom and Dad said to give him time, but that was what they had been saying for months. Their whole family had been saying that to each other for so long the words didn't have meaning anymore. Dad told Mom to give her injuries time to heal. Lavinia told Octavia to give their parents time to consider her apprenticeship. Mom told Augustus to give Dad time before talking about expanding the bakery. Albus just told everybody to leave him alone. It felt like all they did anymore was give each other time to not talk about anything, to avoid the gaping hole at the heart of their family, to ignore the wound that had split them right down the middle.

All they did now was avoid talking about Hana.

As Octavia climbed down the ladder, she steadfastly did not look at the curtain that hung over the doorway to Hana's room. Hana had been the eldest, so she had a room of her own, but nobody had suggested letting Augustus have her room now that she was dead. Sometimes Octavia wanted to whip the curtain open so badly that she ached. Sometimes she came so close to convincing herself that if she did, if she found that courage, Hana would be there, making notations on her maps or sharpening her blades, and she would shout with outrage at the intrusion and chase Octavia away, and the house would ring with the sound of her voice again, and everything that had been broken in their family since last winter would be repaired.

There was no more chance of that happening than there was of righting a tree once it had been felled by a woodsman's ax, or hearing the bleat of a goat after its throat had been cut by a butcher's knife. Hana was dead. She was gone forever. Even though Hana had been the oldest and Octavia was the youngest, she had always been closer to Hana than to her other siblings. They had the same apricot-colored hair and the same freckles, but even more they had the same yearning to explore the mountains outside Vittoria. Hana had always understood Octavia in a way that wasn't shared by Augustus, who at nineteen was growing up to be a more solemn version of Dad, or by Lavinia, who was seventeen and content to spend her days making up songs while fussing over pastries, or Albus, who everybody liked to say had been a sulky teenager since before he could walk. Nothing was the same with Hana gone. Her death had distorted the shape of their whole family. It had left a bruise on Octavia's heart that would never heal.

As far as Octavia knew, she was the only person to have entered Hana's room in many months, and that knowledge churned with a sour guilt in her gut. Going into Hana's private space to steal was worse than not going in at all. She had done it anyway.

Down two more floors, the stairs dropped Octavia into the storage room behind the bakery. The shelves were crowded with sacks of flour and grain, pots of honey, bags of salt, blocks of butter, all the supplies laid by in preparation for winter. Two more cats, both black with white socks, dozed comfortably on a sack of wheat flour, content in their well-earned rest after a night spent chasing mice from the pantry.

In the bakery's kitchen, Octavia's mother sat at a stool beside the long counter; she was stirring a huge bowl of batter with one hand while ticking off items on a list with another. The air smelled of cinnamon and nutmeg.

Mom glanced over her shoulder and smiled distractedly. "Good morning, duckling. Is your brother up?"

"I tried to wake him," Octavia said. "He's being lazy."

"He's fifteen. I'll send Augustus up in a bit."

"What's that?" Octavia asked, pointing at the list.

"Oh, nothing for you to worry about," Mom said. She shoved the paper aside. "I'm just checking our stores, but these buns are more important."

Octavia looked at her mother carefully, trying to read her expression. Mom only ever said there was nothing to worry about when there *was* something to worry about. The pantry was crammed with supplies, but Octavia wondered if it wasn't quite as full as it ought to be. The last harvest was in; there would be no more until spring. Her parents had been spending a lot of time this autumn counting sacks of flour and negotiating with dairy farmers.

"Your father has some deliveries for you to take to River Street," Mom said. "It's busy this morning. Everybody wants their orders before the snow comes."

When Mom smiled, it took Octavia a moment to remember to smile back.

Octavia knew she looked like her mother, as both she and Hana had inherited Mom's unruly orange hair and freckles, but all she could see now were the scars that creased Mom's face. Mom had been badly injured while searching for Hana last winter. There was a long red line down the left side of her face, curving over her jaw to her neck. Two fingers on her right hand were missing their last knuckles. Her nose, once straight and strong, had healed crookedly after being smashed. She kept her hair short now, where once she had worn it long enough to wrap a crown of braids about her head.

The worst of it, the damage to Mom's leg, was hidden beneath her trousers. Her leg was the reason she had to use a cane now. It was the reason she couldn't hunt anymore.

"You don't mind doing the deliveries, do you?" Mom said, when Octavia had been quiet for too long.

"No," Octavia said quickly. "It's fine."

Mom's smile softened. "That's good. I'm glad you enjoy it."

Octavia scuffed the toe of her boot on the floor. She didn't like making deliveries because she wanted to be helpful. She liked it because it was easier to sneak away.

She looked down, afraid Mom would read the truth on her face. "Hey, Mom? I saw some guards outside. Did something happen?"

"Hm? I don't know," Mom said. Then, quieter, she added, "I haven't heard anything."

Not so long ago, Mom would have been among the first to hear any news; the Hunters always knew what was happening before anybody else. But a Hunter with an injured leg was a Hunter in name only. Mom was more of a baker now, tucked away with her batter and bowl and checklist in a warm kitchen. There could be a dozen guards running down the street and she wouldn't know.

Octavia regretted bringing it up. She slipped out of the kitchen without saying anything else.

The bakery was crowded with people sipping tea while they swapped news and gossip. On everybody's tongue was the promise of a snowstorm, the first of the season, due to arrive at nightfall. People had noticed the guards rushing down Fishing Cat Lane, but nobody knew what was going on. Dad was chatting with customers as he filled their orders. Augustus looked grumpy and harried, with flour on his shirt and nose, while Lavinia was humming to herself by the clay oven. The room was warm and humid and full of delicious, familiar smells.

It was always busy at the Silvia bakery these days. Octavia wanted to think it was because the townspeople finally recognized that her father was the best baker in Vittoria, but she knew many customers came to the bakery out of pity. They felt sorry for her family, with Hana dead and Mom injured. Every sad smile, every gentle inquiry, every condoling word put a sickly twist of anger in Octavia's gut.

A familiar shock of blond hair pushed through the crowd. It was Octavia's best friend, Rufus. He stopped before her and held out a still-warm fruit pastry. "Last of the apricots. Your dad told me I had to share."

Octavia accepted the pastry and took a bite. Still chewing, she said, "Last time he told you to share you shoved the whole thing in your mouth anyway."

Rufus shrugged. "They're good. Are you ready to go?"

Getting the deliveries loaded up took a few minutes, as Dad kept getting pulled into conversation with customers and Lavinia kept swapping out loaves and pies as she double-checked the order list, but before long Octavia had a fully loaded cart outside the bakery door. She took one handle while Rufus took the other.

The cartwheels rattled noisily on the cobbles of Fishing Cat Lane. When they reached the end of the lane, where they would normally turn left to head for the town center, a few people ran past them on Juniper Street. One of them, a young man, stumbled as he veered around Octavia's cart.

"Hey!" Octavia snapped. "Watch where you're going!"

The young man righted himself. "Sorry, sorry!"

"What's going on?" she asked, even as the man turned away.

He called the answer over his shoulder. "There was somebody locked outside last night!"

For a second Octavia could not move. All the sounds of Vittoria faded.

Guards rushing down the streets.

People running toward Wyvern Gate.

Now she knew what had happened.

Somebody had been locked outside.

Vittoria was the last town in the world, the only one to have survived the Sorcerers' War decades ago. It was the only place of warmth and light in a world filled with terrible, predatory Ferox and ravaged by cruel, deadly magic. It stayed safe because the town gates never, ever opened after dark. It didn't matter who was outside or how they begged for help. It didn't matter if a guard heard his own mother calling from the other side of those great doors of iron and wood. Once the gates closed for the night, they remained closed, and they never opened before dawn.

Everybody in Vittoria knew that. Everybody knew to be inside before dark.

"Who do you think it is?" Rufus said.

His quiet voice broke through Octavia's muffled, muddy shock. She shook her head; she didn't have an answer. They grabbed the cart handles and turned right instead of left.

A crowd was filling the small square just inside Wyvern Gate, pressing in around the five white stone pillars that honored the explorers lost during the first years after the war, when people still believed there were other cities and towns and survivors elsewhere in the world. A pair of black-clad guards was telling everybody to step back, to wait for the gate to open, to give them space. Octavia and Rufus stopped at the back of the crowd, right beside the pillar for the third expedition.

"Who is it?" Rufus asked the adults around them.

People shook their heads worriedly. They didn't know, and they were afraid to find out. Even if the person caught outside wasn't somebody they knew, it would be somebody their friends or neighbors knew. There were only about five thousand people in Vittoria, and they had been alone in the world for fifty years. Nobody was more than one or two degrees removed from everybody else.

One woman offered, "They think it's the cheesemaker's boy. His mother is there."

The woman pointed. A diminutive woman stood beside a frowning guard. Her face was pale, her hands wringing anxiously, her lips pressed into a thin line. She looked familiar to Octavia, but she didn't remember the woman's name until Rufus gasped.

"Oh, no," he said. "That's Willa."

"You know her?" Octavia asked. Rufus's mothers ran a popular tavern; his family interacted with just about everybody.

"She's Bram's mom," he said.

Octavia went cold all over. She knew who Bram was. He was nineteen, the same age as her brother Augustus, although they weren't friends. She only knew him because there had been a period a few years ago when he had come by their bakery nearly every day to beg Mom for a chance to become a Hunter. Mom had refused him, gently at first, then more firmly when he persisted. Hana said she felt sorry for him, but some people just weren't meant to be Hunters. Bram tended goats for his mother instead.

He went outside the town walls every day.

A goatherd wouldn't have a chance against the Ferox that came down from the mountains after sunset. He didn't know how to hunt or fight. He would have been completely alone, completely helpless, and so very scared.

The guards lifted the massive oak crossbar to swing iron gates open, pulled chains to raise the portcullis, and finally opened the outer steel door.

Three of the guards raised their crossbows while three more moved outside with their long spears hefted. A hush fell over the crowd. It felt like the entire town was holding its breath, waiting in fearful silence, until finally two of the guards returned, dragging a limp body between them.

There was no blood. Bram was not injured. He hadn't been stalked or hunted or attacked; no Ferox had slashed him with great claws or ripped him apart with terrible teeth.

It had been the cold. Only the cold, nothing more.

They could have saved him, if they had opened the gate.

Bram's mother began to wail.

A few people rushed forward as she dropped to her knees and gathered her son into her arms. Everybody else backed away to form an empty space around her, as though they were afraid her sudden outpouring of grief might be contagious. Octavia yanked the cart around, turning her back on the gate; Rufus had to jog to keep up with her. Willa's cries echoed from the high town walls, from the buildings and the cobblestones, filling the cold morning with the aching and inescapable sound of her pain.

2

The Charm Master of River Street

———»»———

Rufus didn't speak until they were several streets away from Wyvern Gate. "Why was he out late? Something must have happened. He knew better."

"He was stupid," Octavia said. "He's not a Hunter. They wouldn't even train him. He was *stupid*."

She glowered at the cobbles of River Street as they tugged the cart along. Maybe she was being unfair, but Bram had been careless. Now he was dead. The truth of it felt like poison welling up inside, acidic and bitter. You didn't stay out after dusk. Not during the summer, not during the winter, not ever. The only people who ever stayed outside Vittoria's walls overnight were Hunters, and they traveled in well-armed groups, moved along Crafter-charmed trails, and took shelter in spell-protected watchtowers. They used to go as far as twenty or twenty-five miles from Vittoria, in carefully planned hunting expeditions, but since Hana's death the town council had decided such long journeys were too dangerous. Now the Hunters never trekked farther than about ten miles from Vittoria, and the herders and foragers rarely ventured even half that.

And nobody who left the relative safety of the Lonely Vale did so alone. Being alone outside the valley meant ending up like Hana, dead on a mountainside, with nothing left behind except scraps of bloody clothes and a single knife.

"Something must have happened," Rufus said again.

Octavia didn't answer. It didn't matter what had kept Bram out late. He was still dead.

They pulled the bakery cart down River Street toward the center of town. On this cold morning, before sunlight reached the bottom of the valley, a heavy mist clung to the river, making everything soft and pale and murky. Half a dozen bridges spanned the River Nyx through town, and on every one of them were dried bundles of flowers, herbs, leaves, and grasses tied up with ribbons and strings, slowly crumbling into the river. The humble bouquets were the remains of the Rite of Remembrance, the solemn night at the end of the harvest when Vittoria gathered to honor everybody who had been lost in the Sorcerers' War. It was their duty and their privilege to remember, as the only survivors in the world. Master Camilla, head of the town council, would read a long list of names of friends and family members the townspeople had lost, while the gathered crowds murmured along with her. There were so many her voice was always raspy and soft by the end.

Octavia and Rufus parted ways at Hawthorn Bridge near the town center. Rufus was apprenticed to the healer Master Cicerus, a tottering old man who had been tending to the sick and injured since before the war. Cicerus's workshop was on the other side of the river, in a narrow waterfront building that smelled perpetually of muddy poultices.

"See you later?" Rufus said.

Octavia shrugged.

Rufus narrowed his eyes beneath the brim of his knitted cap. "You know they'll be watching extra carefully today. The council will have all the guards on alert."

"What do you mean?" She couldn't quite meet his gaze.

"Just be careful, okay?"

"Careful with what?"

Rufus let out a sharp breath. "You know nobody's allowed out without reason."

It was easy to invent a reason, if you knew the right kind of lie to tell. Octavia kicked at the cartwheel. "So? All I do is deliver bread."

"That's all you're gonna do today?"

Octavia could feel him looking at her, steady and knowing, and she felt a pang of guilt. She had never told him about the days she sneaked out of Vittoria to hunt and track on her own, but Rufus knew anyway. He never said anything about it. Octavia reasoned that as long as he kept it secret, they could both pretend he didn't know anything. Kids who went outside when they weren't supposed to were generally left to their parents to punish, rather than getting the council involved, but Rufus was an apprentice now, and Master Cicerus was a member of the council. Trouble for Rufus might mean a lot more than simply being grounded for a few days.

"I'm not going to do anything," Octavia said. "Don't worry."

She hoped he heard a bit of promise in her voice, maybe a bit of apology. Rufus knew why she had to sneak outside the walls. It was the only way to practice her hunting skills. It was the only way to make sure she remembered everything Hana had taught her.

But that was for later. First, she had bread to deliver.

She rushed through the deliveries in Center Square, where the councilors lived with their families, then pulled her cart into the narrow, twisting streets of the Crafters' Quarter, where Vittoria's magic users had their workshops and homes. It was a jumble of mismatched buildings overhanging both sides of river, some so old they leaned against each other. A web of pulleys, troughs, and catwalks crisscrossed the river, while rickety ladders and twisting staircases stretched down to the water. Wind chimes and bells and weathervanes created a cacophony of sound on every railing and balustrade.

None of it was decoration. It was all there to help the Crafters in their work: extracting dangerous, powerful magic that the River Nyx carried down from the ruins of Aeterna, so they could tame it into forms people could use.

All of the magic in the mountains came from Aeterna. The sorcerers had had secret ways of drawing magic out of the world all around them, and they had passed their secrets down for hundreds of years. As their magic became greater, so too did their wealth and power. They filled Aeterna with magic, using it without limits, until it seeped into the very foundations of the city.

Now the sorcerers were dead, except for the few who had renounced their brethren during the war, and the once great city of Aeterna was an empty ruin. The only magic in the world was what they had left behind. The Crafters of Vittoria never created their own magic; they only drew what they could from the river. Nor could they use it however they wanted. After the horrors of the Sorcerers' War, the town council had decided, under the guidance of Master Camilla, that magic could be used for only one purpose: to protect Vittoria.

Octavia's final stop in the Crafters' Quarter was an ancient building of bluish-black stone that loomed over the river. River Street passed beneath the building in a long archway that felt more like a tunnel. The doorway was beneath the arch, in deep shadows where sunlight never reached, and there was no sign outside the door. Everybody knew whose workshop this was.

Octavia knocked and waited. A couple of moments passed before she heard a distant "Come in!"

She grabbed the last bundle of baked goods from the cart and went inside. A narrow stone staircase led to a massive room on the second floor, where tall windows overlooked the river. A fire burned merrily on the hearth, with a cauldron heating over the flames.

At a long workbench a woman of about sixty was bent over a steaming pan of water. She was short and slight, with chin-length silver hair and thin shoulders. She was Master Flavia, the best Crafter in Vittoria. Master Flavia was better at protecting the town than anybody. Her charms surrounded the fields and wove through the walls, encircled the Hunters' watchtowers and lined every forest trail. It wasn't possible to keep the Ferox away entirely—they were too powerfully magical, especially at night—but Master Flavia's craftwork did more than anybody else's.

Master Flavia looked up from her workbench. "Good morning, Octavia. Those smell delicious. Apple this morning?"

"Apple and spice," Octavia said.

Master Flavia's eyes were the color of bright green agate—her mother's eyes, people said. Same color, same sly spark. Octavia had no idea if that was true. She only knew that people did not dare say it where Flavia could hear, because Flavia's mother had been Agrippina, a sorcerer of Aeterna, the woman who had nearly destroyed the world.

Agrippina was the one who had created and unleashed the magical sickness that swept over the mountains and the lowlands, roiling through every city and town and village all the way to the sea. It had been Agrippina's equally powerful sister, Camilla, who had finally stopped her. Camilla had renounced sorcery and turned her back on the other sorcerers, risking their wrath to save so many lives and becoming a hero to all who survived in Vittoria. But she could not save everyone. The plague had still spread across the world, killing everybody in its path. Agrippina was the reason there was nobody else left in the world. She was the reason Vittoria was so utterly, dangerously alone.

Octavia had asked Hana once why Master Flavia's charms were so much better than any other Crafter's. Hana had been teaching her to follow a trail of sigils carved into trees in the forest. Every Crafter had their own symbols, and Hana insisted Flavia's were the safest to follow.

They have to be the best, don't they? Hana had said, after thinking over Octavia's question for a bit. *Nobody would trust her otherwise. If she does one thing wrong, they'll say she's just like her mother. She has to prove she cares about Vittoria more than anybody.*

Now Agrippina's daughter clapped her hands like a child and said, "Apple and spice! My favorite. Let me brew some tea—do you have time to sit for a moment? I'd like to talk to you."

Octavia didn't want to sit and talk. She wanted to get outside the wall and spend the day hunting. But her parents would be angry if she offended a good customer. A good customer who happened to be a powerful Crafter as well as Master Camilla's niece.

"I can stay a bit," Octavia said, reluctantly.

As she was crossing the workshop to join Flavia at a table by the windows, the front door burst open and footsteps slapped up the stone stairs. A teenage girl ran into the room in a whirlwind of dark hair and long scarves.

"I'm so sorry I'm late! Something terrible has happened!" the girl cried.

"I know, Penelope," Flavia said. She lifted a kettle from beside the fire to fill a teapot. "I heard about the boy."

Octavia regretted very much agreeing to stay for tea.

Penelope draped her scarf and coat onto a hook and kept talking. "It's so terrible. They found him this morning at Wyvern Gate."

Penelope was Flavia's apprentice, four or five years older than Octavia, but Octavia knew she had not been friends with Bram. Penelope's father was a member of the town council; she wouldn't be friends with somebody who spent all of his time out in the woods with his goats.

"It's *terrible*," Penelope said again. "That poor boy."

Octavia's hands curled into fists at her side. "Do you even know his name?"

Penelope stared at her like she had turned into a goat herself. "What? He's the goat boy. Of course I know him."

Octavia felt a flush of anger, but before she could say anything, Penelope kept talking.

"The guards are all over town right now, asking to be sure nobody else is missing."

"Why would somebody else be missing?" Octavia asked.

Penelope shrugged. "The guards told my father the goat boy's friends said he'd been meeting somebody in the woods. He brought his goats back before going out again. You know," she said, with a slight smile, when Octavia only stared, "because he was *meeting* somebody. Secretly."

Octavia's face grew warm when she understood what Penelope meant, then even hotter with fresh anger. It didn't matter why Bram had been outside, herding goats or having a secret romance or anything else. He was still dead. It wasn't anything to smile about.

"That's stupid," Octavia muttered.

Octavia hadn't even noticed her approaching, but suddenly Master Flavia was there, standing right beside them, frowning thoughtfully. She was no taller than Penelope but still imposing in her elegant embroidered skirt.

"Idle speculation is not fact," she said. "Come and talk with me,

Octavia. Penelope has to draw water for our work. Eight buckets, please. Watch the cauldron as well. Don't let it boil."

Penelope sprang to obey. "Yes, Master Flavia."

"Then collect what we need to renew the gate charms." Master Flavia set a clanking bundle on the table and unfolded the cloth to reveal four heavy metal keys. Octavia watched with interest as she laid them out in a neat row. Four meant there was one for each of the unused gates of Vittoria, which nobody was allowed to open anymore. "Dried oak leaves, cowflowers, and pyre dust to start."

"Yes, Master Flavia."

Octavia followed Flavia across the room. They passed the workbench, where heated water whirled gently in a shallow copper pan. The water was beginning to show its magic in gentle wisps of gray and green, twisting around and around in a broad spiral. Octavia stared at it for a few seconds before tearing her gaze away. It was always unsettling to see the magic emerge when it had been hidden before.

Flavia led Octavia to a small table by the windows that overlooked the river. She poured tea into both of their cups and sat back in her chair.

"Do you know much about protection charms, Octavia? Do you know why we are always having to invent new ones and refresh the old ones?"

Octavia squirmed at being put on the spot. What she knew was that the trails, fields, and pastures surrounding Vittoria were protected by magical charms in the form of sigils, braided ropes, amulets, or carvings. The charms were never powerful enough to stop the most ferocious of the monsters at night, but during the day the right charms kept the dangerous Ferox away.

The problem was, the charms stopped working after a while, as the Ferox grew used to them, so the Crafters were always having to devise new ones.

The Ferox aren't smart, but they were invented to do just one thing, so they are very good at it, Hana had said last winter, before she died. She had been sharpening her knives by the fire while she told stories about hunting in the mountains. *All they know how to do is hunt us. And they're driven by the same magic we use to fight them.*

Octavia stared into her teacup. "Is it because the Ferox are made with the same magic as the charms? And using their magic to drive them away is like . . . like . . ." She cast around for an example that would explain what she was thinking. "Like using tufts of dog hair to chase dogs from the pastures? It doesn't really scare them."

"We don't know if the Ferox experience fear," Master Flavia said, "but in the broader sense you are correct. The charms work more as a distraction than a barrier. In essence, they persuade the Ferox to look away, and as long as that persuasion is strong enough, the charms can protect us. But the magic that animates the Ferox can change in response, so no charm works forever."

"Why does the magic change?" Octavia asked.

"There are many theories but few answers," Master Flavia said. "What we do know is that the Ferox are what happens when magic runs wild and out of control. The sorcerer who created them probably meant to control them indefinitely. But magic is very hard to tame. It's possible their creator, whoever it was, lost control of them even before they died."

"Did that also happen with the plague?" Octavia asked, before she could think better of it.

Master Flavia's hand stilled with her cup raised halfway to her lips.

"I don't know," she admitted, after a long pause. "But it is likely. My mother used magic as a powerful healer long before she turned to crafting weapons of war. I suspect she probably believed she could control her plague when she unleashed it. But she was wrong, just as the Ferox's creator was wrong." She took a sip of her tea before going on. "In the broadest sense, you are correct. The magic we use is essentially the same magic as that which is running wild, and we cannot use the same magic that animates the monsters to truly defeat them. All we can ever do is push them away. We need stronger charms if we are to expand our farms and pastures."

"Expand?" Octavia said, surprised. "But the council—"

"Has forbidden the Hunters from venturing beyond a very tight perimeter, yes," Master Flavia said. "I believe that is a mistake. We need more land. The harvest this year suggests a need for urgency."

Octavia knew the Lonely Vale well, its cold rivers and broad pastures and mossy forests, but whenever she tried to imagine the world beyond the valley, all she could think about was wilderness and monsters and all the empty cities and villages left behind after the war. The thought of trying to tame that wild land into farms made her shiver with unease.

"Will the council change their minds?" she asked.

Master Flavia let out a short, amused breath. "The council speaks with one mind, and that is the mind of Master Camilla. And my aunt is not often interested in what I have to say."

Octavia shifted uncomfortably in her seat. She knew *why* Camilla and the council never allowed Master Flavia to join them; they were all afraid she would turn out like Agrippina. Everybody knew that—but nobody said it out loud. It was strange to hear it directly from Flavia's lips. Octavia didn't know how she was supposed to react.

She lifted her cup to take a sip. The tea was too hot, though, and smelled faintly of damp soil. She winced as she touched her lips to the cup.

Flavia misunderstood her reaction. "It's quite bitter, isn't it? I've been trying to replicate a blend I remember from my childhood, but I'm afraid it's impossible. I'm not even certain I remember it correctly. I was quite young when I left Aeterna. A few years younger than you are now."

"At the end of the war?" It was so strange to think of silver-haired Master Flavia as a child that Octavia blurted out the question before she could decide if it was rude.

"Well before that, in the midst of terrible fighting in the city," said Master Flavia. "When it became too dangerous in Aeterna, my mother asked a dear friend to take me out of the city. We had no idea what she was planning." Flavia's voice grew soft. "The plague began to spread not long after. I never saw my mother again."

Master Flavia took another sip of the tea, then set it down with a sigh. "There is a small yellow bellflower that grows only on the northern side of Gray Bear Mountain. Without it this tea will never be quite right." Master Flavia looked down at her teacup and folded her hands together. "There is something else I want to talk to you about. You'll be turning thirteen just after midwinter, is that right?"

Octavia sat still with her cup at her lips, suddenly nervous.

"Your parents have asked me to speak to you," Flavia went on. "They suggested that you might be interested in becoming my apprentice when you are of age. Is that something you would like?"

Octavia set her teacup down with a clatter. She swallowed. She didn't know what to say. She knew what she had to say. *No.* That was her honest answer. A clear, resounding *no*. She was not interested. She already knew what she was going to do when she turned thirteen. She was going to become a Hunter. Hana had been training her before she died. Now that Hana was gone and Mom was injured, Octavia was going to take their place. It was all she had ever wanted to do.

"I see," said Flavia, although Octavia did not say anything. "They didn't ask you first, did they?"

Octavia shook her head. Her eyes stung and her face was hot. She didn't trust herself to say anything.

Flavia was quiet for a moment. "I didn't realize. I think perhaps you should speak to your parents before we discuss it further."

She couldn't just keep staring and not speaking. Octavia forced herself to say, "Okay."

"But I want you to know that I would very much like to train you, if you are interested," Flavia said. "I think you would make a good Crafter."

Octavia couldn't stand it anymore. She stood up, the chair scraping back behind her.

"I have to go," she said sharply. "I have—I have deliveries."

"Of course. I don't want to detain you."

"And I—I don't want—"

Flavia gave her a strange, small smile. "Talk to your parents, Octavia. This is a decision you should make together."

Octavia didn't bother to answer. She fled from the workshop.

Flavia was right. It *was* a decision they should all make together.

But Octavia's parents didn't agree. They had already decided that what she wanted didn't matter.

3

Beyond the Burning Ground

------»»------

Octavia broke her promise to Rufus as soon as she left Master Flavia's workshop. She parked the empty cart in the alley behind the bakery, and she kept running before anybody noticed her. She didn't want to see her parents right now. She didn't want to listen to their excuses and justifications for making decisions about her life without asking her. She didn't want to talk to *anybody*. All she wanted to do was get outside the wall.

The guards at Orchard Gate were asking after everybody's business, as expected, but Octavia told them she was foraging for ingredients for the bakery and needed to do it before the snow started. They knew her family's bakery; they liked her father's herb rolls as much as anyone. The guards cautioned her against taking too long and let her pass.

Immediately surrounding Vittoria was a ring of land known as the burning ground, which was kept scrupulously clear of trees and shrubbery. The town set the whole swath of ground alight once a year, during the midsummer Rite of Survival, to ensure there was no place for the Ferox to hide close to town.

She thought about what Master Flavia had said about expanding the farmlands next year. Octavia had never paid attention before to what the adults said about the harvest. She had never asked if there would be enough. She had never had to wonder if the fertile land in the Lonely Vale could support Vittoria forever. It wasn't as though they had never tried to push farther into the wilderness. In the early days after the war, when people had warily ventured out after two years behind the wall, the first group of explorers sent out to search for other survivors had been torn to pieces by Ferox within a mile of town. The second group had made it only as far as the junction of the Nyx and the River Iracundia, five miles upstream. The third and fourth groups vanished without a trace.

Camilla had courageously led the fifth and final expedition herself, eight years after the first. When she returned alone, badly injured and distraught by the horrors she had seen, Vittoria had to admit the truth.

They were alone in the world. They were the last survivors of the war.

Octavia squared her shoulders and crossed the burning ground as quickly as possible. The territory and the harvest were problems for the farmers and Crafters. Octavia was a Hunter. She was outside to hunt.

The orchard terraces were a blazing quilt of red, orange, and yellow, gleaming so brightly in the afternoon sun the vibrant hues stung her eyes. Between the terraces, white stone walls snaked along the steep hillsides, separating each patch of trees into a perfect, vivid gemstone. The sun was warm on her back, the sky blue and clear where the coming storm clouds had not yet encroached. Above the terraces, the orchards gave way to valleys of deep-green pines cut through by streaks of golden larches. Above that, so high above she had to crane her neck to see, the pines made way for the jagged gray slopes and white snowfields of the mountains.

Octavia ran along the packed dirt path, her bag bouncing lightly on her back. When she reached the first terrace wall, she looked around quickly. She could hear the bells on goats or cows somewhere in the distance, but the animals and their herder were nowhere to be seen. To the south she saw the specks of a few workers chopping wheat and corn stubble in the fields. To the north a couple of fishermen cast lines into the River Nyx.

There was nobody nearby. Octavia ran up stone stairs through the first, second, and third terraces. She stopped only when she reached the fourth terrace, where a mixture of plum and pear trees grew in dense, shadowy lines. She stepped through a rusty old gate and into the orchard.

There, for a moment, she did nothing but breathe. She was always both excited and nervous to hunt, but today she felt a little bit more nervous, a little less excited. It was the eerie emptiness of the fields and forests that bothered her. The tiredness in the guards' eyes when they told her to hurry. The darkness of the clouds coming over the mountains. The way Rufus had looked at her when she lied to him.

She pushed her nerves away. She was going to be ready to join the Hunters when she turned thirteen. She would convince her parents to change their minds.

The last of the fruit had been harvested weeks ago, to be dried or boiled into preserves or fermented into wine, but sweet scents lingered in the air. A few flies whirled about, not knowing it was likely their very last day to live, and birds sang brightly in the breeze-rustled leaves.

Octavia chose her steps carefully, avoiding the crunchiest of the leaves, as she searched the sun-dappled ground for Ferox signs. She took her time. She did not let herself rush. She looked for scratches low on the trees, for disturbed dirt and overturned leaves, for tufts of fur or feathers that might indicate small prey had been taken nearby.

Eventually noon came and went, and she stopped to eat food from her pack and drink from a small spring. Because it had gotten a bit boring staring at the ground and listening to the birds, she spent some time searching the stones in the creek for moss freshly scraped clean by unnaturally thin claws. When that too grew boring, she climbed first one orchard tree, then another, at first hoping to spot something interesting from above, then just to see if she could climb even higher.

Hana had always laughed when Octavia complained of boredom. *If you don't like wandering around in the woods trying to decipher every track on the ground, maybe Hunting isn't for you,* she had said. *There's a lot more quiet than excitement.*

So Octavia had forced herself to learn patience, because it was part of what Hana had tried so very hard to teach her. Hana had insisted it wasn't silly to chase after Ferox no bigger than foxes or rabbits, even if they weren't dangerous, because learning to hunt the small ones was the only way to learn to hunt the larger ones. One year of casual training, of stories and advice shared over meals, of cold spring mornings following tracks in the snow, of warm summer afternoons listening to birdsong in dappled forests, it wasn't enough. It would never be enough. Hana was supposed to keep teaching her for years to come. She wasn't supposed to die before Octavia learned everything.

As the afternoon crawled by, Octavia returned to the ground to listen to the sounds of the birds and the year's last insects, to the breeze in the crackling leaves and water flowing gently in a spring. The Ferox could mimic sounds; they might cry like a falcon or bleat like a goat or chatter like a squirrel. But far more dangerous was when they imitated human voices, because they always asked for help. Mom said it was because that was all their creator had taught them to say; Hana said it was because they knew how to hunt people as well as people hunted them. Whatever the reason, long ago, only a few years after the end of the war, a guard had heard what she thought to be her long-lost brother pleading for help from outside Vittoria. She wanted to believe he had survived the war. She could not let him die in the cold. She had opened the gate to let him in.

Twenty-four people had died that night before the Hunters finally stopped the Ferox. No guard ever opened a gate after dark again.

As good as the Ferox were at mimicking sounds, their calls were never going to be quite right. That was, Hana had said, the key to recognizing them. Octavia trusted Hana's teaching.

Hana's teaching was the reason she noticed when the orchard went quiet around her.

Octavia froze mid-step.

Slowly, slowly, she lowered her foot to the ground, taking care not to crunch a single leaf. Her heart began thumping painfully. The orchard trees turned in a breeze that was now more stiff than gentle. The air had gotten colder and grayer. It was late afternoon now; thick clouds had overtaken most of the sky.

She couldn't remember when she had last heard birdsong.

She took a step. And another. Octavia very carefully slid her bag from her shoulder to retrieve her knife. Hana's knife, which Octavia had taken from her room over the summer, and nobody had noticed, nobody had even cared, because nobody went into Hana's room anymore. It was the only thing the Hunters had found of Hana after she was killed, besides blood and scraps of clothes. The only thing that mattered.

One more step and Octavia heard a burst of song from a bird nearby. It was the cheery fluting call of a wood thrush. The trees around her were black walnuts now, and the terrace was bending toward the west, away from town and into an adjoining valley. Far below was the dirt ribbon of Hermit Road, which joined Long Road north of Vittoria. If she listened carefully, she could hear the tumble of Hermit Creek. She had come farther than she realized. It was time to turn back.

But even as she began to turn, the birdsong changed from a wood thrush's happy warble to the harsh cry of a blue jay.

Octavia's heart skipped. That was a mistake the Ferox often made when they mimicked birds; they didn't know the call of one species from another. It was so close she thought she could smell it: rusty, musky, with a hint of peppery spice. She heard a rustle of leaves. The clack of something solid on wood. Metal scraping on metal, in an orchard where no metal should be.

Ferox were not animals in the usual sense. They were weapons, made up of messy collections of bone, metal, wood, skin, vines, stone, and all manner of materials, held together and animated by magic. They had no heart or brain to target, which meant there was no easy way to kill them. The only way to stop them was to take them apart until the magic could not hold the amalgamated pieces together anymore. Many hunters carried spears or machetes or axes to target the monsters' weak joints, but Hana had always used a knife for the killing blows. She said she preferred to rely on speed and precision rather than brute force.

She had also said Octavia wasn't ready to actually kill a Ferox. But that had been months ago, and Octavia had been waiting for a chance. This could be her first.

There was a flicker of motion to her right, against the stone wall that stepped up to the highest orchard terrace. It was a patchy lump of ruddy brown that stood out against the gray and white stone. The Ferox was no bigger than a rabbit, and not even a large one. Small enough that she could catch it in her hands, if its mossy, tattered hide weren't bristling with long, thin bones sharpened to spikes.

Gotcha, she thought.

Octavia picked her way closer to the Ferox as it inched along the base of the wall. She knew the moment it sensed her presence, because its mixed-up birdsong stopped mid-note.

She stilled, and she waited.

In a clattering flurry of motion, the Ferox fled.

Knife in hand, bag bouncing on her back, Octavia ran after it.

With its spines jutting from its small, round body, it looked like a tumbling cluster of blades and sticks, no bigger than a foot wide at its largest but sharp and menacing nonetheless. Its metal parts were a deep reddish-brown that Octavia told herself firmly must be rust and not blood. It sliced through leaves and branches as it ran, leaving telltale scrapes in the trunks of the trees and fresh scratches on the surface of stones. It scurried along the terrace wall so quickly it was a blur of motion, but Octavia could be quick too. There was no need to be quiet now. She followed it through the walnut grove, over a low stone wall at the end of the orchard, across another spring and over a set of crumbling stairs in the hillside.

There the Ferox changed direction to charge up the hill. With a lunge Octavia got so close she felt the air stir as the monster darted out of reach, so close she was *sure* the knife snagged a scrap trailing from its misshapen tail—but that wasn't close enough. The creature leapt upward. One of its spines scraped across her hand and left a fine slice in her skin. Her aim was off anyway. The knife plunged uselessly into the soil.

She needed to get closer before she tried again. She had to dig the blade into one of its joints, where the limbs or head attached to the body. Glancing blows, surface cuts, wild jabs, they did nothing to disrupt the magic holding a Ferox together.

They were outside the orchard now, and the slope was steep and wild, covered with fallen logs and loose stones. Soon Octavia was panting for breath and tasting an unpleasant metallic rasp at the back of her throat. Her legs burned from the effort of sprinting uphill, and the air had grown so cold her breath came out in curls of mist. The Ferox bounded over an outcrop of granite and below a fallen tree, its spines scraping bark from the underside as it passed, but when Octavia tried to climb over the log she slipped and lost her footing.

She fell forward, so surprised she dropped the knife when she threw her hands out to catch herself. She twisted as she fell and slammed her elbow into the ground, right between two stones. The pain was so great she yelped as she rolled onto her side; her bag was a lump beneath her.

"Ow ow ow *ow*." Octavia sat up, cradling her right elbow.

She had scraped her knee on the log and banged her shoulder on a stone, but the elbow was what hurt the most. Tears gathered in her eyes, hot and stinging. She scrubbed them away, embarrassed, even though there was no one to see. She couldn't believe she had tripped over a log. She was on a hunt, she had followed a Ferox for a good long distance, she had come within inches of getting her knife into one of its haunches, and she had *tripped* over a *stupid log*.

She unbent her elbow carefully, wincing. It hurt, but not so badly that she thought anything might be broken. Not so bad that she would have to tell anybody about it or make up a lie to explain it. She got to her knees and retrieved Hana's knife.

The rabbity little Ferox was gone. She couldn't even hear it racing away up the hillside anymore. She had no hope of seeing it in the dim light.

For a second, Octavia forgot to breathe.

She squeezed her eyes shut. She opened them again.

The steep hillside and pine forest around her were a deep, murky gray. She looked up, her heart pounding, hoping against hope it was only the clouds. There *were* clouds, dense and dark and rolling over the valley, but that was not the only reason for the lack of light.

Somewhere behind that thick bank of clouds, the sun was setting.

She had stayed out too long.

Octavia scrambled to her feet and barreled down the hill. She swerved to the west, thinking she needed to reach the orchard again, then she changed her mind and kept going straight down. It would be faster to reach Hermit Road and follow it to Long Road. She had time. Wyvern Gate stayed open longer than the others, to allow the guards time to return from their last patrol of the day, and there would be lamps and torches spilling light from the town walls. The goatherds and shepherds and farmers would still be coming in from the fields and pastures. She could make it. It was her only chance.

She nearly tripped two more times before she sheathed Hana's knife and tucked it into her bag. It wouldn't do her any good to fall and stab herself. The hill was so much steeper and longer than she had thought. The pines growing along the slope were tall and spindly, swaying in the wind of the oncoming storm, and the stones on the ground so broken and jagged they looked like teeth jutting from the hillside.

She was afraid, for a few wild seconds, that she had somehow gotten lost, that she was going the wrong way. But that was impossible. She had not crossed the road or Hermit Creek. She just had to get down the hill without breaking her neck. She had time. She had to have time.

She was breathing so hard every gasp felt like ice scraping her throat. Her nose was running freely and hot tears streaked down her cheeks. She had heard stories of winter nights so cold tears froze as they fell. She thought about Bram curled up outside Wyvern Gate. He would have pounded on the cold metal. He would have screamed for help. The guards in the watchtowers might have heard him.

Octavia dropped into a shallow ditch so suddenly the step jarred every bone in her body. But she didn't fall, and when she looked up she realized she had reached Hermit Road. Up the road, to the east, was a Hunters' watchtower, its tall wooden structure looming at the side of the road.

The sight of it was first a relief—but a new terror quickly chased the relief away. The nearest watchtowers were much farther from Vittoria than she had intended to travel. She was nearly three miles from town. The road was supposed to be lined with charms, but roads were harder to protect than trails; it was almost impossible to trick a Ferox into ignoring a broad swath of well-packed dirt wide enough for two carts to pass side by side.

She still had time. It wasn't even three miles. Closer to two and a half. She could make it. The gates were still open. She turned left, toward the west, and she started running. Vittoria was still hidden behind the curve of the hill.

Then she heard, echoing from the valley, the mournful low sound of the evening bells.

No, no, *no*. It wasn't fully dark yet. She was supposed to have more *time*.

A shape lumbered into the road.

Octavia skidded to a stop, nearly tripping herself in surprise.

The scant dusky light showed the merest gleam of metal and

polished wood. Joints clanked softly, almost bell-like in their sound. The air smelled of pepper and rust.

Octavia could not move. Her feet were rooted to the road. She was frozen in place with terror.

From the hulking creature came a soft voice.

"Help," it said. "Help me."

Octavia began to shake. She pressed her hand to her mouth to keep from whimpering.

"Help," said the voice. "Help me."

It was a Ferox. It was luring Octavia closer with a human voice.

And it was much, much bigger than a rabbit.

4

Danger on Hermit Road

———»»———

There was a grunting in the darkness, low and rough, and the sound of claws scraping through dirt. Octavia felt the hairs on the back of her neck rise. She couldn't move. All she could see of the Ferox was its hulking shape about fifty feet down the road. The strap of her bag was pressing into her shoulder, but she couldn't bring herself to slide it onto her arm to find the knife. The monster would hear her. She dared not make a sound.

"Help me," said the monster. Its voice was hollow and light, singsong in a way that made Octavia's skin crawl. "Help me, please. I'm cold. Please help me."

The Ferox moved toward the center of the road, away from the shadows of the trees. Finally Octavia could see it—and it was big. As big as a bear, or even bigger. It was far too big to be so close to Vittoria at dusk. The protection charms should have stopped it.

"Help me," said the monster. "Can I come in? Help me."

It snuffled on the road, pressing its broad snout into the ground. It didn't look like an animal's snout. It was sharp, more like a horn or a blade, a wicked curve that bent upward from what had to be its mouth. Octavia couldn't see its eyes in the darkness. Not all Ferox even had eyes; some hunted by smell or sound or taste. She couldn't tell if it was looking at her. She needed to know if it was looking at her. Maybe it could smell that someone was near, but it didn't know where she was yet. Maybe it was calling out its horrible mimicry of a human voice to make her reveal herself. She didn't know what to do. She didn't *know*.

Everything Hana had taught her had flown from her mind. All she could think about was how this might have been how Hana felt right before she died. Knowing there was a monster close enough to hunt her. Desperate to avoid being caught. Knowing, even so, how inevitable it was. Octavia had spent countless nights imagining the fear her sister must have felt in her last moments. Now she didn't have to guess. It was so much worse than she had ever imagined.

She began to shiver and clenched her teeth to keep them from chattering. She felt, very suddenly, the desperate urge to pee. And maybe to throw up at the same time. She was going to freeze to death right here, right in the middle of the road, because she was too afraid to move. She was going to freeze to death like Bram.

No more than fifty feet away, the Ferox reached the center of the road, and it stopped.

"Help me," it said. "Please let me in."

The twilight was growing darker and grimmer, with the last pale gray fading into the heavy clouds and cold wind. Octavia's nose was running and her throat felt tight and ticklish. Icy, hard snowflakes stung her face and hands. Her foot was cramping painfully in her boot.

"Help," said the monster.

It sniffed noisily. Nobody knew why the Ferox even needed to breathe. They were magical creatures made up of debris, without any proper organs, but they huffed and snorted like the animals they mimicked.

The monster moved its head from side to side. Still Octavia could not see any eyes, but it was looking for something. It was looking for her.

She knew the exact second it spotted her.

For a long, terrible moment, she stared at the monster, and the monster stared at her, and neither of them moved.

The monster huffed again.

"Help me," it said. "I'm so cold."

Octavia turned and ran.

She ran as fast as she could, feet pounding painfully along the packed dirt road. The monster grunted as it loped closer. This one was fast. She had to be faster. Her chest ached and the cold scraped painfully in her throat. Her legs burned.

She had to get away, but there was nowhere to go. Three miles was too far—it was too late. She would never make it back to Vittoria, even if she could get past the Ferox. She was running away from town, away from the magic-warded orchards and fields. She was running into the wilderness.

Into the wilderness, and toward the Hunters' watchtower.

Her heart leapt with sudden hope.

That was her only chance. She couldn't see the watchtower, but it couldn't be far. Surely she would come upon it any moment now.

There was a loud huff right behind her, and a gust of cold, fetid breath swept over her neck. It smelled of rotting meat and tanned hides and deep, musty cellars, but it was so cold, colder than the night air around it.

She had to look. It was close, but how close? She turned her head quickly.

The monster was no more than three paces away. Its bulky head and sharp snout curled above her. From this close she could see the bones and branches that made up the lines of its neck. She could count its rusted metal teeth.

Octavia stumbled backward, tripped over her boots, and went

down hard. She fell crookedly, one leg twisting as the other gave out. The monster was two paces away. Now one pace. It lowered its head. She rolled and crawled away from it, fingers scrabbling at the dirt, whimpering with fear.

The monster's great jaws opened, and it roared.

The roar blasted over Octavia with icy cold air. It surrounded her and swept over her, reverberating as it bounced from the trees along the road and the rocky slopes of the hills. It made Octavia's ears ache. She jumped to her feet as the monster swiped at her with its claw. It missed her by inches and took a chunk of road instead. Dirt sprayed upward in an arc before raining on Octavia's face and hands.

There was a bright flash, and a whistling sound whisked past Octavia's ear. She barely had time to flinch. The Ferox roared again, then its roar broke off into an abrupt gargle of surprise. It reared back, like a bear rising to its hind legs, and batted at its own head.

Only then did Octavia see the flaming arrow jutting from its snout.

"What?" Octavia spluttered, so stunned that for a second she forgot to flee.

Her shock didn't stop her for long; she backed away from the monster. It had to be a Hunter, somebody already tucked into the watchtower for the night. They had heard the monster and come out to help her. Her heart leapt again, this time with relief.

There was another flash of light, another whistle in the air, and another arrow struck the monster, this time where its massive front leg joined its shoulder. It roared and stumbled backward, biting at the arrow frantically. The fire on the ends of the arrows lit the monster from within, showing the sharp lines of its bones and skull, the twisted metal and charred wood that made up its abominable skeleton. Even as the monster was trying to dislodge the arrows with its clumsy claws, Octavia was running again.

The monster was right behind her, but the Hunters' watchtower was just ahead, standing over a gentle curve in the road. It was as tall as the swaying trees, a dark and delicate silhouette against the night. There was no sign of firelight at the top, no warm yellow glow through the shutters.

The Ferox slashed at Octavia again. Its claws snagged her coat and bag, striking her so hard she lurched to the side. She stumbled again but did not fall.

Somebody was shouting up ahead, and finally she saw them, the dark shape of a person at the base of the watchtower. They had another flaming arrow nocked and raised. She ran harder than she had ever run in her life.

Octavia reached the base of the tower as the other person let their arrow fly. She pounded up the stone steps of the base, then climbed the wooden ladder without hesitation. The monster roared behind her as the final arrow struck home. The other person climbed after her; the ladder trembled with every step.

The entire tower shook when the monster rammed into the base. The other person let out a yelp but held on. The trapdoor leading into the watchtower was already open. Octavia scrambled through the hole and turned around.

"Come on!" she shouted. "Come on, come on!"

The monster, alight with three flaming arrows, circled the base of the tower, snorting and roaring in frustration. The other person reached the top of the ladder and climbed through, and together they pulled the ropes to raise the lower section of the ladder. The pulleys rattled noisily and the rope burned Octavia's hands.

When the ladder was raised, and the ropes knotted and secure, Octavia sat on her heels, panting heavily.

"Thank you," she said. Her mouth was dry, her throat sour and sore. She wiped tears and snot from her face. "I didn't know there were any Hunters out tonight."

The other person settled into a crouch on the opposite side of the trapdoor. They reached up, hesitantly at first, then slowly unwrapped the scarf from their head.

The person was only a girl, about Octavia's age. She watched Octavia through narrow eyes. She didn't say anything.

Octavia felt a sickly cold worry worm through her relief.

She knew all of the Hunters in Vittoria, including the apprentices and journeymen, and this girl was not one of them. She knew everybody her own age as well, and probably everybody for a few years on either side, because Vittoria wasn't that big. There just weren't that many young people.

She didn't know this girl.

Octavia had never seen her before in her life.

She was a stranger.

5

The Impossible Girl

——— »» ———

There were no strangers in Vittoria. There couldn't be, because there was nobody else left in the world. After the lowlanders had rebelled and the sorcerers responded by waging a terrible war, after they unleashed magical weapons so destructive they leveled entire cities, after the Ferox ran wild and out of control, after Agrippina's deadly plague, everything except Vittoria had been destroyed.

For years after the war, explorers from Vittoria had tried to find survivors. Five different expeditions had searched and failed. Master Camilla had returned from the fifth so terrified by the horrors she had experienced that she forbade anybody else from venturing out to endure such hardship. The world was full of empty towns, empty villages, empty farms, and countless monsters. The people of Vittoria had learned to live in the Lonely Vale, in their small, protected territory surrounded by a cruel and deadly wilderness, because they had no other choice. They were the last survivors in the world. There was nobody else.

There were no strangers.

Until now.

"Who are you?" Octavia demanded. "What's your name? Who's your family? Where do you live?"

The girl didn't answer. Octavia studied her face. Her chin, her mouth, her nose. Her wide dark eyes. She didn't look any older than Octavia, but she had to be. She had to be old enough that neither Octavia nor her siblings would know her. Octavia's mind was racing.

The girl was still holding her bow with an arrow nocked, pointing it through the trapdoor toward the Ferox circling the base of the tower.

"Can it climb?" the girl asked. Her voice had a lilt to it, an accent that Octavia didn't recognize.

"What?" Octavia said. "Of course it can't climb. We got the ladder up, and the protective charms will confuse it."

The girl frowned for a moment before raising her bow to aim the arrow directly at Octavia. "Are you a sorcerer?" she asked.

"*What?*" Octavia said again. "No! How could you even ask that?"

There was a roar from below, and the tower rocked as the monster flung itself into the wooden stilts. Octavia pushed against the wall to brace herself. The other girl rose to her knees to aim her arrow out the trapdoor again. She moved it this way and that, tracking the monster as it circled the tower. Octavia waited warily for another blow, but none came.

After a moment, the girl spit through the opening in the floor and sat back on her heels. "It's leaving."

"Good. Good." Octavia had to take a few breaths to calm herself again.

"Why is it leaving?"

Octavia blinked. She didn't understand how this girl could shoot a Ferox with flaming arrows when it seemed like she didn't know anything about them. "The charms in the stones at the base make it forget and lose focus."

"Charms?"

"The protection charms."

"You said you don't do magic," the girl said, her tone accusatory.

"I don't! I didn't make the charms. The Crafters did that. Who *are* you? Why don't you know anything?"

"You don't know what I know!" the girl said, her voice rising. "I don't trust sorcerers!"

"I'm not a sorcerer!" Octavia shouted.

They glared at each other across the open trapdoor for several seconds. The night was growing darker, the very last of the murky gray evening slipping away. It was also getting colder; the wind whistled through the trees and pushed icy pellets of snow through the open shutters. Octavia clenched her teeth to keep them from chattering. All of the sweat she had worked up while she was running was now clammy on the inside of her clothes. Her skin prickled.

"This is stupid," she said. She couldn't think properly when she was so cold. If the girl was going to be stubborn about answering her questions, that wasn't Octavia's fault. She flung her bag to the floor and stood. "Don't shoot me. I'm just going to start a fire. The normal way. Not with magic."

Every watchtower was stocked with supplies the Hunters needed to survive outside of Vittoria, and that included a small iron stove and a stash of wood and kindling. Octavia found them easily enough as her eyes adjusted to the darkness, but she couldn't locate a flint. She should have brought one in her bag.

Hana had always said every Hunter should carry flint at all times, but Octavia hadn't listened. She had never expected to be out after dark.

"Let me," said the girl.

Octavia scowled and clenched her fists. She didn't want the girl to see how much her hands were shaking, but even more she didn't want to have to suffer through another minute of unnecessary cold. She stepped aside and gestured at the wood stove.

"Fine. You light it."

The girl did, swiftly and easily, pulling a flint out of her pack and easily striking a spark that caught the kindling on the first stroke. Octavia tried not to be jealous but failed. She never had to light fires at home; the bakery's ovens never went cold. Hana had promised to teach her properly someday.

As the girl was blowing gently on the flame to coax it to grow, Octavia closed the shutters to keep the cold wind outside, then took one more look through the trapdoor before closing it as well. There was no sign of the Ferox.

When everything was closed up tight and they were as safe from the cold and the night as they could be, Octavia sat down. There was light enough now for her to get a good look at the strange girl.

The girl's skin was brown, as dark as the darkest-skinned families in Vittoria, the ones whose forebears had come from far to the south across the sea centuries before the war. Her brown eyes were wide, her nose straight and strong, her hair black where it was escaping from braids beneath her scarf. The scarf itself was brightly colored, an elaborate weave of red and gold and green and blue that gleamed in the firelight. The finer threads in the scarf looked more like silk than wool, but that was ridiculous. Nobody wore precious silk into the woods. It had once come from seaside cities far to the south, but of course nothing came from anywhere anymore, so what was left was too valuable to ruin.

Octavia dug her waterskin out of her bag and took a drink. Her throat was dry. Even though the watchtower was warming quickly, she couldn't stop shivering. She had heard stories about lone wanderers in the wilderness, feral children or mad huntsmen or isolated hedge witches, people who had missed the end of the war, survived the plague, and escaped all of the ravenous monsters left behind. They were only stories, though, the sort of thing grannies told to children at bedtime for a tickle of imaginary fear. Nobody actually believed those stories. If there were anybody out in the wilderness, anybody at all, the Hunters would have found signs of them long ago.

Besides, the girl didn't look like she had been living wild. Her bow and quiver of arrows were good weapons in fine repair, and her clothes, while well-worn with splashes of mud and damp on the hems, weren't rags. She wore boots with laces all the way up to her knees and a woven tunic dyed deep, deep red; her long coat was blue, with polished bone buttons in a line up the front. Octavia's plain gray shirt, brown trousers patched with pieces of flour sacks at the knees, and ill-fitting leather boots and wool coat—all hand-me-downs from her siblings—felt terribly drab in comparison. None of the spinners in Vittoria dyed wool for everyday use; bright fabrics were reserved for special occasions. The girl wore several layers, but none of them seem particularly padded or warm.

For the first time Octavia noticed that the girl was also shivering.

"What's your name?" Octavia asked.

The girl looked at her sharply. "Why do you need my name?"

"I don't *need* your name," Octavia said. "I just want to know it. I'm Octavia Silvia. My family owns the bakery on Fishing Cat Lane."

The girl showed no sign of recognition. If anything, her expression only grew warier.

"You are from the city of sorcerers?" she asked.

"You mean Aeterna? No way!" Octavia shook her head rapidly. "What kind of question is that? There's nobody there anymore.

There hasn't been anybody there for years. Why don't you know that?"

The girl pressed her lips together stubbornly and did not answer. Octavia sighed. She inched closer to the fire, slowly, so as not to startle the girl. She held out her waterskin.

"Thank you for saving my life," Octavia said. "You're a good shot."

The girl hesitated, then accepted the water. She took a swift gulp before handing it back.

"You're not from Aeterna," the girl said.

"No," Octavia said. "I'm from Vittoria."

The girl's eyes widened. "*Vittoria?*" she said incredulously, as though Octavia had claimed to be from the moon.

"Well, yes," Octavia said.

"But you're not a sorcerer. Your family are not sorcerers."

"That's what I said!" Octavia said, frustrated. "I don't do magic. Nobody in my family does magic. We have a *bakery.*"

The girl's dark eyes did not look away. She barely even blinked. The unease Octavia felt was only growing stronger. She had a feeling that she and the strange girl were having two very different conversations, and neither of them was fully understanding what the other was saying.

"Where are you from?" Octavia said. "How are you here?"

The girl stared at Octavia a moment longer, then she opened the flap of her own bag. She rooted around for a little bit until she found a slender scroll tied up with two neat strings. She unrolled it to reveal a map in black ink. The girl smoothed her hands over it, tracing the long, slender line of a road. The road passed through the jagged hashmarks of the mountains, from the flatlands to a bright many-pointed star surrounded by peaks. The star was rendered in vibrant inks of blue and green and red, the most colorful thing on the entire map. It was labeled in a script Octavia could not read.

And near it, tucked into the mountain terrain, was another star. Smaller, with seven points, sitting astride a river and a road.

Even without being able to read the labels, Octavia recognized Vittoria as the smaller star; the larger, more colorful star was Aeterna. They were linked by the twin lines of the River Nyx and Long Road and surrounded by mountains.

But the mountains were only a small part of the map. They were tucked away in a corner, while the rest was filled with rivers and roads and hills and forests Octavia didn't recognize, with cities and towns whose names she couldn't read, a dizzying expanse of geography that stretched all the way to a swath of blue at the bottom of the map.

The girl ran her hand over the map to press down its curl.

"My name is Sima," said the girl, "and I come from the city of Iberne, by the sea." She pointed at another star, this one perched right on the border between the land and the sea. "Here."

It was quiet in the watchtower, with the crackle of the fire and the moan of the wind outside as the only sounds, but Octavia felt as though the small room had been rocked by thunder from the fiercest summer storm. For a moment everything was muffled and strange, like the reverberations that followed a thunderclap. She stared at the map, at the constellation of stars and the lines connecting them.

It wasn't possible. It couldn't be true. There was nobody left. For fifty years, ever since the war had ended, the people of Vittoria had yearned for any sign that there were others left alive in the world. In all that time, there had been nothing. The only world Octavia had ever been able to imagine was a vast and endless wilderness overrun by Ferox. Vittoria's Hunters never traveled more than two or three days from the safety of town. Octavia had always thought that was a terribly long and frightening distance, the sort of journey only the bravest people could make.

Now, looking at Sima's map, it seemed like no distance at all.

She was afraid to blink, afraid that if she closed her eyes for the slightest second, the girl before her would disappear.

Sima, from Iberne by the sea. A stranger who should not exist.

"But how . . . why are you . . ." Octavia swallowed. "Are there a lot of people where you come from? People who survived the war?"

Sima tilted her head, as though she couldn't decide if Octavia was serious. "Many people died in the war."

"But not everyone?"

Sima let out an amused snort. "Obviously not everyone. There is no war now. It was a long time ago."

Octavia's vision blurred for a second, with shock and the sudden sting of tears. The Sorcerers' War had never felt very far away, even though it had been over before her parents were born. It wasn't possible to feel far from the war in Vittoria, where every part of their lives was shaped by what had been lost—by what they *believed* had been lost, if Sima was telling the truth.

"We didn't know," Octavia said weakly. "We didn't know there was anybody out there."

Sima was looking at her with an expression Octavia couldn't read.

"It was a long time ago," she said again.

They sat in silence for a little while, both of them with their legs crossed and their eyes wide, facing each other across a room that was so small, but seemed to Octavia to be filled with ideas and surprises so impossibly huge there was scarcely air left to breathe.

The people of Vittoria believed the world to be empty. Every year during the Rite of Remembrance they whispered the names of the people they had lost. They honored the five groups of brave, determined explorers who had died trying to find survivors. Hunters patrolled the wilderness every day and never saw anything but monsters.

That they had been wrong all along, that there had always been people out there, it was too big to comprehend. Octavia had a thousand questions. Why Sima was in the mountains. Where she was going, what it was like where she had come from, why was she alone, how she had learned to hunt. How many other people there were in the world. How far they traveled, what roads they walked, what places they had seen that she had never even imagined. How they survived the Ferox.

Why nobody had ever come to Vittoria in all that time.

How everybody in Vittoria could be so very, very wrong about the world.

Octavia's stomach suddenly rumbled. The noise startled both of them, and Sima's lips twitched in amusement.

"I have food," Octavia said quickly, to cover her embarrassment. "And there's food stored here. The Hunters always keep supplies ready."

She hadn't realized how hungry she was before, when all she could feel was panic and fear, but now that she was warm and still and relatively safe, her body was quick to remind her how much she had exerted herself since her lunch beside the orchard creek. She dug into her bag to find two slightly crushed potato and pea pies. They were cold and crumbly, but the smell that rose when she took them out was familiar—and so was the sudden pang of guilt.

By now her parents would be searching for her. They would hear from the guards that she had left town earlier in the afternoon. They would look for her everywhere inside the walls, the same way Bram's mother would have searched for him, going to every shop, every friend, every neighbor, asking again and again if they had seen her. They would talk to Master Flavia and Penelope, to Rufus and Master Cicerus, to everybody they could think of. Rufus would probably tell them she had been sneaking out some days to hunt. Octavia couldn't even be mad at him for that. He had been right all along. She should have been more careful.

Octavia separated the squished pies and handed one to Sima. "Here. My dad made these."

Sima accepted the pie, sniffed at it, and took a single bite.

"Thank you," she said. She reached into her own bag and brought out a small cloth pouch, from which she tipped a handful of dried fruit and roasted nuts. She offered them to Octavia. "This is what I have. This, and some tea, if we have a pan to heat water?"

There was a pan in the Hunters' provisions, as well as a few clay cups and some strips of dried venison. It made for a satisfying, if strange, meal. The watchtower was growing warm, but the wind was still howling outside. Swaying pines brushed constantly on the outside walls.

Octavia hadn't heard the Ferox since they had climbed into the tower. Maybe it had stalked away into the woods to hunt elsewhere. Or maybe it was in the shadows beneath the tower, waiting for them to make a foolish mistake.

Waiting for the trapdoor to open and the ladder to descend.

Waiting for its chance.

Octavia asked, "What are you doing in the mountains, if you're from the sea? Why are you even here? Why are you by yourself?"

Sima was licking flakes of buttery crust from her fingers, but when Octavia spoke, she stopped. Her eyes narrowed with renewed suspicion. "Why do you want to know?"

"I don't have a *reason*," Octavia said, frustrated. "It's just . . . nobody should be out here alone. It's too dangerous."

"You are."

Octavia's face warmed. She ducked her head to pluck at the laces of her boots. "Yeah, but that was a mistake. Are you really traveling by yourself?"

Sima hesitated, then shook her head. "I was with a caravan, but we were attacked by the sorcerers' monsters. It was last night. I've been looking for the others but I . . ." She trailed off and shrugged.

"You were in the woods last night too?" Octavia asked, astonished. "How did you survive? What did you do?"

"I climbed a tree," Sima said. "I tied myself to the trunk to keep from falling out. I didn't know the monsters were so big or so fast. I didn't know they could speak like that."

Octavia stared at her. "Don't you know anything about the Ferox?"

Sima looked at her with a frown. "There are none in the lowlands. They are only in the mountains. The people who drove the caravan, they said we could avoid them or drive them away. But they were wrong."

Octavia's view of the world tilted again. "But that's not possible. The Ferox are everywhere. They overran the world."

Sima's snort was even more disdainful this time. "They are only here. Nowhere else. Everybody knows that."

"I don't believe you," Octavia snapped, even as doubt began to wriggle into her mind. "Why would you even come here, if it's so much more dangerous? Why not stay in the lowlands where there aren't any monsters? Nobody would do that. I think you're lying."

She knew immediately it was the wrong thing to say. Sima's expression turned hard, and she set her clay cup down with a *thunk* to cross her arms over her chest.

"I don't care what you think," Sima said. "You don't know what you're talking about."

After that, she refused to say anything else. They sat in sullen, uncomfortable silence, watching each other with wary distrust across the small room, until they both grew too tired to stay awake any longer.

6
The First Day of Winter

———»»»———

Octavia woke, disoriented and shivering, to an achingly cold darkness. She had fallen asleep slumped sideways against the wall; her entire body was stiff and sore. She tugged the blanket tighter around her shoulders and crawled over to the wood stove to stoke the fire back from the embers.

Sima was still asleep, curled onto her side with her scarf balled up under her head like a pillow. She looked peaceful and pretty, with her black braids tucked over her shoulder and all the fear and suspicion erased from her face. Octavia looked away quickly to add more wood to the fire. She shouldn't be staring.

It felt like a dream, everything that had happened the night before, but Sima was not a dream. She was a real person, right in front of Octavia.

And with a few simple words she had swept away everything Octavia had believed about the world.

When the fire was crackling and filling the watchtower with warmth, Octavia stood, stretched, and opened one of the shutters for a look outside. Snow had fallen during the night. Not a mere dusting, either, but a thick blanket that draped every tree and mountain, changing the entire shape of the forest. Where the pines had been pointed and dark before, now they were softened and pale, glistening gently beneath the last lingering stars. The clouds had cleared, swept away by the night's wind. The sky was brightening in the east with a gentle rosy blush.

There was a grumble behind her. Octavia turned to see Sima sitting up and looking around in bleary confusion, clutching the blanket to her chest.

"It's so *cold*," she mumbled. "Why is it so cold?"

"Because it's winter. It snowed last night."

Sima's eyes widened. "Snow?"

"Well, yeah." Octavia gestured out the open window. "Didn't you notice the storm blowing in yesterday?"

Sima scrambled to her feet and joined Octavia by the open shutter. She leaned out to look around, her long black braids dangling free. Her breath puffed warm mist into the air. There was an expression of surprise on her face, mingled with something like awe.

"I have never seen snow before," Sima said, quietly.

Octavia blinked. "Never?"

Sima glanced at her. "It doesn't snow by the sea. I have heard of it, from places inland, but we only have rain. This is a lot of snow."

"Not really," Octavia said. At Sima's look of disbelief she went on. "I guess it's a lot for a first snow. But there will be more. Sometimes it snows so much it's higher than your head."

Sima looked very much like she wanted to call Octavia a liar, but she kept her doubt to herself. She pointed to the west, down the road. "Vittoria is that way?"

"Yes. This is Hermit Road. It leads into the Lonely Vale and Vittoria."

"And the city of the sorcerers? Where is that?"

"You mean Aeterna?" Octavia pointed to the northeast. "That way."

"How far?"

"It's about thirty miles." Octavia felt strangely sheepish as she said it. It had always seemed like such a vast distance to her, farther than even the bravest hunters dared travel, but Sima had traveled ten times that or more in her journey from the sea. "They're dangerous miles. A lot of Ferox. Why do you want to know?"

Sima didn't answer. She was looking to where Octavia was pointing. As the sun rose, the hulking shapes of the mountains emerged in the gray dawn. Octavia recognized the sharp summit of Gray Bear Mountain over the shoulders of the nearer peaks. Its highest point was already catching the rays of the sun, gleaming with golden light. Octavia thought about pointing it out to Sima, telling her its name and those of the mountains around it, but she didn't say anything. She was afraid if she spoke she would say, *That's where my sister died*, and that was too much for this fragile, cold, glistening morning.

They lapsed into an awkward silence. Sima's shoulder brushed against Octavia's, and Octavia couldn't decide if she should move away or lean into it to show she wasn't afraid or suspicious or uneasy. She didn't even know if she *was* afraid or suspicious or uneasy. She had been the night before, because Sima had been as well, but now she didn't know what she was feeling. Her thoughts were a confused jumble, everything she had believed to be true clashing with everything Sima had told her.

The gray sky faded to pink and yellow, until the sun finally peeked over the horizon and set the snow-capped mountains ablaze with light. It was so bright and so sudden it stung Octavia's eyes. The sound of a single, lonely bell carried up the valley. It rang with a chime so clear and pure it made her heart squeeze in her chest.

Beside her, Sima gasped softly. "What is that?"

The second bell joined the first, then the third joined the pair.

The bells were so much softer than she had ever heard them. Octavia stepped back from the window.

"That's Vittoria. The bells mean it's safe to go now," she said. "The Ferox never hunt during the day."

Sima took one last look outside before she began to gather her things. "I have to find the caravan."

"What? But how? You said you were attacked!"

"But I survived, so others must have as well. I was looking for them yesterday, but I think I took a wrong turn at a crossroads."

This was more than she had told Octavia the night before. "Which crossroads? How far from here?"

"Not far," Sima said, but there was the briefest hesitation in her voice. "It was dark. I don't know how far."

Octavia held out her hand. "Let me see your map again."

Sima gripped her pack like she was going to refuse, then changed her mind. She brought the map out and unrolled it on the floor. Octavia knelt beside her for a closer look. She found Vittoria first, as well as Aeterna, and the faint lines of roads that connected them. What she didn't find was Hermit Road, the very road they were on; it wasn't on the map. She explained this to Sima as she traced the length of Hermit Creek.

"If you didn't pass Vittoria, you must have been on this road," she said, pointing. "We call it East Road. It crosses Hermit Road not far from here. There used to be an inn there, before the war." She frowned, trying to remember the details from Mom and Hana's maps. "I don't think it's that far. But why were you on East Road? It doesn't go anywhere now. It only goes to Aeterna."

When Sima didn't answer, Octavia looked up to find the other girl watching her with narrowed eyes. Her lips were pressed tightly together and the edges of her mouth turned down.

"Wait." Octavia sat back on her heels. "Are you . . . are you going to Aeterna?"

Sima grabbed her map and rolled it up again. "I have to find the caravan."

"But *why*? Why would you want to go that way? There's nothing there!"

Jamming the map into her pack, Sima jumped to her feet and yanked the trapdoor to the ladder open. "What do you know about it? What do you know about anything outside your cursed valley?"

"I know it's dangerous!" Octavia retorted angrily. "There are Ferox everywhere! And you've never even seen snow before! You're just going to get attacked and killed, like the rest of the caravan you left behind!"

Sima whipped her head around to glare at Octavia. "Don't say that."

Octavia swallowed back the sudden guilt.

"You don't say that," Sima said again. "They're not—they're *not*. I'm going to find them."

Sima's voice was quiet and tight, but there was something besides anger in her eyes. It was fear. Fear, and sadness, and a hint of guilt. Octavia's stomach churned. Her face was warm, but she felt the morning chill seeping into the little room, overpowering the meager fire. She looked down and twisted her fingers together in her lap. Sima was still standing beside the trapdoor, but Octavia was afraid to look up at her, afraid to see the hurt painted plainly across her face.

"Who are you traveling with?" Octavia asked.

Sima said, "My mother and brother. And others from Iberne and the lowlands."

Her family. Octavia rubbed at her nose with the sleeve of her shirt. Sima's family had been attacked on the road, and she had been separated from them, and she was scared for them and worried and didn't know if they were okay. And Octavia had yelled at her like it was her fault, when it had only ever been the fault of the Ferox. She took a breath.

"Okay," she said. "The crossroads isn't far, and it's early."

Sima nodded slightly. "Thank you for the food. I will go now."

"You mean we'll go now." Octavia pushed herself up to her feet. "I'm not letting a lowlander wander around in fresh snow. I'll help you find them."

All around the base of the watchtower, the snow was marked by tracks, the deep, broad, gouging tracks of a Ferox with long claws. In some places the footprints were so deep they pressed all the way through the snow to the dirt below, but even those were dusted with snow. Octavia could read the tracks clearly: the Ferox had returned during the night, but it had not come back since the snow had stopped. She hoped that meant it was far away. She hoped it had forgotten about them. It was daylight now. They were safe until dark.

Sima noticed the tracks too, but she only adjusted her pack and quiver firmly and started up Hermit Road.

The clear sky meant the morning was bitterly cold, but slivers of sunlight fell through the tall trees, slicing through the deepest shadows in bold, blinding rays. Here and there snow plopped from the sloping evergreens, sending up puffs of snowflakes that sparkled and shimmered. Hermit Creek babbled cheerfully beside the road as the water carved odd little shapes beneath thin ice and around snow-covered stones.

Octavia had never been in the forest at dawn immediately following snowfall. She thought it might be the most beautiful sight she had ever seen.

She didn't think it was more than a mile or two to East Road, and Hermit Road was broad and easy to follow. But their pace was slow and uneven. The snow was almost up to their knees in some places, and in others it was thin with a hard crust of ice beneath. Sima was especially clumsy, and Octavia found it hard to explain to her how best to walk in snow when she wasn't sure herself. Before long they were both overly warm and quiet and grumpy.

It was about midmorning by the time they reached the cross-roads. They came to a meadow, round and broad and draped with snow. At one side of the meadow was a collection of ruined build-ings. The largest had once been three stories high, but it was a burnt husk now, with no roof and no windows and half of its walls collapsing.

"That was the crossroads inn," Octavia said. It was the first thing either of them had said in a long time. "Did you pass it? Before the attack, I mean, with the caravan?"

"No." Sima looked around thoughtfully. "Which way is Aeterna?"

Octavia couldn't help the small laugh that escaped. "It's still northwest. It hasn't moved since you asked earlier. That way," she said, pointing, when Sima only looked confused.

"In Iberne the sea is always to the south. Without it everything is turned around."

"But you still have the sun in Iberne, don't you?"

"Not when it's raining." Sima huffed and turned away, but not before Octavia saw the slight quirk of her lips. "We came from that way, I think."

There were no tracks in the snow, which was disappointing. Octavia had hoped that maybe Sima's family was still in the area, looking for her as she was looking for them. But the snow on East Road was completely fresh and clean, aside from a few tracks of deer and foxes. Octavia pointed them out to Sima as they walked, describing their differences and what she could guess about each

animal from the tracks they left behind. She knew she was showing off a little, but Sima was so fascinated by everything to do with
snow that Octavia couldn't help herself. The snow wasn't quite
so deep here, so walking was easier. And it was almost fun, even
though it was cold. Octavia hadn't been in the woods with anybody else since Hana had died.

Octavia saw the big, bulky hump on the road first. Her heart
lurched with sudden fear. It was big, bigger than the Ferox from
the night before, and right in the middle of the road. She stopped
abruptly and heard Sima's small sound of surprise behind her.

Only when Sima shoved past her and started running did Octavia realize she wasn't looking at a massive Ferox out in the daytime. It was a wagon, turned on its side and covered with snow,
with two of its wheels sticking up. There were a couple of ravens
perched on the wheels and a couple more picking through the
snow around the wagon. They took flight with raucous squawks as
Sima ran toward them.

"Mama! Pavi!" She cupped her hands around her mouth to call
out. "Mama, are you here? Pavi! Auntie! Is anybody here?"

Octavia followed more slowly. Now that she knew what she
was looking at, she could make out the yellow-painted boards of
the wagon where the snow had fallen away. There were also other
mounds in the snow, smaller ones, around and along the road. She
paused to look at the nearest one. She took a breath and smelled,
beneath the scents of the forest and the morning, something
metallic and foul. Her stomach churned.

"Mama!" Sima shouted again. Her voice was shaking now, even
as her shouts grew louder. "Pavi!"

Octavia kicked the snow away from the mound at her foot. It
was a horse. Not a person, as she had feared. A horse. Another few
swipes with her boot and she could see where the Ferox's claws

had sliced through its neck and throat. The blood was frozen now, seeped into the cold, muddy ruts of the road. One of the animal's big black eyes stared up at her blankly.

"*Mama! Pavi!* Where are you?"

Octavia stared at the dead horse for a moment, her vision blurring until she had to blink rapidly. She started to turn away—then stopped, turned back, and looked down again. Not at the horse this time, but at the road beneath it. A road that had been muddy a few days ago, if the depth of the ruts was any indication. Now the mud was frozen stiff beneath the snow. She retreated a few steps and cleared another spot, then jogged a little ways down the road to do it again.

"Sima!" she called. "Look!"

Sima was running toward her at once. "Is somebody here? Why is nobody here? There are only animals, there are no people! Where are the other wagons?"

"Look at this," Octavia said, indicating the ground at her feet. "Wagon tracks and hoof prints under the snow. The other wagons kept going before the storm."

Sima's expression was hopeful. "Are you sure?"

"Yes," Octavia said. Sima looked so scared and worried. She had to be sure. "They kept going north."

"Then I can follow them," Sima said, and she started striding down the road.

Octavia had to run to catch up to her. "Wait! You can't just go after them. They could be miles ahead by now."

"I walk faster than the caravan travels," Sima said.

"Yeah, but it's been a day and a half, hasn't it? You don't have any food. You barely have any arrows left." Octavia grabbed Sima's arm to slow her down. "You don't even know how to track them! It's too dangerous!"

Sima shook Octavia's hand off. "What do you know about dangerous? You hide inside your walls like cowards! You don't know anything about danger!"

"My sister was killed by the Ferox!" Octavia shouted. "I know exactly how dangerous they are!"

"And my family might be—"

Sima broke off sharply and clicked her mouth shut. They both knew her family might be dead. Saying it out loud couldn't change that.

They walked several steps in silence. Octavia's anger faded as quickly as it had flared. Left in its place was a dull ache, so familiar in the months since Hana's death. She didn't want Sima to feel that same ache. She didn't want to believe Sima's family was dead until there was proof.

"They might be fine," Octavia said quietly. She tugged on Sima's sleeve. "They're headed to Aeterna, right? That's where the caravan is going?"

Sima finally slowed her pace to allow Octavia to walk beside her. She nodded stiffly.

"But why? Why would you ever want to go to an empty city?"

They walked several steps before Sima answered.

"There is somebody there we need to find," she said. "We have been traveling for a long time. Other travelers tell us, go to Aeterna, that's where you'll find the—find what you are looking for."

Octavia bit back her instinctive response that there was nobody in Aeterna. There wasn't supposed to be anybody *anywhere*, but Sima was here, and her family and a caravan were somewhere on the road. If that was possible, then it was also possible there were travelers in Aeterna. Anything was possible now.

"Who are you looking for?"

There was a long pause before Sima answered. "My brother is

sick. We are looking for somebody to help him. Somebody who is in Aeterna."

"Are you sure? There has to be somebody else who can help. Maybe if—"

"The only thing that will help is getting to Aeterna," Sima said shortly. "The rest is not your concern."

Her words stung a little, but Octavia didn't want to start a fight. Sima was scared and worried, and Octavia was just as much a stranger to her as she was to Octavia.

"I can help you get to Aeterna," Octavia said. "But I don't think we should follow the caravan."

"Why not? I need to catch up to them."

"Because we don't have any supplies. You don't even have proper winter clothes. If we go back to Vittoria first—"

Sima stopped walking and narrowed her eyes. "Why?"

"Because it's my home, and we have food and shelter and dry socks, and a whole bunch of people who actually *know* how to travel through the mountains without getting attacked. We can't risk staying out in the woods for another night. We need help."

"My family needs help."

"They're too far ahead now," Octavia said. "But the Hunters can find them and help them. All we have to do is tell my mom what happened and she'll makes sure they get help."

"She will?" Sima asked doubtfully. "The people of Vittoria will help? They would help a stranger?"

In truth Octavia had no real idea how people would react when they met Sima. Vittoria had been alone for fifty years, and now they were not. Trying to imagine the full breadth of reactions was too much, like trying to see the whole of a summer thunderstorm even as it loomed so big it filled the entire sky. She couldn't even make sense of her own emotions, much less guess at everybody else's.

But she knew it was their only choice. She couldn't let Sima stay out in the wilderness for another night.

"We will," she said, with as much confidence as she could muster. "I promise. I will help you find your family."

When Sima finally nodded in agreement, they headed down the road.

7

A Stranger Arrives

———»»»———

The day had warmed considerably by the time Octavia and Sima reached the Lonely Vale. Even on the road, walking in deep snow without snowshoes was a slow, unpleasant slog. Octavia's boots were sodden, her trousers damp to the knees, her shoulders sore from the straps of her pack. Her eyes hurt from the glare of snow in sunlight. The sun shone all day, filling the forest with glistening light and making the slopes of the mountains gleam, but it was still so cold that every time they rested the chill crept into Octavia's coat.

When the walls of Vittoria finally, *finally* came into view, Sima stopped abruptly. Octavia plodded a few steps forward before she noticed.

"What?" Octavia said. She didn't want to stop now. They were so close to fresh food and dry clothes and the warmth of the bakery ovens. "We're almost home."

"That's Vittoria?" Sima asked, with a slight waver in her voice.

"Obviously," Octavia said. "What else would it be?"

"The wall is . . . bigger than I expected."

"Oh. I guess. I never thought about it."

"And they . . ." Sima considered her words. "Let you leave?"

Octavia looked away as her face warmed. "Well, yeah."

She didn't mention the fact that she wasn't supposed to be out, and especially not alone. She didn't think that was what Sima was asking anyway. After a moment, Sima started walking again, but she kept looking up toward Vittoria, as though she expected the town to move unless she was keeping an eye on it.

Octavia fell into step beside her. "I mean, we *can* leave. We're not locked in or anything. It's just too dangerous to go far."

"Because of your monsters."

"They're not *our* monsters. We didn't make them. A sorcerer did that." Octavia itched her forehead beneath the sweaty brim of her hat. "But yeah. They're the reason we don't go far."

It had always seemed like reason enough, before. But now, walking beside somebody who had come from so far away, who had encountered not one but two Ferox at night in the wilderness and survived, it felt more like an excuse than a reason.

Vittoria, from the outside, looked perfectly ordinary, and Octavia was just a tiny bit disappointed by that. She had sort of been expecting that people would be in a panic, after the second night in a row that somebody had been caught outside. But she didn't see any panic—not until she looked closer. There were herders watching animals in the pastures, but they stood in tight groups, glancing uneasily over their shoulders. Foragers were returning from the forest, but they were accompanied by Hunters who had their weapons drawn. There were woodsmen leading carts of freshly felled logs down Long Road, but their carts were only half full and they were hurrying their horses along at an anxious trot.

As she and Sima crossed the burning ground and neared Wyvern Gate, the black-clad guards watched them warily. One of the guards nudged the other, and the second guard's mouth fell open.

"You're the baker's girl," the guard said, her eyes wide. "Everybody's been looking for you! Your parents are frantic! Where have you been?"

So maybe there was a little bit of panic. But instead of feeling relieved that she had been missed, Octavia only felt guilty. She had known since last night that her parents would worry, but it was worse now that she was about to face them. She didn't want to waste time explaining things to the guards. She had to talk to Mom and Dad first. Sima's family, somewhere out there on East Road, was more important.

"Well, I'm here now," she said, trying to sound casual. "I'm going home."

One guard started walking with them as they entered the gate. "I'll escort you. Do you have any idea how worried people have been? The council was ready to call an emergency meeting." The guard looked at Sima and frowned. "Are you the one who found her? Whose kid are you?"

Sima glanced at Octavia, and Octavia grabbed her arm to pull her along faster. "Yeah, she found me. She's my friend."

As soon as they turned onto Fishing Cat Lane, Octavia saw a crowd of people outside the bakery. Everybody was talking and gesturing. Then somebody spotted her, elbowed the person next to them, and everybody was staring, then a man bellowed, "She's home!"

Maybe it was more than a *little* bit of panic.

The front door of the bakery flew open, and there was Dad. He looked around frantically until he spotted Octavia. His face lit up as he ran toward her.

"Octavia! Where have you been? We were so worried!" Dad caught her in a hug so tight he lifted her off the ground. "Are you hurt? Where have you been? What happened?"

"I'm fine," Octavia said, her voice muffled against his shirt. She squirmed, aware of all the people staring at them and murmuring to one another. "Dad, I'm fine. Put me down! I have to tell you something."

Dad released her from his embrace but kept his hands on her shoulders. "What is it? What happened? Are you hurt? Where have you been?"

Before Octavia could answer, the guard spoke up. "Come on, people, give the family some space. I know you're not here to buy pastries." To Dad he said, "Let's move this inside, Julius. Where we can talk."

The crowd grumbled but let them pass. The inside of the bakery was less crowded, with only Mom and a couple of Hunters and guards in the front room. There was no sign of Octavia's siblings; they were probably out looking for her. Mom did not cry out and open her arms like Dad had done. Mom didn't say anything at all. Her expression was grim and stony. A cold, icy feeling filled Octavia's chest.

When they were inside, with the door closed behind them, Dad finally noticed that Octavia had not let go of Sima's sleeve.

"Who is this?" he asked, blinking in surprise. "Do we know you?"

"This is my friend Sima," Octavia said quickly. "She saved my life by shooting a Ferox and now we have to help her find her family."

"She what?" said one of the Hunters, while at the same time Dad asked, "Who is her family?"

"She comes from Iberne, down by the sea," Octavia said. "She was traveling with a caravan on East Road."

For a second—the briefest split second—nobody in the bakery made a sound.

Then everybody was talking all at once. The guards were talking to the Hunters, the Hunters to each other, Dad was trying to talk to Octavia, and Mom—

As fast as a blink, Mom was across the room and standing right in front of Sima. Even with her cane and her injured leg, she was fast and nimble. She grabbed Sima's arm and tugged it from Octavia's grasp. Mom leaned close to Sima, looking intently at her face, staring so hard that Sima tried to back away.

"Let me go," Sima said.

But Mom was holding too tight. "There are no survivors in Iberne."

Sima took another step back, but Mom kept her from moving. Sima said, "Survivors? It's just where we live. We've been there all along. You just didn't know."

"We do know. We know there is nobody out there." Mom paused. "There can't be anybody out there."

"Augusta," said one of the Hunters, "what do we do?"

"How do we know she's . . . what she says?" said another.

Octavia started shaking her head. "She's not lying! She helped me!"

"She's a child," Dad said, but there was doubt in his voice as well.

She hated the way Dad and Mom were looking at Sima, hated the way Sima was trying to hide how scared she was, hated that the Hunters were stepping close and forming a half circle around them.

"This is bad," one guard muttered. "I don't like it. We have to tell the council."

"Octavia?" Sima said shakily. "What do they mean? What's wrong?"

"We can't take any risks," Mom said. "We have to find out what's going on."

"I just told you what's going on!" Octavia cried. "Sima needs help! She needs to find her family! Mom. *Mom*." Octavia tugged at her mother's sleeve. "Mom, she just wants to find her family. I told her we would help."

Instead of answering, Mom nodded sharply. "Take her to the Council Hall. We need more information."

"Don't take her away!" Octavia grabbed her mother's arm, but Mom shook her off. "She can stay with us! She needs our help! Her family needs help!"

"Octavia, what are they doing?" Sima finally broke free of Mom's grasp, only to stumble backward into one of the Hunters, who quickly seized her pack and bow and quiver. Sima tried to fight him, tried to grab her things, but before she could two more Hunters were taking hold of her arms. "Let me go! Let me go, let me go!"

"Don't hurt her!" Octavia lunged forward to help Sima, but Mom stepped into her path to block her. "Mom! What are they doing? Why won't you listen to me?"

"You said you would help!" Sima shouted. "You lied! You said you would help!"

Sima fought hard, but she wasn't strong enough to overpower the Hunters and guards. She was still shouting as they took her out of the bakery and through the gawking crowd on the street.

The door clicked shut. A heavy silence fell over the bakery.

Mom said, "Go upstairs, Octavia, and wait for us."

"But—"

Her father added, "We'll be up in a bit."

"But what are they—"

"Octavia." Dad's voice was sharp. "Go upstairs. Now."

Octavia had never seen her mother and father so angry. As much as she wanted to argue, to shout, to run after Sima, she did as she was told. She climbed the stairs to the second floor and went into the family kitchen to wait. She stripped off her coat and bag, folded them neatly to take up to her room later. She pulled off her boots and set them by the hearth to dry. The room was warm with heat seeping from the chimneys of the bakery ovens, and the midday sun shone brightly through the window. Octavia's stomach was tight with hunger. She hoped the guards would give Sima something to eat. She hoped they wouldn't hurt her.

Octavia tried to hear what her parents and the Hunters were saying downstairs, but all she could make out were murmurs. The longer she waited, the more anxious she grew.

Octavia knew she had made a terrible mistake.

She should never have brought Sima to Vittoria.

Finally there were footsteps on the stairs. Octavia's heart leapt into her throat, and she was on her feet before she could think about it. "Why are they taking Sima? What are they doing to her?"

"Sit down, Octavia," said her father. "This is not a game. This is important."

"I know it's not a game! Why did you make them take her away? You didn't even give me a chance to explain!"

"Octavia. Sit down."

Dad never raised his voice, and he spoke quietly now, every word measured and calm. Mom looked like she *wanted* to shout, but she kept her lips pressed together and said nothing. They both took seats at the table, and Octavia slid into her own chair across from them. Her stomach wasn't so much grumbling now as churning unpleasantly, filled with acid and nerves all wriggling around in a tight, queasy knot.

"Okay," Dad said. "I want you to be quiet and listen for a moment. Can you do that?"

"But I have to tell you—"

"Just listen," said Dad. "When you didn't come home yesterday, we were worried. Nobody knew where you were. We eventually realized you must have gone outside the wall."

Octavia squirmed in her chair.

"We only learned that after it was already dark," Dad went on. "The gates were closed. The patrols were in for the night. It was too late for us to go looking for you. We couldn't do anything but worry all night. We were afraid that when morning came we would find you outside the gates like Willa's son. We were afraid you were lost and caught out in the storm."

Octavia couldn't keep quiet any longer. "I wasn't lost! I was in the watchtower on Hermit Road. I was *fine*, I was warm and safe, because Sima saved my life! She saved my life and we stayed in the watchtower and I promised I would help her find her family! I promised!"

"Why were you that far from town?" Mom asked. Her voice was tense and angry. "You should never be that far out."

Now that Octavia had started talking, she found it hard to stop. "I didn't mean to, but I was in the orchard and it was still daytime, but I was tracking a little Ferox, and it went too far and then it was getting late. I got down to the road, but I was too far from town and there was a Ferox—a big one this time—and I tried to run but Sima chased it away. And we made it to the tower and—"

Mom stood up so quickly her chair rocked back on its legs and her cane rattled to the floor. "Stop. *Stop.* Do not say another word."

Octavia clicked her mouth shut. Her heart was hammering in her chest. Mom leaned forward to rest both hands on the table. She was breathing heavily, as though she had just climbed from the cellar to the attic, and her face was snowy pale except for angry red spots on her cheeks. She wasn't sunbrowned anymore. Octavia hadn't noticed, over the summer, how Mom's face had changed now that she was spending less time outside.

"Why were you tracking creatures in the orchard?" Mom asked.

Octavia didn't know if she was supposed to answer or not, so she said, hesitantly, "I was—it was for practice."

"Practice?"

"Practice hunting," Octavia said.

"*Why* are you practicing hunting?"

She lifted her chin defiantly. "Because you won't teach me! Nobody will teach me so I have to practice by myself!"

"You don't get to play around in the woods whenever you want! It's too dangerous!"

"I'm not playing!" Octavia retorted. She was on her feet now too, even though her knees were shaking so badly she could barely stand. "I'm training! How else am I supposed to become a Hunter if nobody will help me?"

Mom slammed her hands on the table so hard it made both Octavia and Dad jump.

"*You are not going to be a Hunter!*" she roared, her voice so loud it echoed from the walls of the room and stung Octavia's ears.

Octavia gaped at her. "But I—"

"No," Mom said firmly. "Absolutely not. We've already made arrangements with Master Flavia."

"You didn't even *ask* me—"

"This is *not* up for discussion." Mom leaned over to grab her cane, holding tight to the table for balance. "You lost the right to have this discussion when you went out without permission."

"But you decided before that!" Octavia cried. "You never even asked me what I wanted to do! It's not fair, I don't want to—"

"*That is final.*" Mom hit the table again, not quite as hard this time. "You lied to the guards. You broke the rules. You worried your father and your brothers and sister. You endangered yourself and everybody who went to search for you. And, worst of all, you brought something back that might endanger the entire town. You have risked the lives of everybody in Vittoria for your whim."

She whirled away from the table and headed for the stairs.

Octavia couldn't help herself. "Sima's not a *something*. She's a person. She needs help."

"You don't know that," Mom said, without turning around. Her voice shook as she spoke. "You don't know what's out there. You don't know how easily the sorcerers' magic can lead you astray. You don't know how good it is at tricking us."

"Sima isn't tricking us," Octavia said. She hadn't noticed when she started crying, but she felt the tears hot on her face now. She couldn't even yell anymore. It was hard enough to talk. "She's not. She saved my life. I promised I would help her."

"You're a child. You're easy to manipulate."

"But she's not—"

"The rest is not up to you, or to any of us. The council will figure out what is really going on and decide what to do. And you will not—"

"Augusta," Dad said, interrupting Mom. "She understands."

Mom plodded heavily down the steps, leaving Octavia and her father in the kitchen.

Octavia wiped at her eyes, scrubbing away the tears she wanted to hide. "Why is she saying that? What are they going to do to Sima?"

Dad's eyes were dark and sad. He let out a slow breath and slumped back in his chair. "There are no people left outside Vittoria, Octavia. You know that."

"How do you know? How does anybody know, if we never go far enough to look?"

"We did look. We looked for years after the war. But we never…"

Dad started to say something else, then stopped and shook his head slightly.

"We didn't look hard enough," Octavia said.

"It's more complicated than that. The council will know what to do."

"She just wants to find her mom and her brother. I told her I would help." Octavia's breath caught. "I just wanted to help."

"I know. But this is bigger than what you want." Dad sounded tired and frustrated, and Octavia felt a fresh pang of guilt. "What do you think people are saying and thinking right now? A stranger after fifty years? Somebody who shows up out of nowhere? We can't just decide what to do on our own. This is for the council to handle."

"Is anybody at least going to look for her family?"

"The Hunters will scout the roads, when the council approves it," Dad said. "What do you think they will find? Will it be what you expect?"

A toppled wagon. A dead horse. Ruts in the road beneath the snow. And somewhere deeper into the mountains, closer to Aeterna, a traveling caravan of people who didn't know Sima had survived.

The answer to her father's question was obvious, but Octavia found herself hesitating. Dad wasn't shouting like Mom; he wasn't angry or aggressive like the Hunters and guards. His calm was what made Octavia doubt herself for the first time.

For fifty years they had believed themselves to be the last town in the world, the last warm fire in the cold wilderness the war and plague had left behind, the last survivors of so much incomprehensible violence. To learn that they had been wrong, that there were other survivors, it should be reason for celebration. People might have long-lost friends and family out in the world. All the memorial bouquets drying to dust on the bridge, all the names they whispered during the Rite of Remembrance, those people might still be alive. Vittoria could trade with the lowlands and coastal cities again. They wouldn't have to hide away behind their wall forevermore, never venturing farther than a few days' cautious travel, never daring to look beyond the Hunters' watchtowers. Everybody had given up hope. Octavia wanted to believe they had been wrong.

But it had been fifty years, and Octavia was just one girl. One girl who had never spent a night outside the wall before last night. That's what Dad was trying to tell her, in his quiet way. She was only one girl, who had been through one strange night, against fifty years of history.

"Sima did save my life," Octavia said. "And there was a wagon on the road, and wagon tracks. I'm not making it up."

"I know you're not," Dad said. "But I also know that magic can be tricky, especially the kind of magic the sorcerers used. It can make us see and hear and believe things that aren't true. That's why we have to leave it up to the council. They'll know what to do." He stood and gently touched the top of Octavia's head. "Go upstairs and get changed into dry clothes, then come down for some food. There are fresh meat pies."

He headed for the stairs.

"Dad?" Octavia said.

"Yes?"

"I don't want to be a Crafter. I want to be a Hunter."

Dad looked back at her and shook his head. "Not now, Octavia. Your mother is afraid of losing you the way we lost Hana."

He went back down to the bakery, and Octavia was left alone.

8

The Difference between Magic and Mayhem

——————»»——————

Three days later, Octavia was finally allowed to leave the house again.

She had been grounded since she returned to Vittoria. She spent her time helping in the bakery, but only in the back, where she couldn't talk to anybody. Rufus wasn't allowed to visit; he had stopped by twice only to have Dad send him away with a pastry and an apology. Mom wouldn't speak to her at all. Octavia knew she was meeting with the Hunters and the council and the guards and *everybody*, but she didn't share any of what was going on with Octavia. The first time Mom said anything to Octavia since she had brought Sima back was to tell her that she would be starting an apprenticeship with Master Flavia.

That was why Octavia finally left the house, but she wasn't allowed to go alone. Her parents said, bluntly, they didn't trust her anymore. Albus had to walk her to and from Master Flavia's.

"I don't know what you expected," Albus said. "Of course they're not going to let you run around by yourself."

"I'm not going to *do* anything," Octavia muttered.

Albus huffed a sound that was almost a laugh. "Your idea of not doing anything and their idea of not doing anything are very different."

"I just wish they would tell me something," she said. "They won't even tell me what's happened to Sima."

"I don't know if Mom and Dad know," Albus said. "I think the council isn't telling the Hunters much of anything. They won't even let them scout beyond the usual perimeter. That's part of why Mom is so angry."

He was trying to make her feel better, but it didn't work. She knew the truth: Mom was angry because of Octavia.

As they turned onto River Street, Octavia saw a few people murmuring and pointing. She ducked her head and tried to ignore them. One man stepped right into her path; Octavia could have walked into him if Albus hadn't grabbed her arm.

"What did you bring back?" the man demanded, jabbing a finger in her face. "It's bad enough that the monsters are out there, but you have to bring them inside as well?"

"I didn't!" Octavia protested, but the man only scoffed.

Albus hauled her away by the elbow. Octavia tugged her scarf up to hide her face, but it didn't do any good. The angry words and suspicious murmurs followed her all the way to the center of town.

Everybody knew she was the one who had brought a stranger into Vittoria. Mom wasn't alone; the whole town was angry, worried, and very afraid.

The morning was chilly but not bitterly cold, and there was a strange, heavy feeling to the air. There was no snow falling, but the sky was gray, a muted and low ceiling of clouds that make everything feel close and muffled and grim. It made Octavia yearn for the clean white snow and blue skies and deep green of the forest outside. It had felt so peaceful and simple when she and Sima had been on the road together, breaking trail through fresh snow with sunlight glistening all around. She couldn't stop thinking about it.

She had gone over her night outside the walls a thousand times in her mind, but she couldn't figure out why Mom was so convinced Sima was some kind of magical monster instead of a girl. She couldn't see what Mom saw, and it bothered her. Mom was an experienced Hunter who had spent countless days in the wilderness outside Vittoria. Mom knew more about hunting the Ferox than just about anybody. She knew the tricks they played to lure people after them, the ease with which they mimicked calls for help, the danger they presented to even the wariest of Hunters. If a Ferox could do it, Mom knew about it.

And nobody had ever heard of a Ferox that could disguise itself as a person.

Octavia kept thinking about Sima's worry for her family. Her bafflement upon seeing snow for the first time. The way her hand had smoothed carefully over her map. How quick she had been to shoot flaming arrows at the Ferox to save Octavia's life. Octavia didn't know how anybody could think Sima was a monster. It made no sense.

When she and Albus reached the archway on River Street, there were two guards in black jackets standing outside Master Flavia's workshop. Just as Octavia was trying to figure out what to say to them, the door opened and a tall, slender woman with pure white hair stepped out. Around her waist, neck, and wrists she wore delicate chains of different kinds of metal, with charms of metal, wood, and bone dangling from their links, all of which made her jingle slightly with a soothing, tinkling song when she moved.

Octavia stopped short, her mouth open in surprise. She recognized the woman immediately.

She was Master Camilla, one of the oldest and most respected Crafters in Vittoria, and Flavia's aunt. Camilla had been a sorcerer before the war, until her sister Agrippina—Flavia's infamous mother—created the Sorcerers' Plague. After that, Camilla renounced both sorcery and her sister, and she had devoted herself to stopping the war. The plague had spread anyway, but Camilla's heroism was the reason so many refugees from Aeterna and the surrounding mountains were able to escape to Vittoria and survive. She was a member of the town council now, supposedly no more powerful than any other councilor, but everybody knew that wasn't true. Because of her age, because of how courageous she had been to kill her own sister in battle, because of the expeditions she had led searching for survivors after the war, because of all she had done to save the people of Vittoria, Camilla was the council's leader in all but name.

Master Camilla was more than eighty years old, and her dark eyes were sharp and knowing, her smile perfectly pleasant. A long scar crossed her right eye; rumor had it her sister Agrippina had tried to cut it out during their last battle. Those same stories claimed that Agrippina had died with a mirrored wound on her own face, where Camilla had blinded her left eye before dealing the killing blow.

"Ah!" said Master Camilla, as her gaze fell upon Octavia. "Here is my niece's new apprentice now! You had quite an adventure, haven't you?"

Octavia didn't know what to say, so she mumbled, "I didn't mean to cause trouble."

"Oh, we know that. Not everybody would have been able to keep their wits about them to survive a night outside the walls."

Octavia was unsure of what to make of Master Camilla's words. Part of her wanted to preen under the praise, but a bigger part of her felt guilty for enjoying it, because she had only survived because of Sima. Even worse, everybody seemed to have already forgotten about Bram, who had died because he had been alone, and the gates had been locked, and the guards had not let him in.

Before she could decide how to respond, Master Camilla went on. "As for the trouble you've caused, we're well on our way to a solution. Why don't you come by the Council Hall tomorrow for our next meeting? We do very much want to talk to you before we proceed."

Octavia was so surprised by the request that she didn't answer until Albus nudged her.

"Okay!" she burst out, then she blushed. "I mean yes, Master Camilla! I'll be there."

"Very good. I'll see you in the morning, Octavia. We'll get this sorted out," Camilla said.

The door to Master Flavia's workshop opened again, and Penelope came out, wrapping her scarf about her. "I'm ready, Master Camilla! Sorry to keep you waiting!"

Camilla smiled. "Not to worry, Penelope. I'm glad to have run into Octavia."

Penelope gave Octavia a hard glare before looking firmly away.

"Let's go now," Master Camilla said. She took a few steps, her guards and Penelope trailing behind her. She stopped and looked back at Octavia. Her charms swayed and clinked. She was still smiling. "Go on up now, Octavia. My niece has much to teach you. She is nothing like her mother, for which we are all thankful." A brief shadow passed over her eyes; it looked, for a second, almost like fear. "We take care of each other in Vittoria. We always have, and we always will, no matter what dangers find their way here."

With that, Master Camilla swept away, out of the archway and toward the town square.

"Ugh, Crafters are so strange," Albus said, when she was out of earshot. "And soon you'll be one of them."

"Not by choice," Octavia grumbled.

"Yeah, yeah. I'll be back this evening to walk you home."

"I know."

"Don't get into any trouble."

"I *know*."

Albus shoved her shoulder playfully. "See you later."

Octavia rolled her eyes at her brother as he walked away. She pulled open the door to the workshop and climbed the stairs.

Master Flavia was standing by the window, looking out on the river and the gray morning. She didn't turn around when Octavia entered, so Octavia awkwardly shed her coat and scarf and hung them on hooks.

"Master Flavia?"

Flavia finally turned from the window. "Good morning, Octavia. Thank you for coming."

As though Octavia had any kind of choice. "I saw Master Camilla and Penelope outside."

"Ah. Yes. I was not expecting a visit from my dear aunt this morning. She wants Penelope's help making visits around town. I suspect she wants to sniff out anybody who might be fibbing about their winter supplies, and having Penelope fluttering about is a good cover."

Octavia felt both uncomfortable and strangely proud that Master Flavia would speak to her so frankly about Master Camilla—and about Penelope, who really did flutter.

Without waiting for a reply, Master Flavia nodded sharply. "Never mind them. Let's get started, shall we?"

Master Flavia gave Octavia a quick tour around the workshop, showing her the workbenches where she prepared her charms, the endless shelves of ingredients gathered in jars, the washroom for scrubbing all the supplies clean, the hearth with its crackling fire, the library teeming with books, and the buckets and pulley system for lifting water from the river. Octavia tried to take it all in, but she knew right away that she would never be able to remember where everything was supposed to go.

"Now." Flavia began to collect ingredients and piled them on the workbench. "I'm going to show you how to extract magic from the river. Draw a bucketful and bring it here."

Octavia fetched a bucket of river water, sloshing a little onto her trousers and boots as she carried it across the room. Master Flavia helped her lift it onto the workbench, then patted the stool beside her and invited Octavia to sit. The four metal gate keys Flavia had brought out the other day now hung along a string over the workbench, gleaming brighter than they had, with a bluish-black sheen that was uncomfortable to look at. Octavia tore her gaze away to focus on what Flavia was saying.

"We'll start with a very small sample. This pan is copper, but any metal would work just as well," Flavia said. She ladled some of the water into a pan over a hot brazier and began to stir it slowly. She glanced at Octavia. "Do you have a question? Go ahead and ask. I know you don't want to be here, but that doesn't mean you should be bored."

"I was just wondering . . . Where does the magic come from?" Flavia lifted an eyebrow, and Octavia hurried to explain. "I mean, I know it comes from the river, and the river carries it from Aeterna, and the sorcerers made it, but how did they do that? Didn't it have to come from somewhere first?"

"Ah." Flavia continued to stir; the wooden ladle made a soft scraping sound as it brushed against the copper pan. "The short answer is that we don't really know how the first sorcerers created magic. They kept it secret and only passed it to their own apprentices, and those secrets have been lost over time."

"Since the war?"

"Oh, it started long before that," Flavia said. "By the time the war began, most sorcerers were simply reusing the magic their forebears had created, although some, including my mother and aunt, still knew how to create their own. The more complicated answer is that, as far as we understand it, magic can only be created by sacrificing something else, something important and valuable to the sorcerer. I don't mean valuable in the way of riches or belongings. I mean valuable in the way that has meaning and power only to the person who chooses to sacrifice it."

"Like what?" Octavia had trouble imagining what such a thing would be.

"Another good question. The answer would vary depending on which sorcerer you asked. But, of course, they wouldn't answer, even if you did ask. I asked my mother once, when I was a child."

Octavia's breath caught. She had not expected Flavia to bring up her infamous mother so casually.

"She was able to create her own magic. So was Camilla, before she turned her back on sorcery. They learned together, when they were young, from their own mother."

"Your grandmother?" Octavia said.

"Yes, although I never really thought of her that way," Flavia said. She was still stirring the water, still watching it whirl with a thoughtful expression. "I only met her a few times. She was a strange, cold woman. When she spoke, it was as though she didn't really see you, as though you were nothing but a distraction. My mother said she had not always been that way, that she had once been warm and loving, but then she had devoted herself to sorcery. I always wondered . . . Hand me that blue pot there, the small one."

Octavia passed her a small clay pot with a wooden stopper.

Flavia opened it with one hand and tipped a bit of its contents into the water.

"This is pyre dust from a butcher's bonfire. We use it because it is made up of something that used to be alive," said Flavia, as she stirred the dust into the pan of water. As Octavia watched, the heated water began to shimmer with a strange, oily sheen. "Because magic was created by living things—by people—it is best drawn out by something that also has the memory of being alive."

"What did you always wonder about?" Octavia asked. "About your grandmother?"

"Ah, yes. I never knew for certain, and I certainly could never ask her, but I wondered if that was what my grandmother had sacrificed to create her magic and gain power as a sorcerer. The warmth she used to show to her daughters. The love she used to have."

Master Flavia spoke calmly, as though she were discussing nothing of great importance, but there was a hitch in her voice, one that gave Octavia a cold, quivering feeling. She had grown up hearing endless stories about the greedy sorcerers of Aeterna and how they had dedicated themselves to the pursuit of absolute power. But she had never thought before what it would have been like to know a sorcerer who was doing just that, to watch somebody cut away parts of themselves to become stronger. It was a horrifying thought. She wanted to push it away.

"My grandmother's specialty was controlling the weather—a type of magic that requires both immense power and immense hubris, and one she did not pass on to her daughters. As you've probably heard, my mother was a skilled healer," Flavia went on. "Camilla was a talented artificer, before she gave up sorcery. She could use her magic to build things and create contraptions," Flavia explained, at Octavia's questioning look. "She used to devise and play the cleverest musical instruments. She loved music with all her heart. But she doesn't anymore."

"Is that what she gave up?" Octavia asked.

"It is at least part of it. But there was probably more. She and my mother were quite close before the war, you know. The best of friends as well as sisters. But once the fighting began, everything changed. At first, the sorcerers of Aeterna were in agreement about how to subdue the rebellious lowland cities. But that agreement didn't last, and the sorcerers began to fight amongst themselves—and that included my mother and aunt. As their methods and goals diverged, so did they. They both gained so much power, but in doing so it became easy for them to turn against each other."

"They . . . they gave up *each other*?" Octavia asked, horrified. She tried to imagine wanting magic and power so much she would give up her love for Hana, or for any of her siblings or her parents, or even for Rufus and his family. It was impossible. There was no prize great enough. She felt guilty just thinking about it. "They chose that? Just to do more powerful magic?"

"I don't know for certain," Flavia said. "But I have always suspected. They were not the only ones to make such extreme choices during the war. The sorcerers had been in power for so long that when they felt they were losing even a small part of that power, they were willing to do anything to keep it." Flavia tapped the metal pan gently and watched the water ripple. "The look on your face tells me you have another question."

Octavia blinked. She recognized that Flavia was changing the subject, and it took her a second to remember what she wanted to ask.

"What's the difference between using magic like you do and the way sorcerers used it?" Octavia asked. She was thinking about how Sima hadn't seemed to know the difference between Crafters and sorcerers. "Isn't it still magic?"

Flavia lifted the ladle to peer at the water, which was now faintly blue and gray. "As Crafters we agree to follow the rules decided upon after the war. Do you know the rules?"

Everybody in Vittoria knew the rules. They were recited every summer at the Rite of Survival, while the land around Vittoria burned. Octavia repeated them dutifully. "We do not use magic to wage war. We do not use magic to cause harm. We do not use magic on ourselves or our fellow townspeople. We do not use magic to create weapons. We use magic only to protect Vittoria and its people." She frowned thoughtfully as she finished. "That's the only difference? The rules?"

"The rules themselves are only words," Flavia said. "The sorcerers of Aeterna did not have even that. They did as they pleased, to whomever they pleased, and never cared for the consequences until the lowland cities rebelled."

"So it's the same magic," Octavia said slowly, "but the difference is in how you use it. It's different if you use it to protect people."

"Precisely. The difference is entirely in the choices we make. We decided, after the war, that magic was a tool to be used for the common good, not a way for individuals to gain power. That is what separates us from the sorcerers who wrought so much destruction." As she spoke, the water in the pan grew cloudy, then filled with long threads of filmy black material. Flavia sighed. "That's what we get for allowing ourselves to be distracted. We've heated the pyre dust too long. Let's discard this attempt and try another."

By the end of the day, Octavia had managed to successfully extract magic from river water using pyre dust, bone meal, and dried pine needles. None of the magic was stable enough to be used for a charm, but Flavia assured her that was normal for first extraction attempts. She sent Octavia home just as the evening bells began to ring.

Albus hadn't arrived yet. Octavia would get both of them into trouble if she walked home alone, so she waited, hopping from one foot to another to dispel the cold. Darkness fell quickly, as there were heavy clouds sitting low over Vittoria.

"You. You're the baker's girl."

Octavia twisted and turned mid-hop, startled by the voice behind her. She landed awkwardly and had to catch the wall to keep her balance. There was somebody standing at the entrance to the arch. In the darkness, all Octavia could see were stooped shoulders and a sagging hood.

"Yes?" She hoped her sudden fear wasn't apparent in her voice. "What do you want?"

The person stepped closer and pushed their hood back. It was Willa, Bram's mother.

"Is it true what they're saying?" Willa said. She was a small woman, not much taller than Octavia, and her face had the gaunt, pale look of somebody who had not been eating or sleeping properly. "Did you find people outside the wall? You brought them back?"

"Um." Octavia took a step back. She didn't like the angry, intense look in Willa's eyes. "Yeah. No. I mean, yes, I did? But just one girl. Not a whole group."

Willa's hand snapped out quickly to grab the front of Octavia's coat. "This girl, is she the one my Bram met?"

"He met someone?"

"He told me he met somebody outside the walls," Willa said. "He was watching them. He wanted to know what they were doing."

Octavia tried to step away again, but Willa's grip on her coat was strong. "He saw the caravan on the road?"

"He didn't mention a caravan. He saw a solitary stranger. He first spotted them weeks ago."

"Weeks?" Octavia repeated. Sima's caravan would have been miles away in the weeks before Bram died. But Octavia remembered what Sima had said about searching for somebody in Aeterna, about how other travelers had told her family where to go.

Willa nodded. "Since before the harvest. They were hiding in the mist."

"What do you mean, hiding in the mist? That sounds like . . . like some kind of magic. Was he sure it was a person?"

"Quite sure," said Willa. "Because eventually they saw him as well. He spoke to them. More than once. He wanted to tell everyone there was somebody out there. But I made him keep it a secret." Willa looked at Octavia steadily. Her eyes were rimmed with red and watery with tears, but there was no vagueness or befuddlement in her expression. "I thought it would keep him safe, if he didn't tell anybody else. I only wanted to keep him safe."

Octavia's heart was beating so fast she was sure Willa could hear it. "Did you tell the council?" she asked.

Willa shook her head. "I tried. I tried to tell Camilla what Bram had told me, but she told me I was confused. She told me I had misunderstood. She told me my *own son* had lied to me. My son did not lie to me." The anger in Willa's voice echoed through the archway. "Once a sorcerer, always a sorcerer. No matter how well she's fooled everyone."

Octavia stared at Willa in shock. She had never heard anybody speak about Master Camilla like that. People who came into the bakery sometimes murmured that she was too old to lead properly or had held power for too long, and the Hunters sometimes grumbled that she didn't fully understand the dangers outside the wall, but nobody ever accused her of still using sorcery.

Or if they did, Octavia realized, they did it in secret.

Willa spat on the street. "My boy told me what he found outside the wall. I couldn't make them believe me, but you can. You brought back proof. You can make them—"

"Octavia?"

Willa released her coat, and Octavia jumped backward. Albus was standing at the entrance to the archway.

"Uh. You ready to go?"

"Um, yeah, I was just . . ."

But Willa was already drawing her hood up and hurrying away. She didn't look back as she faded into the gray twilight.

"Who was that?" Albus asked.

"Bram's mom," Octavia said.

Albus lifted his eyebrows. "What did she want?"

Octavia thought for a long moment before answering. "She misses Bram."

9

In the Chamber of Truth and Lies

———⟩⟩⟩———

Octavia had never been inside the Council Hall before. She hunched her shoulders as she passed through the tall wooden doors, which were carved with intricate images, symbols, and words in ancient languages that nobody spoke anymore. She didn't like the way the black wood looked oily and slick in the gray morning.

She didn't know who she was expecting to greet her inside, but it definitely wasn't Penelope. The older girl gave Octavia a weak smile and said, "My father told me to show you the way."

Octavia nodded. She wished she hadn't eaten breakfast. She wished Mom or Dad or even Master Flavia could be here with her, but Master Camilla had been very clear: Octavia was to speak to the council alone.

"You don't have to be scared," Penelope said, as she led Octavia down a long, dim hallway.

"I'm not scared," Octavia said.

"The councilors act all stern and important, but really they're not so bad. Just tell them the truth. That's all they want. Then everything can go back to normal." Penelope walked a few steps in silence, then said, quietly, "Everything needs to be normal again."

Octavia didn't know what to say. She was going to tell the truth, but the truth meant that nothing could go back to normal. The truth meant that everything the people of Vittoria believed would have to change.

Penelope led her to the entrance of a chamber at the end of the corridor. She didn't go inside or announce Octavia's presence. All she did was whisper, "Good luck," before pulling the doors closed.

The room was long, narrow, and windowless, with a high ceiling and dark floors. The only light came from dozens of metal sconces with fat, dripping candles and tall braziers filling the room with smoke. At the far end of the room was a curve of seven wooden chairs with high backs, and in the chairs sat the members of the council.

Master Camilla was in the center. Beside her was Master Etius, the man some people called Camilla's sheepdog, although never where he could hear them. Octavia recognized the others by sight even if she didn't know their names. There was an empty chair at the end of the row. Octavia felt a pang of dismay, because the missing councilor was Master Cicerus, the kindly old healer who was training Rufus. She had been hoping to see at least one friendly face on the council.

"Good morning, Octavia!" Master Camilla called out. She raised her hand, as though she was waving to Octavia on a busy street. The charms on her chain bracelets jingled faintly. "We're so glad you were able to join us."

She said it like Octavia had had a choice, like anybody could refuse a request to speak to the council. Octavia kept her head high and her shoulders straight, trying to walk like Mom or Hana would walk, unafraid and unhesitating. But her boots clomped on the polished wood floor as she crossed the room, and she felt small and clumsy and round in her winter coat. Her knitted hat was itching her hair; she didn't know if she should take it off or not. She finally decided to remove both her hat and her gloves, and she did so nervously, stuffing them into her pockets and smoothing down her unruly hair as she approached the council. She couldn't stop thinking about Willa's words the night before: *Once a sorcerer, always a sorcerer.*

"Good morning," Camilla said again. "We're going to get started, even though Master Cicerus isn't yet here. He was called away to tend to an emergency."

"Not that he ever does anything but nap anyway," one councilor said, and the others snickered.

Camilla ignored them. "There is no reason to be nervous. We only want to ask you some questions about that terrible night you spent outside the walls."

"It wasn't that terrible," Octavia said.

Camilla laughed, and a few of the others chuckled politely. Octavia flushed with embarrassment.

"I told you she was very brave," Camilla said. "Now, Octavia, all we ask is that you tell us the truth. Our only concern is protecting the people of Vittoria. Do you understand?"

She knew what Camilla wanted to hear. "Yes. I understand."

"Very good! Then let us begin. Master Etius will ask the questions." Camilla nodded to the bearded man who sat beside her. "Answer everything he asks honestly, Octavia. We will know if you are lying."

Master Etius was a man of moderate height, with gray hair and gray eyes, dressed in an impractical white jacket and boots that looked like they had never stepped in a puddle of mud. Octavia didn't know much about him besides his unkind nickname, only that he was the councilor in charge of enforcing Vittoria's rules and laws, and most adults believed he would be the most powerful councilor when Camilla retired or passed away. He dealt with people who made serious trouble. She didn't know anybody who got into the kind of trouble Master Etius handled.

Until now, she thought. She swallowed nervously.

Master Etius stood and walked over to Octavia, stopping only a few paces away.

"You must not lie to us," he said. His voice was higher than Octavia had expected, a bit wheezy and hoarse, as though none of his words had quite enough air. "Do you understand?"

"Yes," said Octavia.

"You must tell the truth."

"I will."

"You must answer every question with complete honesty."

"I will," Octavia said again.

"Oh, just get on with it, Etius," another councilor said. "We haven't got all day."

Etius didn't take his eyes off Octavia. "Begin with why you were outside the walls."

Octavia told her story again. It should have been easier now, as she had already told her parents everything, but Master Etius's pale eyes and the watchful silence of the other councilors made her so nervous she stammered and backtracked and confused herself. She told them about wanting to practice so she might become a Hunter, about tracking the little Ferox through the orchard terraces, about realizing that darkness was falling only when she was far from Vittoria and high above Hermit Road.

"I wanted to run back to town," Octavia said. "I started to run. But there was a Ferox. A different one, I mean. Not the one I was chasing. A big one."

Master Etius said, "You say it was dark, yet you saw this larger Ferox clearly. Describe it."

"Oh. Oh, okay." Octavia thought about it a moment, remembering the horrible creature as best she could. "It was about the size of a bear—a big bear, fully grown. It was made mostly of metal and wood, but there was some kind of hide over the outside. Its snout was a long, curved piece of metal."

"And it spoke to you?"

"Yes. It was saying 'help me' and some other things."

"How did it speak?"

Octavia hesitated. "I don't understand."

"Was it crying? Shouting? Pleading?"

Was that what Ferox were supposed to sound like? Octavia felt a rush of doubt as she looked over the listening councilors. "It was, well, it was just talking. Like a regular voice. It kept repeating itself."

"Are you quite sure the voice came from the Ferox?"

Octavia looked at Master Etius in surprise. "Yes. It was right in front of me."

"How far was it?" The question came from another of the councilors, an older woman. "What do you mean by 'right' in front of you?"

"Oh, um, about . . . maybe about thirty feet when it came out of the woods, but closer when it started to chase me?"

"You don't know?" Master Etius said.

"It was—it was getting dark, and I was really scared," Octavia said. "It might have been forty feet. I started to run."

"Was it thirty feet or forty feet?"

Octavia was getting flustered. In her memory, the Ferox was so big and so close, its bulk and its smell and its eerie, horrible human voice surrounding her so completely the woods and the mountains had all but faded away.

"I don't know," she said. "I started running right away."

"Did you think you could *outrun* it?" another councilor asked, incredulous.

"I—no!" Octavia looked from him to Etius, growing more and more nervous. "I just wanted to get away!"

"Trained Hunters with much more skill and speed than you have tried to run from Ferox and failed," Master Etius said. "As you well know, as your own sister foolishly perished in just such a manner."

It was like a punch in the gut. Octavia wasn't expecting him to bring up Hana. She stared at Etius, her mouth open, her eyes stinging. She didn't know what to say.

Etius looked at Octavia impassively. "Did you think you might survive where she had not?"

"I didn't—I was just—I didn't think anything," Octavia finally managed to say. Her voice was small, little more than a whisper. "I was scared. I don't think I would have been fast enough if Sima hadn't shot the Ferox."

"Did you see when the arrow was shot?"

Octavia started to nod, then shook her head. "No, I mean, I only saw it when it hit, it was flaming and caught the Ferox in the—I don't know, maybe it was the throat? Or the mouth?"

"You aren't certain? But you said you saw it," said Etius.

"I'm—I'm not sure," Octavia admitted. In her mind, the Ferox was a looming dark shape over her, then it was aflame, and it was roaring, and she had a chance to get away. "It was so fast. I just wanted to get to the tower."

"Did you not think it strange your apparent savior showed up right when you reached the watchtower?"

"It wasn't—I was running for the watchtower," Octavia said. "And Sima was there, but she was coming down the road, she was—she just happened to be there, it wasn't like . . ."

"Like what?" Etius said. "Like she was trying to lure you to the watchtower?"

"No! She wasn't luring me anywhere! She saved my life."

"Are you quite sure of that?" Etius said. He stepped forward; Octavia shuffled backward. "It sounds to me as though you were successfully lured into a trap. A true Hunter would have seen the trap for what it was, but as you are a child, and inexperienced, you fell for the clumsiest of ruses."

"No, it was—it wasn't like that!" Octavia said.

"And because of your ignorance and naivete, you have endangered all of us," Etius said.

"Sima's not dangerous! She didn't hurt me! She helped me!"

"You would taunt those you have endangered with your rashness by proclaiming your own good fortune?" Master Etius said.

"No! That's not what I meant, I only meant—"

"That is enough, Etius," said Camilla firmly. "You've upset the poor girl."

Etius's eyes were as narrow and pale as shards of glass. There was the slightest hint of a smile upon his lips. He stepped back from Octavia. "I am finished. It is obvious what happened. The child has been deceived by an unusual Ferox."

"*What?* What do you mean?" Octavia demanded. "You can't mean—"

"We have never known one to disguise itself so well before," Master Etius went on, "but there is no other possibility."

"You can't mean Sima," Octavia said, her voice shaking. It had to be a misunderstanding. Master Etius couldn't mean what she thought he meant. "Sima's not a monster. She's a person!"

But none of the council members were surprised by Master Etius's words, nor did they pay any attention to Octavia's protests.

"It was always very unlikely that a girl could have survived a Ferox attack," said one of the council members, and the others murmured in agreement.

"By herself? It's impossible," said another.

Then they were all speaking at once.

"The creatures were designed to be deceptive."

"We've never truly understood the extent of magical forms."

"We should dispatch the Hunters right away."

"The creatures' creator was more clever than we want to give them credit for."

Octavia realized, with a horrible sinking fear in her chest, that they had already known what Etius was going to say. They were only discussing it now to reassure themselves and each other. They were all decided.

"Sima saved my life!" Octavia cried, but nobody was listening to her. "It wasn't a trap! She's not—she's helped me! She's a person! There are people out there! I promised I would help her! You have to—"

The chamber doors banged open. Octavia spun around as the councilors fell quiet.

A guard rushed into the room. Her face was pale, her eyes wide. "Councilors! I'm sorry to interrupt, but there's been—there's a—" She gulped in a breath. "It's awful, there's been—"

Master Camilla rose from her chair. "My dear, calm yourself. Tell us what has happened."

"There's been an attack! There are Ferox in Vittoria!"

The councilors erupted into a flurry of exclamations and shouts, with questions and demands echoing from the high walls of the chamber. Octavia's mouth was open, but she couldn't say anything, even if she could be heard over the clamor. She felt as though a heavy stone had dropped into her stomach.

Ferox in Vittoria. It was daytime. The gates had been locked all night. It wasn't possible.

Unless, she thought, with a new, queasy sensation, *unless they're right. Unless the Ferox can disguise themselves now.*

"Quiet!" Master Camilla called out. She clapped her hands loudly, making the charms on her wrists clink like tiny bells. "Quiet! Councilors, calm yourselves!"

The other councilors stopped talking at once.

"We will *not* panic until we have all the facts," said Camilla.

"If I may," said a new voice. It was quiet and accompanied by the slow shuffle of footsteps. Master Cicerus came into the chamber behind the guard, leaning on his cane. His expression was troubled, his gray hair messy. "I think gathering the facts is indeed the best approach, before we leap to conclusions."

"You know what this is about?" said a councilor hotly. "Tell us what's going on!"

"Has there been an attack?" another asked.

"Is the prisoner secure?"

"Is there still danger?"

The guard said, "I saw the victim myself! All the blood, there was so much—"

Master Cicerus touched her arm gently. "Thank you for accompanying me. You can go now."

The guard looked to Master Camilla for her approval before hurrying away; she shut the doors behind her.

"Tell us what this is about, Cicerus," said Master Etius.

"Yes, yes, of course." Cicerus tapped the floor with the tip of his cane. He looked worried and thoughtful, but he didn't have the look of a man who feared Ferox were running loose inside Vittoria. "Before you ask, yes, the young stranger is still secure in her cell downstairs. I asked just now, and the guards confirm she has not gone anywhere since being locked in."

Octavia pressed her lips together to keep her surprise from showing. Sima was downstairs in this very building. And if she was locked away, she couldn't have hurt anybody.

"Yet somebody was attacked," Master Camilla said.

"I'm afraid so," said Master Cicerus. "The victim is Willa, mother of the boy who died the other day. I was summoned this morning when her neighbors discovered her in her home. But it was too late. She was already dead."

"No!" Octavia gasped.

"How did she die?" asked Master Etius.

Master Cicerus nodded gravely. "It does appear to have been a violent attack. Her wounds were extensive."

"No," Octavia said again, weakly. Willa had been so strong and fierce when she approached Octavia last night.

"Another Ferox must have sneaked in while we were distracted by the first," Master Etius said. "It is hiding somewhere in the town as we speak. We must arrange a search."

Master Cicerus held up his hand. "I said it was a violent attack. I did not say it was a Ferox attack."

One councilor scoffed. "What else could it be? A particularly angry goat?"

"No," said Master Cicerus calmly. "It might have been a person."

The councilors all burst into argument at that, talking over one another again in voices that grew louder with every moment. It was impossible, they said. That didn't happen in Vittoria. Nobody would hurt a grieving woman. It had to be a beast. A monster. The torrent of words drummed against Octavia's thoughts. Willa had wailed with heartrending misery when they brought Bram's body through Wyvern Gate. And last night her eyes had blazed when she spoke about her son. She had gripped Octavia's coat with so much strength in her hands, so much anger in her eyes. So much love and grief for her son who had died so unfairly. It was hard to believe she could be gone.

"Our duty is clear," said Camilla. Her voice rang through the chamber; the councilors fell quiet. She alone had not jumped to her feet when the guard burst in. "We will find the monster behind this attack and stop it. But first I think we should be thanking Octavia. She has done a great service for Vittoria."

"What?" That was the last thing Octavia expected to hear.

"Is that so?" Master Etius said skeptically.

"Indeed. We have long theorized about how the Ferox might be changing, but we have never had proof until now. We have known they could mimic human speech, acquire new forms, and apply a rudimentary sort of cunning to seek their prey. But thanks to what Octavia has brought back to us, we know exactly how far their abilities have evolved. We know they can now disguise themselves so thoroughly they can fool a child, at least. And we know they can cooperate with one another to infiltrate our defenses."

"We don't know that," Master Cicerus said, a stern edge creeping into his mild voice. "As I said, it might have been—"

"We heard you," snapped Master Etius.

"And we will consider your theory, because it would be irresponsible not to," said Master Camilla. "But we all know that our friends and neighbors do not go about slaughtering each other for no reason. The Ferox are now, as they have ever been, the only true enemy we face. To deny that danger is to be disloyal to Vittoria and all that we stand for as survivors."

Camilla rose to her feet and stepped forward. She smoothed one hand over the delicate chains of charms that hung around her neck.

"Master Etius, you will arrange for the guards to search Vittoria thoroughly. A creature in disguise will not go unnoticed for long, but there are many places for an infiltrator to hide. Find it immediately. Find out where it came from. Stop it before it harms anybody else."

"Yes, Master Camilla," Etius said.

"The danger is very real," Camilla said, "but good can come of this tragedy. It is a marvelous opportunity to study them so that we will be prepared the next time the creatures attempt such a ruse. We are in agreement, yes? We'll begin tomorrow. We will study the aberrant Ferox we have in captivity before disposing of it."

The words shook Octavia to her bones. She meant Sima. Octavia didn't understand why none of the councilors were arguing, nor how they could accept so easily what should have been impossible. Wouldn't the Hunters have noticed if the Ferox could change like that? Why weren't they asking more questions about how Willa had died? Everything was happening so fast, all of their doubts swept away as soon as Camilla spoke.

What Octavia did understand was that even if there was a monster hiding in Vittoria, it wasn't Sima. Sima was a *person*. She had saved Octavia's life and grumbled about walking through the snow and curled onto her side while she slept. She was locked up and alone and she couldn't have hurt anybody.

"Wait," Octavia said, Camilla's words catching up to her. "What do you mean? What does 'disposing of it' mean?"

Nobody answered. The meeting was over, and the councilors were already leaving.

"What are you going to do to her?" Octavia demanded. She darted forward, but a hand clamped onto her arm to stop her.

Master Etius tugged her back. "It is not your concern anymore."

"Are you going to hurt her? What are you going to do?"

Master Camilla walked by without even looking at Octavia. "The meeting is adjourned," she said. She smiled at her fellow councilors as she neared the door. "I am so proud of this council for taking swift action. We will protect Vittoria."

The councilors hurried after her, including Master Etius. The last to leave was Master Cicerus, who shuffled over to Octavia and said, in his papery old man's voice, "Help an old man outside, Octavia, if you will."

"What are they going to do to Sima?" Octavia asked.

Master Cicerus's only answer was, "Walk with me outside."

Master Cicerus didn't need her help, but she offered her arm and stayed by his side until they emerged from the Council Hall into the gray morning. As soon as they came down the steps, Rufus fell into step beside them; he had been waiting right outside. His blond hair stuck out from under the edge of his knitted cap, his bright green scarf was knotted around his neck, and he would have looked completely normal if it weren't for the tiredness in his eyes and the anxious look on his face. "Is the meeting over? What did they say about Willa? What are they going to do?"

"Master Etius will lead a search through town," Cicerus said.

Rufus frowned. He rubbed his hands together—he wasn't wearing his gloves—and Octavia spotted a ruddy smudge on his sleeve. Blood, she realized with a start. It was blood. He had gone with Master Cicerus to Willa's home. He had seen what happened to her.

Octavia said, "Willa came to see me—"

She stopped as the door to the Council Hall opened and two of the other council members came out. They nodded politely to Cicerus, glanced warily at Octavia, and ignored Rufus entirely.

When they were several steps away, Octavia said, "She came to see me last night."

But then she paused. She looked around nervously. She bit her lip. It wasn't like she could get Bram and Willa in trouble, but she didn't want to say more out in the open where anybody could hear.

Master Cicerus said, "Let us walk you to Master Flavia's workshop. Come along, Rufus."

As the three of them made their way toward the Crafters' Quarter, Octavia asked, "Was it really a Ferox that killed her?"

"It was certainly made to look that way," Master Cicerus said. He sounded troubled and distracted. "There was a great deal of damage inside her home, suggesting a violent confrontation. But the timing of the attack is in question. One neighbor claims to have heard a commotion just after the evening bells. Another claims to have heard a shout just before the morning bell. But the first was at work in her own cellar and the second was asleep in his bed, so both might be mistaken. It makes more sense to me that such a brutal attack would have happened under the cover of darkness, when there were no witnesses."

"It was awful," Rufus said quietly.

They reached the archway on River Street. Master Cicerus did not knock on Flavia's door; he opened it and climbed the stairs, with Octavia and Rufus trailing behind. When they reached the workshop, Flavia was seated at her workbench. She did not look surprised to see them.

"The meeting is over already?" she said.

Master Cicerus removed his coat and sat on one of the benches. "It doesn't take very long for everybody to acknowledge what they have already decided," he said.

Master Flavia pursed her lips, unsurprised. "I heard about Willa. Penelope brought the news, but I've sent her home for now. Are you okay, Octavia? I know that being questioned by the council is never pleasant. I've been in that position myself more than a few times."

Octavia shrugged awkwardly. It had been awful, that was true, but it was nothing compared to the horror of Willa's death and the danger Sima still faced. She looked from Master Cicerus to Master Flavia, then at Rufus, who was watching her with a worried expression. She wanted to take Rufus aside and ask him if they could trust Master Cicerus. She wanted to know what both Cicerus and Flavia were thinking.

"Sima isn't a Ferox," Octavia said to Master Cicerus.

Master Cicerus raised one of his extremely bushy eyebrows. "We know that. The Ferox have not spontaneously developed the ability to perfectly mimic humans. But what we know carries little weight when Camilla has made a decision, even if her decision is driven by fear rather than sense. What Camilla decides guides the council's actions. They rarely want to question that her choices are what is best for Vittoria."

"Is she . . . is she lying on purpose?" Octavia asked.

Cicerus and Flavia exchanged a significant look. They did not look surprised by her question, only worried and uncertain.

"My aunt keeps her true thoughts to herself. She has always placed the protection of Vittoria above all other considerations, but her judgment might be clouded. Without proof, it would be reckless to make an accusation about her motives." Flavia stood and began to pace in front of her workbench. She picked up jars and set them down, touched her notes absently, tapped at the four black gate keys still hanging on a string. "This is unfamiliar territory. We have trusted in Camilla's protection for so long, we are like travelers without a map when it comes to doubting her. But . . . there is a child that needs help. That we cannot deny, whatever my aunt is thinking."

"Camilla will send the Hunters out to scout the road tomorrow," Master Cicerus said. "She's stalled them as long as she can get away with. They're already upset about that."

"Why didn't she send them already?" Rufus asked. Octavia's mother had been asking the same thing for days; the Hunters didn't like when the councilors, who never left Vittoria, told them how to do their jobs.

"I suspect she wanted more information before she did so."

"Part of the caravan that was attacked is still in the road," Octavia said. "It's not even that far for Hunters. They'll find it."

"I wonder if they will," Cicerus said.

"Or admit to finding it," Rufus added darkly.

Octavia wanted to argue that the Hunters wouldn't *lie*. But while she would have been certain of it only a week ago, she couldn't claim the same now. She didn't know what the Hunters would say. Her own mother didn't even believe her.

"What is she going to do to Sima? Is she going to hurt her?" Octavia had to stop to take a breath. "Is she going to kill her?"

Master Flavia turned to face Octavia. "My aunt won't call it that, as the Ferox are not truly alive."

"Sima isn't a Ferox!" Octavia cried. "We have to help her. We have to—she didn't even want to come here. It's my fault she's here."

She should have let Sima go to Aeterna, no matter how dangerous the journey would be. Sima could be with her family now, instead of locked away by people who believed her to be a monster.

"Let's not waste time debating what Camilla is going to do," said Master Cicerus. "Camilla will do what she wants. She is predictable in that way, if nothing else. A more important question is what are we going to do."

"We have to help Sima," Octavia said again, her voice very small. She rubbed tears from her eyes and cleared her throat. Master Flavia and Master Cicerus were listening. They were trying to help. She straightened her shoulders. "We *are* going to help her."

"But what can we do?" Rufus said.

Master Flavia reached out again to tap at the gate keys hanging above her workbench. They swung together, clinking softly. "Do you remember when I was a child," she said, with a small smile directed at Master Cicerus, "and we had to hide in barrels to sneak past the patrols and escape Aeterna during the war?"

A dear friend, she had said, when she told Octavia about her mother sending her away. That friend must have been Master Cicerus.

Master Cicerus raised one bushy eyebrow. "Are you thinking about barrels again?"

"Not quite," said Flavia. "But I think we can make a plan."

10

Octavia's Promise

---»»—

That evening at dinner, Mom was more energetic than she had been all week.

"Everything will be back to normal before long," she said. She spoke with a firm, decisive voice that Octavia hadn't heard her use in months. "The Hunters will move quickly. They'll find the danger."

News of Willa's death and the council meeting had spread, and most of the town was anxious and worried. Even though it hadn't yet been dark when Octavia headed home from Master Flavia's, most of the shops and houses were already closed up, with the doors locked and curtains drawn. People had crossed the street to steer clear of Octavia and Albus. At first Octavia had thought they were avoiding her, but then she noticed that they were all avoiding each other too. Everybody was wary of anybody they didn't know well.

Octavia stared at her plate. She felt eyes on her but she didn't dare look up. She was being good. She was being agreeable. She was doing everything she could not to raise her parents' suspicion.

To her surprise, it was Lavinia who asked, "But are there really Ferox in Vittoria? How is that even possible?"

"Now that we know they can disguise themselves, we'll find them," Mom said.

It was not an answer to Lavinia's question. And Mom kept saying *we* like she was heading out there with the Hunters to search.

"But . . ." Lavinia trailed off. Octavia risked a glance up to find her sister looking right at her. "But Octavia said . . ."

"Octavia made a mistake." With determined casualness, Mom reached over to run her hand over Octavia's frizzy braids. Octavia flinched. "It's easy to do when the enemy changes tactics and you don't have the training to adapt."

"We'll learn what the Hunters find soon enough," Dad said. "Until then, it's best that we stay together and safe."

Mom blinked. "Yes. Right. The Hunters will deal with the problem, and there won't be any harm done."

"Except Bram's mother," Augustus said. He was staring at his plate too. Bram had been the same age as him; although they weren't friends, there weren't so many young men in Vittoria that two of the same age could avoid crossing paths.

Mom's hand dropped away from Octavia's head. "Of course. That's why we need to trust the council."

The rest of the dinner was quiet and uncomfortable. Octavia didn't speak. She didn't know what the Hunters would find when they searched Vittoria, but she did know that they would find evidence of Sima's caravan on the road. They would find the tracks. They would look up East Road and know the wagon ruts led to Aeterna. They would know Octavia had been telling the truth.

What they would do after that, Octavia had no idea.

She asked to be excused as soon as she was finished eating. Dad nodded tiredly and told her to go to bed early.

Octavia climbed upstairs and paused outside the curtain to Hana's room. She listened for several seconds, her heart pounding in her chest. Nobody followed. They were still at the table. She shoved the curtain aside and stepped into the room. As quickly as she could, she grabbed Hana's old pack and began stuffing it with gear for winter travel. Warm clothes, good leather gloves, flint and rope and a tattered map. One of Hana's old bows that she had restrung for Octavia just weeks before she died. Octavia had Hana's knife already in her own pack upstairs. She added an extra waterskin. She stopped to listen and heard the clatter of dishes as her family cleared the table.

Octavia stashed the pack under Hana's bed and pushed the curtain aside to find Lavinia standing right outside.

"Oh, Octavia," she said.

The surprise on her face softened into something sadder as she looked past Octavia into Hana's room. It was all Octavia could do not to snap the curtain closed to block her sister's view. She had hidden the pack. There was nothing to see. But if Lavinia saw anything—if she suspected anything—the whole plan would be ruined.

Lavinia sighed. "I miss her so much. She always knew what to do when Mom gets like this." Lavinia smiled sadly. "I just wish . . . it's stupid. I just miss her."

"Me too," Octavia whispered.

Lavinia reached out and caught Octavia in a tight hug. She was warm and smelled of fresh bread and cinnamon. "It'll be okay. We'll be okay."

She went to her own room, humming a soft, sad song, leaving Octavia alone at the doorway to Hana's. Octavia stood there for several seconds, so surprised she couldn't make herself move. They didn't talk about how much they missed Hana. Nobody in the family ever said it aloud. Octavia had started to believe she was the only one. She wondered, now, if Lavinia had believed the same thing. And their brothers. If Mom did too. And Dad. If they had all been hiding their grief and their sadness away from each other so effectively that they forgot it was something they shared.

Voices rose from downstairs. Mom and Dad, and they sounded like they were arguing in the way they did sometimes, when they spoke in low, tight tones while pretending they weren't angry. Octavia couldn't make out what they were saying. She didn't want to. Feeling shaky and a little shivery, with the warmth of Lavinia's hug fading from her shoulders, she climbed upstairs to the attic room.

Octavia was in bed, fully dressed with the blanket pulled up to her chin, when Albus joined her in their room. Her eyes were closed, but she could still see the flicker of warm light from the candle.

He whispered, "Octavia? You asleep?"

She didn't answer. She didn't move. She didn't let herself relax when he blew out the candle and settled under his blankets. She heard him murmur something to one of the cats that always slunk into his bed, and she waited while his breathing softened. Even then, she kept waiting. She heard Augustus go into his room. Mom and Dad's voices finally fell quiet. Their bedroom door closed. The house was silent.

Octavia slipped out of bed. She grabbed her own pack from her chest, then climbed down the ladder to Hana's room to fetch the other one. She had tried to pack them the same way the Hunters did when they went out for long excursions, but they were lumpy and uneven. There was no time to fix them. She went down to the storeroom behind the bakery. She gathered nuts and dried fruit, cured meats and cheeses, stuffing as much as she could into the packs. She had no idea how much she needed. When she had fit as much as she could, she put on her coat, pulled a hat over her hair, and wrapped a scarf across her face.

It was time to go. Nobody had woken up.

Nothing was stopping her.

Octavia took a breath. She was growing warm, standing inside in her coat. The packs already felt heavy. She took another breath, held it for several seconds, and pushed open the back door.

Vittoria at night was always quiet, but tonight it was even quieter than usual. Octavia had expected there to be guards and Hunters about, searching for the Ferox supposedly lurking in the shadows, and every corner she turned, every alley she darted down, she was terrified of running into somebody. But she didn't see anybody. If there were people out, they weren't in this part of town.

She found the narrow alley that ran behind the building on Center Square. It was very dark there, with no light in any of the windows above, and Octavia nearly yelped in shock when she and a cat startled each other in the shadows. The cat fled, and Octavia waited just long enough to catch her breath before continuing. She crept along the alley until she was behind the Council Hall.

Once she was there, she tested every window and door she passed. Master Cicerus had told her there was one with a latch broken in such a way the guards never noticed if it was unlocked. When she had asked how he knew, he had only said everybody who regularly attended dull council meetings wanted a secret way to slip away unnoticed. She found the broken window halfway down the building, and her heart leapt with excitement. She left the packs lying on the ground in the alley and wriggled through the window. It led into a cool, dark room, illuminated only by a sliver of light beneath the door; it was some kind of storage room. She didn't hear anything outside the door, so she opened it carefully. She was beneath a broad set of stairs. There was nobody around.

She found the staircase leading into the basement. It was quiet downstairs as well. There was a long hallway, lit by a few candles in sconces, empty except for a single guard seated in a chair about halfway down.

Octavia jerked back around a corner when she saw him. Her heart was hammering. She held her breath. He wasn't that far away. Maybe fifteen feet. He could have seen her. She had been expecting at least one guard; she just hadn't known he would be *right there*. She squeezed her eyes shut, held her breath, and listened.

She heard a quick intake of breath down the hallway, then a loud, grating snore.

The snore was followed by another. And another.

The guard was asleep.

Exactly as planned.

Octavia let out her breath slowly and leaned out to look again. The guard was slumped in his chair with his legs stretched out and his head lolling to the side. A clay mug sat on the floor beside his chair. Octavia silently thanked Rufus and Master Cicerus for their sleeping draught and the council for sending the other guards out to chase shadows.

Octavia crept around the corner and down the hallway. Master Cicerus had warned her that the guard could still wake up, even with the sleeping draught in his blood, so she moved quietly, so very quietly, until she was right in front of him. There was a ring of keys at his belt, half hidden under one of his arms. Octavia looked around, hoping to see another set of keys hanging on a hook or something, but there were no others. She had to take them from his belt.

She reached for the keys but froze when the man snorted in his sleep and shifted his position. Octavia nudged his arm away from the keys. Carefully, carefully, she lifted the ring from the hook on his belt. The keys jingled, and the man shifted again. He mumbled a few unintelligible words. But he didn't wake.

Octavia tried a few keys before she found the right one. It clanked loudly as she turned it; she looked at the sleeping man. He didn't stir as she turned the metal handle and pulled the door open. The room beyond was dark and damp and smelled a bit stale, as though it hadn't been aired in several days.

"Sima?" she whispered.

No answer. It was the kind of darkness that felt like it had something waiting in it, the silence of held breath and wariness.

"Sima?"

There was movement—a rasp on stone—and, without warning, something burst from the shadows and knocked into her. For a panicked moment, she thought: she was wrong, the council was right, they *did* have a monster locked up here.

Then she felt hands on her shoulders and heard the angry splutter of words. A familiar voice. A whip of braided dark hair. It was Sima. Angry, shouting, striking at Octavia's front with rapid blows, but not a monster. Only Sima.

"Wait!" Octavia said. She tried to grab Sima's hands. "Wait, wait, wait, stop!"

"*You!*" hissed Sima, as she batted at Octavia's arms and kneed her in the side. "I should never have trusted the people of Vittoria! I knew better!"

"Sima! We have to be quiet! I'm trying to—"

There was a loud snort from the guard. Both turned to him. He shifted in his chair and crossed his arms over his chest, hugging himself. He was still asleep.

"We have to be quiet," Octavia whispered. "My friend gave him something to keep him asleep, but he still might wake up."

Sima was motionless for a second, then she shoved past Octavia and into the hallway. She looked in both directions.

"That way," Octavia said, pointing toward the stairs.

Sima hesitated. "What do you want?"

"I'm going to get you out of here. We have to go."

"Why?"

"Because it's not safe to stay!" Octavia said. The guard was mumbling in his sleep again. "We have to go!"

Sima didn't move. Octavia reached out, but Sima whipped her hand away quickly. Octavia closed her fingers into a fist and said, "I know this is my fault. I shouldn't have brought you here. They're going to—" The words caught in her throat. "They think you're a Ferox. They think you're attracting other creatures to Vittoria. We have to get you out of here."

"You lied to me," Sima said. "I don't believe anything you say."

The guard made another noise and raised his hand to scratch his nose.

"You don't have to believe me!" Octavia whispered. "Just let me get you out of here! We can find your family!"

"Why? What do you—"

"What?" said the guard. "Who?"

His eyes were open slightly, still bleary with sleep. He yawned loudly.

"Nothing," Octavia said, softly. "It's nothing. You can go back to sleep."

"Mmm. Okay." His eyes closed again.

Octavia glared at Sima, and Sima nodded. Together they crept down the hallway. Octavia only realized when it was too late that she had left the keys in the lock, but it hardly mattered now. The guard would know Sima was gone as soon as he woke. She just had to make sure they were far away by then.

She led Sima up the stairs and into the storage room, where the window was still hanging open. Octavia helped Sima through the window then scrambled out after her.

"What are we doing?" Sima hissed. "Tell me!"

Octavia dug warm clothes out of one pack and shoved them at Sima. "Put these on. We have to go. I'm going to get you out of Vittoria so you can go to Aeterna and find your family and warn them! We have to hurry!"

"Warn them about what?"

"The council. The Hunters. Everything! I promise I'll explain it, but we have to go!"

"Your promises mean nothing," Sima said.

Octavia was on the verge of tears. Sima had every reason to distrust her. She believed Octavia had lied and led her into a trap. She had spent days locked up because of Octavia. Octavia had no idea what she could say to get Sima to trust her again. She didn't even know if it was possible—but she did know that if they didn't run, she would never get the chance to try. There were guards searching the city. The council would not let Sima escape twice.

"I know you don't trust me. But we have to go anyway." She picked up Hana's old bow and held it out. "This is for you too. You're better with it than I am."

Sima pulled on the coat and hefted the pack before taking the bow. "Fine," she said. "We'll go."

Octavia led her away from the town square and across the river. They didn't see any guards on the way, although twice they heard voices and footsteps from the far end of a road. In the quiet northwest corner of Vittoria, a narrow irrigation canal flowed beneath the wall beside Oldgate, the smallest of Vittoria's seven gates. Oldgate had been locked up and unused since before Octavia was born.

Octavia slowed as she approached the gate. Sima was close behind her, looking around warily, starting at every sound.

There was a hiss of a voice in the darkness. "Octavia?"

Rufus, exactly where he was supposed to be.

"Good, you're here," Octavia said. "We have to hurry."

"Octavia," Rufus said.

He wasn't alone. Standing right beside him was her brother Albus.

11

Shadows and Ice

————»»————

"Octavia," Albus said, "what are you *doing*?"

Rufus said, miserably, "I'm sorry. I didn't know he followed me."

"I shouldn't have to be following anybody!" Albus said. "But then you were sneaking out and I lost track of you and I saw Rufus and *what are you doing*?"

His words echoed. Sima stepped back, glancing around quickly, like she was thinking of running away before they even made it beyond the wall. This was all wrong. Albus wasn't supposed to be here. He was supposed to be home, in bed, sleeping without a thought for anybody or anything except himself, the way he had been for months. Yet here he was, blocking their way out, ruining everything.

"Be quiet!" Octavia snapped. "It's got nothing to do with you! You shouldn't be here!"

"*You* shouldn't be here," Albus retorted. "None of you. Haven't you caused enough trouble—is that the stranger?" His gaze fell upon Sima for the first time. "But I thought—they said something attacked Bram's mom—"

Octavia stepped forward and shoved Albus with both hands. Albus rocked backward but caught Octavia's wrists before she could shove him again. "It wasn't Sima! They lied and I'm trying to keep her from being killed!"

"Who is that? Who was killed?" Sima asked, alarmed. "I've been in that room. They never let me out."

"We know," Rufus said quickly. "Master Cicerus tried to argue with the council and tell them she had nothing to do with it, but they've made up their minds."

"I don't understand," Albus said. "Something did kill Willa, didn't it?"

"Something or somebody," Octavia said, "but it wasn't Sima. Even Master Flavia thinks Master Camilla is wrong. What if . . . what if Camilla doesn't want anybody to think there are people outside the wall?" she asked. "Bram told his mom he saw people outside, and Willa told Camilla." Octavia paused to suck in a cold breath. "Now Willa is dead."

The same horror Octavia felt was plain on Albus's face. "You can't mean—you think Master Camilla is why Willa is dead? You think she did something?"

"I don't know!" Octavia cried.

"But that's . . ." Albus closed his mouth, opened it again. "But that's not possible. Is it?"

"I don't know," Octavia said again. It was such an awful thought, that the woman all of Vittoria had always trusted to keep them safe could have done something so terrible, but Octavia couldn't shake it. She just kept thinking about how angry Willa had been. How she had thought Camilla hadn't believed her.

Albus turned to Rufus. "Is that what you think too? Does your master think that?"

"I don't know," Rufus said. "But . . . if there was a Ferox loose in town, why would it kill just one person, who had one secret? It doesn't make any sense."

"All I know is that Willa tried to tell people that Bram saw strangers outside, and now she's dead so she can't tell anyone else," Octavia said.

"None of it makes sense," Albus said.

Sima made a frustrated noise. "Yes, it does. Your Master Camilla killed this woman to keep her from speaking out. You are all thinking it. You just don't want to say it out loud."

There was a long, heavy silence after she spoke. Nobody contradicted her, because she was right. As soon as the suspicion that Camilla was responsible for Willa's death had entered Octavia's mind, she had been unable to shake it.

"Nobody will believe us if we try to tell people," she said. "Everybody already thinks Sima is a monster. They'll just keep blaming her. Nobody will help."

"But you will?" Albus said. He was still holding her hands. His voice was low and earnest. "What are you going to do?"

"I just want to help Sima find her family. Her mom and little brother are out there somewhere. She wants to find them."

Albus abruptly let Octavia go. "You're going to send her out there by herself in the middle of the night? It's too dangerous!"

"Vittoria is too dangerous," Sima said sharply, although there was a waver in her voice. "I knew better than to come here. I would rather face monsters than sorcerers."

Albus rubbed his hands over his face. "We can talk to someone. We'll talk to Mom. She'll know what to—"

"She won't listen. You know she won't. She hasn't listened to anything I've said."

"We did talk to someone," Rufus added. "Master Flavia and Master Cicerus are going to try to talk to people, but it will take time. We can't leave Sima with the council."

"We're wasting time now," Sima said, stepping closer to Oldgate. "This is the way out? I'll go. You can all go home to your beds."

"You're not going alone," Octavia said. "I'm going with you."

"What?" said Sima.

"*What?*" said Albus. "You're not going anywhere!"

"I don't need your help!" Sima said. "I was fine before you ruined everything! I saved *you*, remember?"

"I know! That's why I'm helping you," Octavia said. "You don't know the way to the watchtowers or where the protected trails are. You didn't even know what road to take! That's how you ended up here in the first place. I have to show you the way. You can't stop us," she said to Albus. "And if you try you'll be just as bad as the rest of them. It will be your fault if they hurt Sima."

Albus let out a huge sigh. "Fine. Fine! What about you?" he said to Rufus.

Octavia began, "He's not—"

"I'm going with them," Rufus said.

"No, you're not!" Octavia replied. "That wasn't the plan!"

"It's the plan now," Rufus said. He was trying to sound calm, but his voice was shaking. "I gave the sleeping draught to the guard. Everybody's going to know it was me, and if I stay Master Cicerus will try to protect me, even though it will make everything harder. It's better if they think I disobeyed him to run away."

Octavia pushed past him and walked stubbornly to Oldgate. She dug the four keys out of her pocket; Flavia had told her to take all of them, so the guards would not immediately know which gate she had opened to escape and the Hunters would not know which direction to start searching. They would figure it out eventually, but any time she could buy was worth it. The first two keys did nothing, but the third scraped in the lock. It didn't turn yet, but there was the soft ting of something clanking, and the key tingled in her fingers. She held her breath. The shadows around the gate quivered and there was, faintly, a sound like a trickle of water that faded almost as soon as it began. The magic keeping the gate secure fell away, and finally Octavia was able to turn the key.

The lock clunked loudly. The gate's hinges creaked.

"Master Flavia's charms are amazing," Rufus whispered, echoing Octavia's thoughts. He pulled the gate open, tearing away the curtain of dried vines that hung across the archway. "We can go."

Sima was already shoving past Octavia and Albus to hurry outside. Rufus went after her, and Octavia moved to follow. She stopped when Albus put his hand on her arm.

"Where will you go?" Albus asked.

Octavia suddenly didn't want to leave him behind. "The closest watchtower."

"I mean after that."

Octavia looked beyond the gate to the snow-covered expanse of the burning ground with the dark canvas of the forest spread out beyond. It was starting to snow again, large whirling flakes that would cover their tracks. Octavia felt that no matter how many layers she wore, she would never be warm enough.

"Wherever Sima needs to go to find her family."

Albus started to say something, then shook his head. "You'll come back? In, what, a day or two? How long will it take?"

"I don't know," Octavia said. "Not too long."

"I'll close this behind you. So they won't know right away how you left."

"Okay," Octavia whispered. She couldn't say goodbye. That felt too big, too final. So she only said again, "Okay."

She hurried to join Sima and Rufus. The gate clanked closed behind them, and the dried vines crackled and crunched across the archway.

Octavia stepped in front of Rufus and Sima to lead them. The ice beneath their feet was hard and crusted, the air so cold it hurt to breathe, and everything was a bewildering patchwork of dark shadows and pale snow. She had to show them where to go. She had to show them that she wasn't scared.

But she couldn't move.

It struck her, all at once, the enormity of what they were doing.

She hadn't let herself think about it all day. She had focused only on the plan, only on how to get Sima out of the Council Hall and out of Vittoria. How to get past locks and guards and gates, how to trick the adults who would stop her if they suspected anything. She had kept herself fixated on this single goal: get Sima out. Everything after that point had remained somewhat vague in her mind, not ignored but not what she had spent the day puzzling over, the next steps as indistinct as figures moving just out of sight in a snowstorm.

She couldn't ignore it anymore. Sima was free. They were outside the wall.

At night. As fresh snow began to fall.

And beyond the frozen width of the burning ground and the barren winter fields was a dark, dense forest filled with monsters.

Octavia felt a shiver begin in her core and spread outward to her arms and legs. What was she *doing*? She had barely survived a night in the wilderness before, and now she was heading back out with two other people. Panic reached into her throat, and it was all she could do not to whimper. They shouldn't be out here. She looked at Rufus, his face pale and his eyes wide. She looked at Sima, who was hunched beneath Hana's old pack and looking around nervously, like she expected something to jump out of the shadows. She wanted one of them to say it, to decide this was a terrible idea, because something *could* jump out of the shadows. They were outside the wall, in the dark, with only knives and an old bow to protect them. Octavia didn't know how to make her feet move.

She didn't know how to unfreeze herself from the terror she felt.

You're always going to be scared.

She heard the words clearly in her memory, as though Hana were standing right beside her.

The wilderness is dangerous, Hana had said. *The Ferox are always watching. The weather can change in an instant. If you aren't afraid, you aren't paying attention. On days like this, especially, the danger can feel closer than ever.*

On that day, not quite a full year ago, Hana had taken Octavia into the forest west of Vittoria to teach her how to follow Hunters' trails and track small Ferox in the snow. It had been a grim, cloudy day, without the least hint of sunlight to lessen the shadows, and Octavia had been wary of venturing into the woods.

But if you let the fear stop you, Hana had said, *then you might as well stay home in your bed.* She had smiled playfully. *You go first. Find the trail.*

"Find the trail," Octavia whispered.

"Octavia?" Rufus said.

Octavia took a breath. She raised one hand and pointed. "This way. There's a Hunters' trail across that field that leads up to the high pastures and the watchtower. It's protected by charms. That's our path." She adjusted the straps of her pack. She hoped they couldn't hear the fear in her voice. It was bad enough that she felt it quivering throughout her body. "Let's go."

They hurried across the crusted, windswept snow of the burning ground, climbed over a low stone wall, and ran along the edge of the field until they reached the opposite side. The forest waited dark and tall ahead of them, like a wall of shadows where no light could penetrate. With Rufus and Sima right behind her, their boots crunching as noisily as hers, Octavia followed the field wall to a wooden gate. There she paused to look back. Vittoria was a block of dark stone, almost featureless against the gray night sky except for the tiny spots of light shining from the guard towers atop the wall. The snow was beginning to fall more heavily, but the flakes were still light, small and icy and stinging.

No guards shouted down from the towers. No bells rang. No torches flared. Nobody had seen them.

She took a breath and started walking. One step at a time. Into the forest.

"Do you see the blazes?" she said, keeping her voice low. She gestured to the wooden sigils cut into the trunks of a pair of trees. "That's where the trail is charmed. Stay between them."

"But the charms don't stop the Ferox," Rufus said. "Nothing stops them."

"No, but they . . ." Octavia tried to remember how Master Flavia had explained it. "They persuade them to look away."

"It didn't look away on the road," Sima pointed out. "Were there no charms there?"

"There were, but it's hard to make them ignore a whole caravan, or a person stepping right in front of them," Octavia said. "So we still have to be careful. It's less than a mile to the watchtower. We can make it." She took a step through the field gate, then stopped to draw her knife. She wasn't going to tell them what Master Flavia had said about the charms losing their effectiveness over time. It wouldn't help them now. "But we might want to be ready just in case."

Sima nodded and nocked an arrow to her bow. Rufus had a knife as well; he didn't draw it, but he placed his hand on the hilt.

The Hunters' trail was narrow, steep, and uneven with roots and rocks beneath the snow. The blazes were not easy to see in the dark, but as they climbed the hillside Octavia grew accustomed to looking for them. Rufus stayed right behind her, so close she could almost feel his breath, while Sima brought up the rear.

Less than a mile through the woods. In the daytime, with Hana right behind her, it had felt like no distance at all. But now, with every step she took, with every breath she took, with every whisper of wind and creak of the branches, Octavia was waiting for the monsters.

By the time the slope of the ridge eased and the trees thinned into an open forest, Octavia was struggling for breath and pushing through a burn in her legs and lungs. Where her face was exposed, her skin was stinging with cold, but where she was covered by clothing she felt overheated and sweaty. She had worn too many layers, or the wrong layers, or the wrong clothes; everything was damp and uncomfortable. Every breath tasted metallic, like blood, and she desperately wanted to stop to dig her waterskin out of her pack. Her tongue was tacky, her throat sore. But she didn't dare rest. They had to keep moving. They could rest when they reached the Hunters' watchtower. The snow was falling steadily now, filling in their footsteps behind them.

When she heard the cry of a blue jay, the sound was so unexpected that her first reaction was confusion.

Her next, a second later, was pure terror.

Octavia stopped so suddenly Rufus bumped into her.

"What—" he began.

She held up a hand to silence him. Sima stopped behind Rufus but didn't speak. Octavia kept her hand raised and hoped they understood. Not a word. Not a sound.

The blue jay's call sounded again. Octavia couldn't pinpoint where it was coming from. She looked in every direction, staring into the woods for any sign of movement, any hulking shadow that did not belong. She stared so hard her eyes watered, and she had to wipe them dry to look again. She could hear Rufus and Sima breathing, hear the sound their boots made when they shifted their weight. The wind turning through the treetops. The snow pattering faintly around them. The cold had sunk into her clothing, into her boots and around her cuffs and collar, filling her with a deep, deep chill that made every part of her skin prickle. They couldn't stand here all night. She didn't know where the Ferox was, but she knew they couldn't stand here for long. It was too cold. They needed shelter.

She took a step, then another, placing her feet carefully on the ice-hardened snow. She checked the trail to make sure they were between the blazes. There was no way to move silently on snow that had been freezing and hardening for several nights. She looked back to see Rufus staring at her with wide eyes, while Sima was aiming her bow this way and that, turning swiftly from side to side, her hands shaking so much Octavia was afraid she would loose an arrow by accident.

After only a few steps she heard the blue jay again, but before it even finished its call it shifted into the rattling sound of a woodpecker. Octavia started and looked sharply to the left. The falling snow and the wind made it look like everything was moving, shifting, creeping. Was that a log or a Ferox slinking low along the ground? She couldn't tell. The clattering woodpecker sound faded, and in its place rose the gentle hoot of an owl. The Ferox was trying to confuse them, trying different sounds to trick them and make them panic.

Somehow knowing that steadied Octavia's nerves. It knew they were here, even if the charms kept it from finding them. They knew it was there, hidden in the darkness. She picked up her pace a little, glancing back only to be sure Rufus and Sima were following close behind. They couldn't get separated.

The owl's call followed them through the woods—soft and so

very menacing—until it too faded, and there came the loud caw of a raven. But that came from the right, from the opposite direction of the previous sounds. It was another Ferox. Maybe a little farther away. Octavia's heart skipped, and her moment of steadiness ended. Two Ferox. Both of them nearing the trail. She tried to find them in the woods, but she couldn't see anything. Everything looked like a creature, and nothing did, and her breath was shallow and frantic, and she didn't realize she'd stopped until Rufus touched her arm.

She whipped around to look at him and saw that both he and Sima were pointing ahead on the trail. Rufus mouthed something silently, a single word. Octavia faced forward again.

The watchtower was just ahead. No more than a hundred feet away. It sat alone in a small clearing, its long ladder climbing up from a square stone foundation. With a jolt of excitement, Octavia quickened her pace to a fast walk, then a jog, no longer trying to be quiet. Her pack bounced on her back, and she could hear Rufus's and Sima's gasping breaths and boots crunching through the snow behind her.

The bird calls ceased, only to be replaced by a metallic clicking. Claws, she thought, and she broke into a run. Claws clacking together from the left—or was it the right?—and the sound of heavy limbs punching through snow and something rasping against tree bark. She was almost there. Almost there. She glanced left and saw a dark shape darting through the forest alongside the trail, too swift for her to make out its shape. It wasn't that big, maybe the size of a fox, but it was *fast*. A glance to the right and she saw the other one—did they work together?—and it was tall, spindly and skinny with uneven long legs that clattered like kindling when it ran. It was loping alongside them, and she looked away for one second, then looked back, and it veered toward them, ducked its head, and charged.

Octavia stumbled against the foundation of the tower and slid to the side.

"Up, up, up!" she shouted. She grabbed Rufus's pack to shove him up the ladder, then gave Sima a boost. "Go! Go!"

The ladder quaked as they climbed, and she scrambled after them, so close behind Sima she had to dodge to the side to avoid being kicked.

One of the Ferox warbled a strange, fluting sound, nothing like any real bird Octavia had ever heard, right before it struck the base of the tower. It reared back with a noisy clatter of claws. Octavia climbed and climbed, her lungs burning. The last thing she saw before they slammed the trapdoor closed was the dark shapes of two Ferox circling the tower below.

12
The Valley of Ghosts

After a cold, restless night, during which every noise outside the watchtower had jolted Octavia from sleep, morning arrived gray, snowy, and bitterly cold. The fire in the woodstove had died down, so Octavia revived it to warm them up before they started.

"You're all mad to live in a place this cold," Sima said, her teeth chattering as she dug through the Hunters' supplies in search of food.

Rufus was bent over another storage chest, digging through blankets and weapons until he found what he was looking for. "Ah! Here. We're going to need these." He lifted out three sets of snowshoes. At Sima's baffled look, he said, "They're for walking in the snow when it gets deep."

Sima frowned, like she thought he was joking with her. "How deep?"

"Deep enough that it's hard to walk," Octavia said. "It can get really deep higher in the mountains."

"Which is where we're going, right?" Rufus accepted a handful of nuts and dried meat from Sima and shuffled closer to the fire. "Octavia said you want to go to Aeterna?"

Sima gave Octavia an annoyed look, but Octavia only rolled her eyes. "He's helping you. Of course I told him."

"But she didn't tell me why you want to go there," Rufus said. "I mean, I know we're taking you to find your family, and we want to do it before the Hunters catch up to them, but why does your family want to go to Aeterna in the first place? It's just an old ruin. There's nothing there."

Sima took a bite of dried meat and chewed. She looked sallow and anxious, now that Octavia was finally getting a good look at her; her dark hair was messy, her eyes shadowed with exhaustion. But she wasn't dirty or hurt, which was a relief. Octavia hoped that meant the guards at the Council Hall hadn't been treating her like an animal, even if that's what the council had decided she was.

"You can tell him," Octavia said. "You can trust him."

Finally Sima swallowed and said, "My brother is sick. None of the healers in Iberne could help him. So we left to look for somebody who could, and my mother heard about a healer who can cure any disease. This healer has been in Aeterna for some months. So that's where we are going."

"How can a healer cure all diseases?" Rufus asked, skeptical. "Is that even possible?"

"And why would they be in Aeterna?" Octavia added. "Isn't that a strange place for a healer to go?"

To her surprise, Rufus said, "Oh, that's obvious. It's all the magic there."

"What do you mean? Healers don't use magic."

"They used to," Rufus said, while at the same Sima said, "Yes, they do."

"It's not allowed anymore, because of Agrippina's plague. In Vittoria, that is. Our Crafters can only use magic to protect the town," Rufus said, then he shrugged. "It's going to be hard to get used to there being other places to think about. Master Cicerus told me healers used to be Crafters too. I guess they still are where you come from?"

"We don't call them Crafters," Sima said. "They are only heal-ers. In Iberne they are the only ones who use magic. Since the war it is forbidden for any other purpose."

Rufus rested his chin on his hand. "It's so strange, isn't it? That's the exact opposite of our rules in Vittoria. We can't use magic for healing because that would mean using it on people. But you're only allowed to use it on people. And both groups decided that way because they thought it was best after the war."

Octavia nodded, because she understood what he was saying, but she felt a prickle of unease. *We will protect Vittoria*, Master Camilla had said, and the council had believed her, as the people of Vittoria believed her. They had been trusting her to do just that for fifty years. But Camilla's idea of protecting Vittoria had been to imprison Sima, tell everyone she was a monster, and lie about what she had revealed about the world outside.

It made Octavia wonder just how much of Camilla's protection had been lies all along.

Sima said, "We heard from travelers that this healer is using the sorcerers' magic to cure diseases. So people are going to Aeterna to be cured, but also to help search the ruins for ways to help oth-ers. There were people in the caravan going because they heard there was work—digging up the ruins, searching the city, looking for what the sorcerers left behind."

Octavia dug into her pack to find the map she had taken from Hana's room. She unfolded it on the floor and knelt beside it; Sima and Rufus leaned over for a closer look.

"This is where we are," Octavia said, pointing to the watch-tower immediately west of Vittoria. "And this is where we have to get to before dark."

She traced her finger along the faint line of the Hunters' trail as it followed the crest of a long ridge and descended into a broad river valley. The trail crossed the River Iracundia and climbed a hill on the opposite side to another watchtower.

"So we're going through the Valley of Ghosts," Rufus said.

Sima narrowed her eyes. "Ghosts?"

"There used to be a city there," Rufus said. He pointed to a shaded part of the map at the very edge, beyond the territory patrolled by Vittoria's Hunters. "It was called Ira. It wasn't as big as Aeterna, but I guess at some point it was bigger than Vittoria."

"Vittoria is not very big," Sima said. "Iberne is ten times its size."

"Well, anyway, the city is empty now. It has been since early in the war. The people of Ira tried to fight the sorcerers, but they failed. The sorcerers had this weapon that let them smash right through the city walls with a single arrow."

"They used that in the lowlands too," Sima said. "It was how they broke through in many cities. They would send the monsters in after."

"They used it in Ira first, and everybody died."

"Everybody?" Sima said.

"Everybody."

"Like how everybody died outside of Vittoria during the war?"

"Um." Rufus made a face. "Okay, you're right, maybe not *every-body*. But there's nobody from Ira in Vittoria. If there were sur-vivors, nobody knows where they went. We call it the Valley of Ghosts because people say ghosts are the only ones who stayed. But also because it's a weird valley. There are all these hot springs, so it's always misty, no matter the weather. I think that's probably the real reason people think it's spooky."

They were hiding in the mist, Willa had said, of the people Bram had seen. Octavia's breath caught. Maybe Bram hadn't been near East Road at all. Maybe he had been looking in the opposite direction.

She didn't think Bram would have spent weeks watching ghosts.

"Ghosts or not, we have to get going," Octavia said.

They set out as Vittoria's morning bells were ringing and the sun was rising, although it was hidden behind thready, patchy clouds. Octavia took the lead again. The night's snow had covered any sign of the Hunters' trail on the ground, but she was still able to follow the blazes in the tree trunks, as well as the spots where the trail had been cut through fallen logs or thick underbrush. It was so much easier in the daytime, yet she still watched the shadows and listened. The Ferox's creator had made them to attack only under the cover of darkness, but Octavia couldn't stop thinking about what Master Flavia had said about the magic running wild and changing over time. Daylight had always meant safety in the past. But a lot of things people had always believed in the past were turning out to be untrue. Octavia was no longer willing to trust what people had always believed.

Even so, it was pleasant to walk through the open forest as it filled with a light, low mist. She enjoyed the challenge of finding the trail and the little triumph she felt every time she spotted the next marker.

Hana would be proud of her, she thought.

If things were different, maybe Mom would be as well.

Around mid-morning, they passed a cluster of abandoned buildings tucked into the trees. Most were half collapsed, with no roofs or windows anymore; woodsmen from Vittoria had taken any salvageable logs years ago and left lonely stone chimneys behind.

"What happened here?" Sima asked.

"Same as happened everywhere else. People left because of Agrippina's plague," Octavia said.

"That's not what happened everywhere else," Sima pointed out. "That's just what you think happened."

"Right. I know." Octavia kicked through a fresh drift of snow. She was already feeling tired from breaking the path, but she couldn't ask Rufus or Sima to take the lead. It wasn't even noon yet. She couldn't admit to being tired so early in the day. "So what did happen everywhere else? What happened when the plague reached Iberne?"

"Many people got sick. Many people died." Sima walked in silence for a few seconds. "Some other cities sent their sick out to sea. Some put them into prisons. Some cast them out. But there were healers who tried to help, and people who took care of the ill, and after many years there was no more plague. So many people died that it couldn't spread anymore. But not everyone."

"I don't think Vittoria even tried anything except shutting themselves away," Octavia said.

"It's still hard to imagine," said Rufus quietly. "How many people are out there. All the things they know that we don't."

Sima made a noise, like she wanted to start listing all the things they didn't know, but she held her tongue.

They walked all morning and did not stop until midday, and then only for a quick break and a look at Hana's map. The ridge was sloping steadily downward now, the forest growing thicker around them, but the Hunters' trail was still marked clearly with blazes and occasional stone cairns. Octavia had hoped that by this point they would be able to see the next watchtower, but the Valley of Ghosts was broader and deeper than she had realized.

"How much farther is it?" Rufus asked. He looked even more tired than Octavia felt; he hadn't spent his summer and fall sneaking out to practice tracking in the woods like she had. His face was paler than usual, and he kept adjusting his pack like it was hurting his shoulders and back.

Octavia said, "We just need to cross the River Iracundia and go up the hill a ways. We can make it before dark."

She hoped she sounded more confident than she felt. In spite of her words, she knew they weren't moving fast enough. Breaking trail in the deep snow was so much harder than she had expected. She wanted to rest—to let Rufus rest—but she was afraid of wasting any more time. She packed away the map and food, stood, and pulled her pack on.

As she did so, she heard a chittering sound from the trees. She turned to stare into the woods. All she could see were dark tree trunks, white snow, and green pine boughs. She held her breath to listen more carefully. She watched for any flicker of motion.

"What is it?" Sima asked. She stepped up to stand beside Octavia. "Is it the monsters?"

"I don't know," Octavia said. "It might have been a squirrel."

Sima gave Octavia a skeptical look. "Do you think it was a squirrel?"

"No," Octavia admitted. She listened for another few moments. "It's still daylight, and we're staying on the trail. They won't come close."

She said it like she believed it, even told herself she believed it, but as they set out again, Octavia had lost the sense of enjoyment that had carried her through the morning. She was only tired now, tired and cold and damp, and every creak of wood, every chirp of birdsong, every brush of branches had her peering nervously into the woods, searching for a glimpse of the Ferox. They wouldn't approach. Not in the daytime. For all her doubts, she hadn't seen anything yet to prove that wrong. She just wanted to know where they were, but without being able to venture off the trail to track them, she never saw more than the swiftest hint of motion, such as a twitching branch or a falling clump of snow.

As the afternoon wore on, clouds rolled over the western peaks to slowly overtake the sky, swallowing up the highest summits and obscuring the broad flanks of the mountains. The mist rising from the hot springs around the River Iracundia grew denser as the day became colder. Soon the entire Valley of Ghosts was swathed in fog.

Only when the ground began to level and the trees dropped away did Octavia realize they had reached the valley floor. Sima was in the lead now, forging the trail through the snow, and Octavia was bringing up the rear. It became harder to follow the trail as they emerged from the forest and entered what must have been Ira's farmland. In places there were no blazes, nor even trees to mark them on, only rock cairns set atop or beside crumbling stone walls that had once enclosed pastures. Here and there springs burbled from the ground, surrounded by barren shrubbery, all obscured by the fog. The mist felt warm on Octavia's face sometimes, but never warm enough to offer real respite from the cold. Everything was cold and quiet and gray.

"I think I hear the river," Rufus said. He sounded uncertain but hopeful as he tilted his head. "We must be close."

Octavia paused to listen as well. She thought she might hear it too, the sound of water coursing through a rocky riverbed, but it was hard to tell. The wind was picking up, whispering over the empty land and across the hillside behind them. She started walking again, not wanting to fall behind.

Nobody was saying it aloud, but Octavia knew they were all thinking the same thing.

It was late afternoon, and they weren't even across the river yet.

After a few steps she heard another sound: the gentle hoot of an owl.

It was followed quickly by a coarse blue jay's call.

Several steps ahead, Sima paused and looked to the side. "Is that...?"

"Yes," Octavia said, barely more than a whisper.

"They sound close," Rufus said.

Octavia had to agree, and dismay washed over her like a flood. She had hoped, foolishly, that the Ferox would not follow them out of the woods. She hadn't heard them for a long time. But they were still there, somewhere in the mist, calling out in their cruel mimicry of birdsong. Following. Stalking.

Waiting for dark.

Sima started walking faster, and Rufus and Octavia followed her lead. The owl calls kept pace with them, just loud enough to be heard over the crunch of their snowshoes. Octavia kept looking to her right, into the fog. Once or twice, she was certain she saw a dark shape slinking low to the ground. It wasn't a big Ferox, no larger than a fox or a small dog, probably the same one that had followed them last night. She didn't like to think about that, how it had been with them all day. She tried to reassure herself that it was small enough that they could fight it off, if it was alone.

She didn't know if it was alone.

She drew Hana's knife. She looked again to see the dark, shadowy shape bound over a stone wall. She heard the scrape of metal claws on stone and a soft rasping noise as the creature landed in the snow. The fog drifted and she couldn't see it anymore.

She was falling behind again. She jogged a little to catch up, only to find that Sima and Rufus had stopped in the middle of the trail.

"This is bad," said Rufus.

Octavia stepped up beside him to see what he meant.

They had reached the River Iracundia. But the bridge was gone.

The ground dropped away in front of them, slanting down a steep riverbank that was covered with rocks, dead branches, dried brush, and the broken remains of the bridge. The stone foundations were still standing on both sides, the far one just visible through the heavy fog, but the wooden structure that was supposed to span them had collapsed. Most of it was gone, probably washed away in a storm or a flood; all that remained were the logs and boards that had been caught in the rocks on the riverbank.

"Can we cross it?" Sima asked.

Octavia considered it, then shook her head. There were ways to cross rivers safely, techniques that Hana had taught her, but none of them were any use on a river as big as the Iracundia, on a day as cold as this.

"Even if we made it to the other side, we would be soaking wet and frozen," she said. "We have to find another crossing."

Sima and Rufus both looked at her. Rufus said, "But that means . . ."

"Leaving the trail. I know. But we can't stay here. We have to keep moving."

"The creature is following us," Sima said.

"I know it is! I don't know what else to do. It won't attack during daylight. We have to cross the river and get back to the trail before dark."

"What if we can't? It's getting late," Rufus said.

Octavia had no answer for him. They didn't have a choice.

Sima drew an arrow and nocked it. "Which way?"

"The Ferox is downriver," Octavia said. "So we head upriver. Putting the trail between us might distract it."

She turned resolutely and headed upriver. Her skin began

crawling at once with a feeling of vulnerability. She hadn't heard the owl hoot in a while. She walked faster, moving as quickly as she could along the rocky, uneven riverbank. The fog remained impenetrable, but as long as she followed the river they wouldn't get lost. She looked at every boulder, every cluster of rocks, every fallen tree stuck in the current. They just needed to find a crossing. The Ferox might not even follow them across. She had no idea if Ferox could swim. It wasn't something Hana had ever taught her, and she had never thought to ask.

She felt dismayed but not surprised when she heard a blue jay's call to their left. She didn't say anything, just quickened her pace, and when she saw a shadow moving at the corner of her vision she broke into a run. She was looking so hard at the river, searching for any way across, that she wasn't watching her step, and she didn't see the stones until the toe of her snowshoe caught and she tipped forward, slamming into the ground so hard it knocked her breath away.

"There's two of them!" Sima called.

"Get up, get up, get up," Rufus said. "Octavia! Are you hurt?"

She had tripped on a pile of stones at the base of a tree. The tree was tall and thin and empty of branches, except for a single small knot at the very top. Octavia stared at it in a daze as her vision cleared.

It wasn't a tree. It didn't have an oddly shaped knot at its crown.

It was a wooden pole with a large wooden ring on top. Hanging in the center of the ring was a skull.

A human skull.

It turned and twisted in the slight wind, knocking against the ring with a hollow tap.

Octavia scrambled to her feet and backed away, only to bump into Rufus, who was panting heavily and saying, "Where is it?

Where did it go? Where is it?"

Octavia turned in circle. "Sima! Sima, where are you?"

Her answer was a noisy racket as Sima burst from the fog, her snowshoes clacking on the exposed rocks. She had fired her arrow and didn't have another one ready. The nearest Ferox was right behind her. The other one was coming closer, closer, close enough now that Octavia could see its long, curved metal teeth and the misshapen form of its head. It had horns made of burnt, twisted sticks, and its claws were long and pale, and it was *fast*. It moved with startling elegance, every limb graceful, its purpose clear. It was gaining on Sima easily.

Octavia raised her knife, but before she could even take a step something swished past her ear, so close to her face she felt it tug at her hair.

A long wooden spear embedded itself in the Ferox's neck. Another spear flew and struck the second Ferox in its chest. The air quivered with a high sound, like a chime from the tiniest bell, before the fragile note faded quickly into the mist.

Both monsters stumbled, stopped by the weapons.

And they began to crumble.

The creatures' patchwork shapes started to collapse in on themselves. The scraps of skin and hide withered, and the wooden pieces darkened and broke like branches turning to ember in a fire. The metal teeth rusted and flaked away to harmless chips. The bone parts were the last to break apart, and they didn't disintegrate like the others, but they did fall to the ground in a heap.

It took only a moment. It was so fast Octavia blinked, certain she had to be imagining it. The Ferox were gone. A single spear strike had made them fall apart. They hadn't merely been taken apart at the joints, the way Hunters destroyed them. They had been obliterated entirely. They were nothing more than heaps of debris and bone now.

Something nudged her back. She let out a surprised yelp and spun around to find herself staring down the length of another spear. There was one trained on Rufus as well.

Holding them were two people dressed in coats and tall boots lined with thick fur. Their heads were entirely swathed in scarves, obscuring everything except for bright, suspicious eyes.

13

In the City of the Furious Dead

———»»———

The tip of the spear was cold and sharp beneath Octavia's chin. She stepped backward quickly and raised her hands. "Wait, wait! What are you doing? We're not Ferox! How did you do that? What did you do to them?"

The person holding the spear snorted. "We know you're not Ferox, little girl." It was a woman's voice, mocking but not particularly alarmed.

Sima ran up beside Octavia, with another arrow finally nocked to her bow, and pointed it at the woman. "Lower your spear. Don't hurt them."

The woman didn't move. She inclined her head toward her companion. "Do you know them? You didn't say there would be three."

"There shouldn't be. I've never seen them before," said the other person. A man or boy, by the sound of his voice, and very annoyed.

"How did you do that?" Octavia demanded again, her voice rising. "Is it your spears? What did you do? How did you destroy the Ferox so easily?"

"What are you doing out here if you can't do that?" the boy retorted. He lowered the tip of his spear away from Rufus's neck. "That's a good way to get yourself killed. Did one of them get you?"

Octavia didn't know what he meant until Rufus said, "Oh. Um. I think so?"

Blood was seeping through his trousers low on his left leg. Rufus leaned over to touch the wound, and as he did so his leg crumpled beneath him. Octavia caught him and lowered him to the ground.

The Ferox's claws had slashed four long cuts on the side of his leg. His trousers were shredded, his skin open, and the wound was bleeding freely. Octavia felt suddenly, sharply queasy looking at it.

"What do I do?" she said. She knew what to do. She knew how to tend injuries. She paid attention when Rufus talked about all he learned working with Master Cicerus. But her mind was a white blank. She couldn't remember a single thing. "Tell me what to do!"

"We need to stop . . ." Rufus hissed and sucked in a sharp breath. "Stop the bleeding."

"Move." The strange woman knelt beside Octavia and shouldered her aside. She unwound her long scarf, revealing a round face with wind-chafed cheeks, framed by wisps of brown hair. She straightened Rufus's leg and peeled back the torn trousers for a look at the wound. "It's pretty deep. You need a healer."

"I know," Rufus said, his voice breathy. "The bleeding—"

"I'll do what I can here." The woman wrapped her scarf tightly around his leg. "Where are you from? What are you doing in our territory?"

Octavia and Sima exchanged a glance. Sima shrugged, which Octavia took to mean she wasn't quite sure how to answer either.

"Um, we didn't know this was your territory," Octavia said. "Sorry."

She wasn't about to admit that she didn't even know people had territory in the Valley of Ghosts. Or that there were people here at all. A small, hysterical part of her wanted to ask if they were ghosts, just because it seemed like she ought to check. The larger, more rational part of her was racing through a series of thoughts: they weren't ghosts, they were just people, because there were people outside of Vittoria, people hidden in the mist from the hot springs around Ira, people who could destroy the Ferox with a single blow, and they were nearby too, and Rufus needed help, and she wanted one of their spears. She really wanted one of those spears. But not until Rufus got help.

She couldn't think of a good reason to lie, so she said, "We were trying to find a way across the river, because the bridge is out. Do you know a healer? Can you help him?"

The woman looked up at her, then looked up at her companion. "Looks like your secret is going to get out."

The boy groaned and thumped his forehead against the long spear, which he was now holding upright. "I'm in so much trouble. I don't even know these people!"

"They were on the Vittoria trail," the woman said.

"Yeah, but they're not—" The boy stopped. "We should get back. It's getting dark."

Octavia and Sima helped Rufus to his feet, while the woman and boy collected their thrown spears. The woman took the lead, taking them upriver through a treeless expanse of land dotted by several more skull-topped poles. Not all of the skulls were human. Some were animals like bears or wolves or horned mountain goats, but there were also the misshapen remains of Ferox, looming from the fog with rusty bones and crooked teeth. The strangers hadn't even checked or looked at the Ferox they had destroyed, or the debris they left behind.

Octavia and Sima supported Rufus, who limped along as well as he could, while the boy brought up the rear. The woman said her name was Brianne, and the boy was Piper, her cousin.

When Octavia asked where they were going, Brianne said, "Home. It's not far."

"I hope home is warm," Rufus said. He was clearly trying to put on a brave face, but every step caused him to hiss with pain, even with Octavia and Sima supporting most of his weight.

"Can we trust them?" Sima asked, her voice low.

"I don't think we have a choice," Octavia said. "They don't seem to want to hurt us."

Sima hummed thoughtfully. "Will they help us? How far are we from Aeterna now?"

Octavia felt the now familiar twinge of guilt, the one that reminded her that she had convinced Sima nobody in Vittoria wanted to hurt her, and look how wrong she had been about that. She was supposed to be helping Sima, but it kept going wrong. Beneath everything Sima said, there was the fear that her family was already dead. Octavia didn't know what she could say, because every reassurance felt false until they learned for certain what had happened to the caravan.

There was something else teasing at Octavia's mind, something she didn't want to say aloud just yet. It was obvious Piper had been expecting to find somebody else out here. Somebody from Vittoria. Somebody he had encountered before.

For days Octavia had been assuming that the person Bram had told his mother about must have been another traveler on East Road, following the same route as Sima's caravan. What Sima had said about several people heading to Aeterna to find some great healer had only convinced her more.

But maybe she had been wrong. She hadn't asked Willa where Bram had met his stranger. Maybe Bram had met somebody out here, near the River Iracundia northwest of Vittoria. Maybe that somebody was the boy walking behind them right now, carrying spears that could stop a Ferox in its tracks.

She wanted to ask, but first she wanted to know more about Piper and Brianne and their home. She wanted to know what kind of people they were before she told them Bram was dead.

The mist grew even thicker as they traveled upriver, but the two strangers didn't seem worried. Their path took them to the remains of a high stone wall that had once spanned the river and stretched across the valley. Most of the wall was destroyed now, as though it had been smashed by giant fists. They passed through tall, open gates and into a twisting warren of streets. All around there were collapsed buildings, piles of rubble, plazas overtaken by trees, and arches where fat woody vines had snaked between the stones to become part of the walls. All of it was draped in a thick layer of snow, and very quiet.

Octavia asked, "Is this Ira?"

"Were you expecting some other city here?" Piper said.

Brianne glanced over her shoulder. "Stop being a jerk, Piper. Yes, this is Ira. This is the City of the Furious Dead."

Octavia mouthed the words to herself. She had never heard Ira called by such a name before.

Finally, Brianne led them down a narrow street, through a series of archways, and down a set of stairs into the basement of a large building. The first room was long and cold, and on every wall there were hooks and shelves filled with winter clothing and gear.

"Leave your snowshoes here," said Brianne. "Piper, go fetch Marta." To Rufus, she said, "She's a healer. Hurry up and get inside where it's warm."

The doorway at the end of the long room led into a hallway lit by candles on the walls. It didn't feel like they were walking through a basement, with weak outside light filtering through high, snow-covered windows. Octavia smelled a hint of smoke and something meaty and spicy that made her stomach grumble with hunger. That hallway in turn led into a large, long room with a tall ceiling and three fire pits beneath three stone chimneys, each one filled with a blazing fire that filled the space with air so warm Octavia almost wept with relief. She wanted to race over to the fires to warm herself, but she had to help Rufus first. He was grim-faced and pale, with sweat on his brow and tears in his eyes.

Brianne led them over to a bench against the wall and told them to stay put. There were about twenty people in the room, mostly gathered around the fires with cooking pots and kettles. Clay vents in the floor brought heat up from the hot springs. Many people turned to look at the newcomers curiously, but they didn't seem concerned or the least bit frightened by strangers appearing among them.

Octavia helped Rufus sit, and Sima helped him take his coat and boots off. The blood had seeped through the makeshift bandage of Brianne's scarf, and every time Rufus bent his knee or moved his foot he grunted with pain. He noticed Octavia looking at him worriedly and tried to smile.

"At least it's warm," he said. "And I can smell food."

"They're getting a healer," she replied, even though he already knew that. "You'll be okay."

"If their Hunters can destroy Ferox so easily with magic, I wonder what their healers can do."

Octavia was wondering the same thing, with a strange, fluttering excitement in her chest. She had never seen magic like what had taken apart those Ferox. She had never even known it was possible. For all the protective charms and repelling spells the Crafters of Vittoria devised, they didn't have anything so powerful. It made her jealous, and curious, and angry, because if such incredible magic was possible, *why* didn't they know about it? If

Master Flavia could craft such weapons, Vittoria would have no trouble expanding its fields and pastures for better harvests, or traveling farther afield to encounter other people, or sending its Hunters into the wilderness and trusting that they would return.

"Why do they call this the City of the Furious Dead?" Sima asked.

"Because we never want to forget," came the reply, "all those who turned their backs on us when the sorcerers of Aeterna started their war."

All three of them startled and looked up. The woman who stood over them was the largest woman Octavia had ever seen. She was so tall her head nearly brushed the wooden beams spanning the room, and she was as broad as a barrel from shoulder to foot. She wore leather and furs, like the others, and her hair was black streaked with gray and plaited into a long coil atop her head. Beside her, looking positively diminutive in comparison, was a white-haired old woman with brown skin and brown eyes carrying a roll of bandages. Behind both of them was Piper, his arms full of small clay pots and leather pouches.

The old woman knelt beside Rufus's leg and began tutting over the wound while holding out her hands for Piper to pass her things, but Octavia could not take her eyes off the tall woman. The woman grinned, revealing a crooked set of teeth. She leaned against the wooden post beside their bench and crossed her arms over her chest. One of her hands was tanned and calloused and missing the smallest finger.

It was the other that Octavia could not stop staring at, because it was not a hand at all.

It was the massive paw of a bear, with thick, dark fur and long claws.

"Like that, do you?" the woman said with a laugh. She tugged her sleeve up to give them a better look. "They're all so used to it around here, nobody admires it anymore."

Octavia knew her mouth was hanging open. She couldn't bring herself to speak.

Sima stammered, "Are you—did you—is that—"

It was Rufus who managed to ask, with his eyes wide, "How is that possible?"

The woman didn't seem at all bothered by his question. "It was Marta here who managed it."

The white-haired woman smiled gently. "That was a tricky wound, to be sure."

"It was about fifteen years ago now—Piper here was just a baby."

With her other hand, the tall woman ruffled Piper's hair; he scowled and ducked away with a muttered, "Gran, *don't*."

The woman went on. "I lost my arm in the fight, but I took one from the beast to take its place. But don't worry. Marta only takes your limbs if there's no hope of saving them." The woman tugged a stool over and sat down facing them. "My name is Ursa. I'm the leader of the Clan of the Furious Dead, and I would very much like to know who you are and why three children from Vittoria are trespassing in our territory."

Sima quickly said, "I'm not from Vittoria."

Marta looked up from Rufus's leg. "Ah! I haven't heard that accent in a very long time. You're from the south, yes?"

Sima looked surprised and pleased. "Yes. My name is Sima. I'm from Iberne, by the sea."

Piper's eyes widened. "You mean . . . the sea? All the way down south? The actual sea?"

"Yes," Sima said, with an exasperated sigh. "Yes, I am from the sea. Yes, there are people there. No, we didn't all die or turn into monsters. No, we don't have snow. Yes, it is very cold here."

Marta laughed. "Don't mind Piper. We always knew there had to be lowlanders out there still, we just don't meet any of them in this part of the mountains."

"But you two," Ursa said, nodding at Rufus and Octavia, "you are from Vittoria."

They introduced themselves and told her that, yes, they were from Vittoria. Octavia added, "We didn't know we were trespassing. We were looking for a way across the river, to get to the watchtower on the west slope of Gray Bear Mountain."

"You're not the usual scouts from Vittoria. We keep our distance, but we recognize most of them from afar. And none of them are children."

Octavia shifted uncomfortably under Ursa's knowing gaze. She didn't know what to make of that, the revelation that these people had watched the Hunters on their patrols. She supposed it was inevitable, with how close they were to the Hunters' trail, but she didn't like that Ursa and her clan knew more about her than she knew about them.

Sima was looking at Octavia. After a second Octavia nodded slightly. Sima was the reason they were out here; she was the one who was fleeing trouble. So she was the one who got to decide how much to share with strangers.

"I'm looking for my family," Sima said. She told them about traveling to Aeterna in search of a healer for her brother, and how she had been separated from her caravan on the road. When she got to the part where she had to explain why they'd had to escape from Vittoria, she hesitated and looked at Octavia.

"We, um, we helped her," Octavia stammered, thinking quickly. "The council didn't want us—they weren't going to let her go."

Ursa gave them a level look. "We know that Vittoria does not interact with outsiders."

"You mean they hide behind their walls and their monsters, too afraid to look outside," Piper said darkly.

"Not everybody," Octavia blurted out. "Are you the person Bram met?"

Piper's eyes widened in surprise. "What? No, I don't—I don't know what you're talking about."

Ursa gave him an unimpressed look. "Piper?"

Octavia was even more certain now. "It was you, wasn't it? He told his mom he saw somebody hiding in the mist."

"Piper," Ursa said.

"It was an accident!" Piper said. "I didn't think . . . I was just doing patrols like normal. I didn't mean for him to see me."

"But you didn't tell us," Ursa said. "And you spoke to this boy."

Piper looked down at the floor and shrugged. "Just a few times. And I told Brianne, after she figured it out."

"So that's why you've wanted so many patrol shifts lately."

Another shrug. "It wasn't dangerous, Gran. All he ever did was ask a bunch of questions." His shoulders hunched lower and his voice was small. "It was fun to talk to him."

Octavia felt a pang of sudden sadness, imagining Piper and Bram first spotting each other from afar through forest and mist, both of them fascinated, before finally finding the courage to approach. Bram, who had tried so hard to become a Hunter to explore beyond Vittoria, would have wanted to know everything Piper could tell him.

Ursa shook her head. "I'll talk to your mother later about your punishment for breaking the rules. Is there also trouble for this boy in Vittoria? You must have rules about keeping your distance," she asked Octavia.

The others looked at Octavia expectantly, but she didn't know what to say. Sima had not known much about Vittoria before she arrived, whereas Ursa and Piper already knew that Vittoria was completely isolated. But they seemed to think the people of Vittoria were hiding on purpose, like rodents tucked away in a burrow while a fox prowled outside, small and frightened and insignificant within the larger world. It was so different from how Octavia was used to thinking about Vittoria that she didn't know how to begin explaining the truth to Ursa. The truth was that Vittoria's rules had gotten Bram killed, and Vittoria's isolation had gotten his mother killed, and their deaths made Octavia feel guilty and angry and ashamed.

The people of the lowlands had made up stories about the people of the mountains; the clans outside Vittoria had made up stories about the people within its walls; and Vittoria had made up stories about the whole rest of the world, stories that were more wrong than any of them, more removed from the truth than Octavia knew how to reconcile. It was too much to explain to strangers when she couldn't even make sense of it herself.

"Ah!" Rufus said suddenly. "That feels odd! It sort of tickles. Does that stop the bleeding? It barely hurts at all anymore."

He glanced at Octavia quickly before turning to Marta, and she knew he had spoken up so she wouldn't have to try to explain about Willa and Bram. Everybody's attention turned toward his leg, where Marta had spread a pale, shimmering slurry over the wound. There was only the smallest seep of blood flowing out now, although it hadn't scabbed over. Rufus peered at it curiously.

Marta chuckled. "Stops the bleeding, lessens the pain, and helps clean a bit. Next I'm going to use a poultice to help the skin close back up."

"You can do that without stitches?" Rufus said.

"For cuts like this, yes," said Marta. "Any deeper and we would have had to help the poultice along a bit. This way is cleaner and less painful."

"What's in it? How does it work?"

Marta's entire face creased when she smiled. "Let's see. Hareweed, spring pansies, a bit of lichen from a northern slope, and some wild mint to make it nice and soothing. The trick is harvesting and mixing it all at the right time, so the magic is strongest. Hold still, now, so I can make sure to cover all the cuts."

"You don't have to extract magic from the river?" Octavia asked.

"Why make things harder than they need to be?" Marta said. "That same water that flows in the Nyx is what makes the grasses and flowers grow and fills the clouds with rain and snow that fall on the high peaks. The magic that's gone wild in these mountains ebbs and flows with the seasons, but once you learn its patterns, you can collect it anywhere."

She dabbed the poultice onto Rufus's leg. It was bright green in color, the same as hareweed when it grew alongside rivers and springs, and smelled brightly of mint. It didn't have any of the whirling shadows that Octavia associated with the magic she had seen in Master Flavia's workshop, but there was a mesmerizing sheen to it, like the faintest ripple of calm pond water.

"There," Marta said. She had finished wrapping a clean bandage over the poultice. "You'll have to rest it for a few days."

Rufus wiggled his toes and bent his knee. "It barely hurts at all."

Marta patted his other knee and stood up. "The muscles will be sore and the skin tender. Even magic can only do so much."

"You can stay here until you're ready to travel again," Ursa said. "We won't put children out in the cold, even children from Vittoria. Piper will show you where to get cleaned up, then you can join us for some dinner."

They thanked her before she and Marta left.

"I've never seen healing like this," Rufus said, his voice full of awe. "I had no idea it was even possible."

Piper, his arms still full of Marta's supplies, scowled. "What do you know about anything? Vittoria is full of cowards." He turned on his heel and jerked his head toward a doorway at the far end of the room. "The washrooms are through there. You smell like you need them." Then he strode away.

Octavia's first reaction was to be angry at his words, at the insult he had offered with so much certainty in his voice.

"He seems friendly," Sima said wryly.

And just like that, the anger faded, and Octavia snickered. "He's like Albus, only grumpier."

"I would say we should lock them in a room together," Rufus said thoughtfully, still staring at his bandaged leg as he twisted his ankle this way and that, "but they would probably just glare at each other and fall asleep. Like cats."

Octavia laughed, and the annoyance she had been feeling gave way to something more like giddiness.

A wild new thought suddenly came into her mind: the people of Vittoria did not have to keep living as they had been for fifty years. Vittoria had a lot of rules, but rules could change. There were people, like Master Cicerus and Master Flavia, who already understood that. They might not be as powerful as Camilla, but that, too, could change. Before the war, people all the way from the mountains down to the sea believed the sorcerers of Aeterna were all-powerful, dangerous to cross, impossible to defeat. In comparison to that, challenging one woman and her obedient council didn't seem like such a daunting task.

Octavia had been so intent on helping Sima that all of her plans had been focused outward, beyond the walls of Vittoria. But now, sitting in this warm room, surrounded by kind and helpful people while magic healed Rufus's leg, she looked around, and she wondered. There were a few young women and men carving intricate designs into spears in one corner, boasting and chatting as they worked. Children tumbled in from the outer entrance, covered with snow and giggling, and nobody scolded them for being outside after dark. The Clan of the Furious Dead had no fear of the Ferox.

For the first time, Octavia allowed herself to think about what she would do after Sima was reunited with her family.

What she wanted, she realized, was to go back to Vittoria. And she would not slink home with her tail between her legs, ready to accept whatever punishment her parents and the council decided. No, she would go back with her head high, armed with all she had learned outside the wall. She wanted to tell everybody about the cities and clans and caravans, so their town would not be alone anymore. She wanted to topple Camilla from power.

She wanted everybody in Vittoria to learn the truth.

14

Different Paths

———»»———

O ctavia woke with a start, disoriented and confused. She wasn't in her attic bedroom with Albus snoring on the other cot. There were no bells ringing outside to announce the start of the day. She wasn't on a bed at all, and she felt overheated from her neck down while her face was chilly. But she wasn't in a small, drafty watchtower either. The space around her felt too big. There were murmuring voices nearby.

Then she remembered. The washed-out bridge. The Ferox and the spears that made them fall apart. Ira and the Clan of the Furious Dead.

She sat up, yawned, and rubbed her eyes. The large room was quiet, with only one fire at the far end stoked high and bright and a small group of people gathered around it. Octavia recognized Ursa by the size of her silhouette; Brianne, the woman who had saved them from the Ferox, was also there. Rufus and Sima were with them, huddled under a blanket and drinking steaming tea from wooden mugs. From elsewhere in the building there came the sounds of footsteps and voices. The City of the Furious Dead was already awake and starting its day.

Octavia sat up stiffly and untangled herself from the blankets. She was sore from her neck down to her feet. She didn't think she had ever been so exhausted. It was a completely different sort of tiredness than what she experienced from working in the bakery for long hours, or even from the long summer days she had spent with Hana in the woods. She rolled her shoulders and stretched. She had to relieve herself, so she pulled on her sweater against the chill and hurried to the washrooms. It was even colder outside the long room; she could hear the wind groaning through the roofs and rafters. A glimpse through the windows showed that it was just after dawn, and the sky was cloudless and bright.

When she returned to the long room, Ursa gestured for Octavia to join them by the fire. Octavia squeezed onto the bench and felt a glow of pleasure when Sima lifted the edge of the blanket to share.

"Our night patrols have just returned," Ursa said.

"They have *night* patrols," Rufus murmured, with awe in his voice.

"We never go into the Nyx Valley proper," Brianne said, "because the monsters are so much stronger there, but we can get a pretty good look from a distance."

"What do you mean, the monsters are stronger? You mean stronger close to Vittoria?" Octavia asked.

Brianne nodded. "We don't know why it is, but we know about how far we can go without running into danger we can't handle. Piper definitely went too far when he was spotted."

There it was again, the pang of guilt Octavia felt for not telling Piper what had happened to Bram. She knew she had to tell him, but for now she was relieved he wasn't around.

Octavia had never considered that the Ferox might not be as powerful elsewhere in the mountains. Even when Sima had told her there weren't Ferox everywhere in the world, she hadn't fully understood what that meant.

For her entire life, Octavia had imagined Vittoria as the one bright, safe spot in a world overrun with monsters. But that was wrong. Vittoria was not a light but a dark spot, a dangerous and deadly zone where Ferox prowled, one last long-festering war wound in an otherwise healing world.

"What did you see on your patrol?" Rufus asked Brianne.

"Smoke," said Brianne, "from your scouts' watchtower at the confluence of the rivers. Somebody took shelter there last night."

The watchtower that stood where the Rivers Nyx and Iracundia met was directly north of Vittoria on Long Road. If there were Hunters there, that meant that not all of them were searching for the caravan to the east. It might be a normal patrol, Octavia thought, but she didn't quite believe it. Nothing was normal right now. Any Hunters outside Vittoria would be looking for Sima.

"What is it?" Sima said, nudging Octavia in the side. "You're worried. What does that mean?"

"Are they going toward Aeterna?" Rufus said, putting voice to what Octavia was thinking. "Are they even checking East Road?"

"There might be another group to the east," Octavia said. "They might be searching in every direction."

"Will there be people on your trail?" Ursa asked.

Octavia thought about it before answering. She recalled how, a few years ago, a very large, particularly bold Ferox had been stalking shepherds in a high summer pasture south of Vittoria. It never attacked during the daylight, but its presence so worried the shepherds that Mom had taken a group of Hunters out to find it. When they returned, successful and triumphant, Mom had been happy to spend the long evening talking about how they had split into two groups, one to startle the Ferox out of its daytime hiding place, the other to predict where it might try to flee and block its path.

That might be what the Hunters were doing now. The group on East Road would be trying to flush out Octavia and her friends, while the group on Long Road was waiting for them to stumble out of the mountains in search of another path.

"I don't know if they're tracking us," Octavia said. She rubbed her face tiredly. "Maybe."

Ursa's expression was grim. "We keep our distance from Vittoria. We take care to be sure our scouts never cross paths. As I said before, we would never turn children out into the cold, not even children from Vittoria. But if your scouts follow your trail here, we will protect ourselves."

The Hunters, like Octavia, would be stunned to learn there were people living in the remains of Ira. She wanted people to know the truth, the whole truth about everybody outside Vittoria, but not like this. Not when the Hunters were looking for monsters they believed had slaughtered an innocent woman within Vittoria's wall. Not when they had orders from Camilla to suspect that every person they met was an unusual Ferox in disguise. If the people of Vittoria and the Clan of the Furious Dead were to meet, it couldn't be under such dangerous circumstances.

"We'll leave," Octavia said. "We won't draw them here. We'll retrace our steps and set a false path, one that leads away from you."

"I have a better idea," said Rufus, lowering his wooden mug. He looked better than he had the night before, with color in his cheeks and only the slightest wince of discomfort when he moved his leg. "I'll retrace our steps alone. I can walk a little, but I definitely can't keep up with you all the way to Aeterna. So I'll go back and find the Hunters in the watchtower and tell them we got separated and I got lost and you're going somewhere else."

"South, to the lowlands," Sima said. "Out of the mountains. Away from my family."

Octavia nodded. "And away from here."

Brianne was skeptical. "Are your Hunters so easily fooled?"

"Not really," Octavia said, "but they'll have to check it out. They're not stupid, but they are proud. They won't go back without investigating."

"What will you say if they ask about your leg? About how the wound is already healing?" Sima said to Rufus.

He shrugged. "I'll tell them it was only a scratch. They won't check, and I won't unwrap it to show them. I'm the healer's apprentice—they're all used to me scolding them not to let wounds get dirty anyway."

"This is what we'll do." Ursa's tone was decisive and allowed no room for argument. "Rufus will head back downriver, but we won't send you alone. Don't worry," she said, raising her bear paw when Rufus started to speak, "our scouts won't go so far that they'll be spotted. We're only going to accompany you to keep you safe until you can find your people. We're not turning an injured boy out alone on a cold winter day."

Rufus's cheeks colored. "Oh. Thank you."

"As for you two." Ursa looked at Octavia and Sima. "You still plan to head for Aeterna?"

They both nodded.

"We know a route that will get you there more quickly than your Hunters' trails, without bringing you close to the River Nyx. It's not an easy path, so you better leave soon. Brianne will show you the way."

And just like that, before Octavia had time to think about it, it was time to say goodbye. Ursa offered them food and supplies, including a quiver of charm-tipped arrows for Sima and a spear for Octavia.

"You're heading away from where the Ferox prowl, but these will keep you safe from any who have ventured farther out," Ursa said.

"You're just … giving them to us?" Octavia asked, stunned. She touched the gleaming tip of the spear. It was forged of two types of metal, bound together in an intricate pattern that flowed seamlessly into the carvings on the wooden shaft. "How does it work? What kind of magic is this? Do all of your weapons—"

Ursa interrupted her. "There is no time to explain all of that now." She softened her words with a smile. "Already this winter is a strange one. Lowlanders making their way to Aeterna. Children from Vittoria sneaking past the wall and the monsters. Things are changing, don't you think? Perhaps, in the future, we will be able to share our knowledge."

It wasn't an invitation to return, but neither was it an admonishment to stay away. Octavia gripped the spear firmly and nodded.

"Thank you," she said.

Rufus was already outside, bundled up and ready to leave. "I can't believe she just gave them to you," he said, when Octavia and Sima showed him their weapons. "Can you imagine our Crafters just giving their magic away like that?"

"No," Octavia admitted. She leaned the spear against a stone wall to adjust the straps of her pack. "You know you're going to get into so much trouble."

"I know," Rufus said. "I'll just tell them you tricked me." Octavia glared at him, and he laughed. "I'm going to tell Master Cicerus and Master Flavia everything."

"Good. They'll know what to do."

They were both quiet for a moment. The River Iracundia flowed nearby, swift and cold. The morning was clear and bright, without a single cloud in the sky, and the mountains were a beautiful, dappled expanse of deep green and gleaming white beneath the blue. Sima, Brianne, and Piper waited for Octavia in a patch of sunshine several feet away, while another two members of the clan were waiting for Rufus in the opposite direction.

"What do you want me to tell your parents?" Rufus said.

Octavia considered several responses, but in the end she said, "I'll tell them everything when I get home. That's all."

Rufus nodded. "Okay." He started to turn away, then stopped himself. He stepped forward quickly to give Octavia a hug. "I'm jealous that you get to see the sorcerers' city soon. I hope Sima's family is safe."

They parted ways then, with waves and farewells, and set off in different directions.

Brianne led their group across a broad stone bridge that spanned the River Iracundia in the center of Ira, then turned to the west to follow a snow-covered road upriver. It was so cold they all kept their faces wrapped in scarves, making conversation difficult. Octavia focused on moving quickly and tracking where they were going. A drumbeat of excitement in the back of her mind reminded her with every step that she was venturing farther from Vittoria than she had ever dreamed of traveling. The frost-rimmed hemlocks, the barren oaks, the towering pines, the birds and the boulders and the sounds of the wind through pine boughs, they were all familiar to her, but it was also new, and she took it all in with hungry eyes.

West of Ira they turned to the north to follow a trail along a tributary river, and from there they began to climb.

And climb.

And climb.

The trail switchbacked away from the river and just kept climbing. It was all Octavia could do to keep up with Brianne, who didn't seem at all affected by the exertion. Sima was huffing and puffing even more than Octavia; more than once she looked back at Octavia with a commiserating grimace. They didn't have any breath to spare for talking; their breaks were few and brief, only long enough for a sip of water before they continued. They wound up through a thick, shadowed forest of dense pines, cutting back and forth along the steep hillside so many times the turns made Octavia dizzy.

It was midday before they reached the timberline, where the trail joined an old road that showed signs of recent travel.

"This road is neutral territory," Brianne explained, when Octavia asked about the tracks. She stopped and leaned on her spear for a rest. "No clan can claim it, so all the clans are safe using it. It's rarely used this late in the year because the pass is covered with snow, but if what you said about people gathering in Aeterna is true, maybe the other clans want to keep an eye on it."

They had mentioned other clans before, but it was still hard for Octavia to wrap her mind around there being groups of people living in the mountains, traveling without fear of the Ferox, interacting with one another, make agreements about territory and roads.

"They're probably keeping an eye on Vittoria," Piper said. "That's where the real danger is."

Sima glanced at Octavia, eyebrows raised, and Octavia realized she could read that expression perfectly: Sima was wondering if she was going to respond. If Octavia wasn't already panting and sweaty from the climb, she would have blushed at that look, both pleased and embarrassed that Sima already knew her so well.

What Octavia ended up asking was, "Why do you hate Vittoria so much?"

Piper laughed roughly. "Why are you so stupid about the world?"

"Piper," Brianne said in warning.

He rolled his eyes. "It's not my fault she doesn't know anything. The real question is why don't *you* hate it, after everything they did during the war?"

He shoved past Octavia and Sima on the road to continue up the pass.

Brianne let out a slow breath. "Ignore him. He's being difficult."

"What did Vittoria do during the war?" Octavia asked. "I know what *we* say happened, but most of what we're taught is . . . it's . . ."

"Lies?" Sima offered.

"Well. Yes. Or at least, it's not the whole story. I don't know what Piper is talking about."

Brianne started walking again, slower than before, giving space for Piper to get ahead of them. The road was wide enough that they could walk side by side. "You saw our forest of the dead outside the city."

"Um, yes," Octavia said, shivering as she remembered the skulls turning in their rings atop the wooden posts. "It was hard to miss."

"They are our reminder. As long as the dead stand watch, we cannot forget what happened to Ira at the start of the war."

"The sorcerers attacked it, didn't they?" Octavia said. "They were testing their magical weapons. We learned that everybody died."

Brianne glanced sideways at Octavia. "It looked at first like they only had arrows, which the walls would have repelled easily. The leaders of Ira offered to talk with the sorcerers, to avoid a siege or unnecessary bloodshed. But the sorcerers had no interest in talking. They used magical devices to change the arrows into something else. The devices looked only like rings atop tall poles, but when arrows were fired through the rings they became strong enough to break through the stone as though it were paper.

Not everybody died, but a great many were crushed immediately. Then the sorcerers created monstrous creatures out of the rubble to drive the survivors from the city."

Octavia felt as though she had been punched in the gut. "I didn't know they had Ferox that early in the war. I thought they came later."

Brianne shrugged. "I don't know. We only know what we have been told in stories, and those stories say that wherever the sorcerers smashed Ira to rubble, a monster rose from the wreckage. There were few survivors, all of them frightened and confused. They went to Vittoria for help, but they were turned away. The people of Vittoria closed their gates. The survivors from Ira were told that what the sorcerers were doing was their own problem to deal with, and Vittoria would not interfere."

"That's awful," Octavia said softly. "That's cruel."

"Yes. It was. Nobody in our clan was there that day. We only know what the elders have told us. The sorcerers turned our own city into monsters to drive us out, and Vittoria chose to protect itself rather than help. That's what we won't forget."

They walked on in silence, their snowshoes pressing into the road. The day remained clear and bright and cloudless. Octavia had never been so close to the sharp, snow-capped peaks. The awe she felt when looking at them was muted, however, and more than once she turned to look back. They were high above the broad valley of the River Iracundia, but she couldn't see Ira anymore, hidden as it was behind the shoulder of a mountain. Nor could she see Vittoria. This high in the mountains, there might have been no cities at all, neither living nor ruined, neither walled nor welcoming.

"Do you know the name of the sorcerer who created the Ferox?" Octavia asked.

Brianne looked at her, surprised. "No. That name has been lost. Why do you ask?"

"A lot of things that were lost are turning out not to be," Octavia said.

"It's not something anybody in our clan knows. Nor any of the other clans." Brianne took a few steps in silence. "We have to cross the pass before nightfall. There's a shelter on the other side where we can rest for the night."

15

The City of Magic

——»»——

When the next morning dawned, the sky clear and ablaze with golden light, Octavia got her first glimpse of Aeterna.

They had passed the night in a small stone hut just below the northern side of the pass. They doused the fire and replenished the firewood for the next travelers, packed their things, and once again dressed for the cold. Brianne and Piper were going to head back to Ira, while Octavia and Sima continued on their own.

When they left the hut, Brianne set her pack down in the snow and said, "I want to show you something. This way."

She gestured for Octavia and Sima to follow along a shadowed, twisting little trail through the trees. The air felt like icicles in Octavia's nose and throat. Brianne stopped several feet ahead, where the trees ended and the land dropped away.

"Come look," she said.

Below, already alight in the morning sun, was Aeterna. It filled the valley, blooming like a brilliant white flower upon the stem of the ice-encrusted river. A long, unbroken city wall stretched across the valley from west to east, extending up the slopes and cutting into the forests with sharp lines, then winding along the foothills to the north before curving into a point farther up the valley. Outside the wall the floor of the river valley was carved into fields and terraces. Inside the wall, Aeterna was a sea of buildings of every size and shape, most of them built from the same white stone as Vittoria. There was a massive, broken dome in the center of the city; Octavia knew that had to be the forum, where the ruling sorcerers used to meet. Its gleaming prism roof had been shattered during the war. Surrounding it were several towers of different heights, some of which were damaged and toppling, although a few remained unbroken.

It was impossibly big, a maze of buildings and streets and plazas and parks. Even with the broken dome and damaged towers, it didn't look like a ruin left empty after a war. It looked like a city that would wake at any moment and once again fill with life.

"Look," Sima said quietly, and she pointed. Tendrils of smoke rose from an area in the southern half of the city, between the shattered sorcerers' dome and the wall. "That's where they are."

"That's not a small gathering, whatever they're doing there," Brianne said. "Ursa will want to know. Now, look."

She turned to face the east, where the sun sliced into the valley through a gap in the mountains. Octavia could just make out the winding line of what had to be East Road, the road Sima's caravan had been traveling on. It joined Long Road beside the River Nyx at the bottom of the valley.

"Just follow this road downhill," Brianne said. "If you're going down, you're going in the right direction. It'll take you to a bridge over the Nyx. Cross that bridge and you're on Long Road. But really, you can't get lost. The city is right there."

The city was, indeed, right there, and it was hard for Octavia to tear her eyes away. But while it looked close enough to touch, it was still several miles ahead, so she reluctantly turned her back on the view and followed Brianne back to the hut, where Piper was waiting.

Only after they had said goodbye and began to walk in opposite directions did Octavia find the courage to speak.

"Piper," she said. She swallowed and licked her lips. "I have to tell you something."

Piper scowled. "What?"

"Bram is—Bram is dead."

Piper's mouth dropped open. "What? How—"

"He was late coming back to town. He was out in the cold all night." Octavia spoke quickly, afraid that if she hesitated she wouldn't get the words out. "The guards closed the gates. They still close the gates—Vittoria still closes its gates to people who need help. They should have helped him. They should have let him in. His mom tried to make them listen—he told her about you—but she's dead too now. I think . . . we think one of our leaders had her killed. Because of what he told her. To keep her from telling anybody about people outside of Vittoria. I'm sorry." The apology felt hollow and inadequate, but Octavia couldn't find any other words. There were none big enough. "I'm sorry."

She made herself meet Piper's eyes and wait for his response. Brianne reached for his arm. Piper made a noise in his throat, a choked half word, then jerked away from her and turned. He started walking quickly up the road. Brianne watched him for a moment, then looked back at Octavia and Sima.

"I hope you find your family," she said. "Travel safely."

She hurried to follow Piper up the trail.

Octavia and Sima were on their own.

Sima looked like she wanted to say something, but she changed her mind. She started walking in silence. Octavia felt relieved, then felt bad for feeling relieved, but she didn't want to talk about Bram and Willa anymore. She fell into step beside Sima. She took several deep breaths to ease the ache in her chest.

There had been no sign of Ferox during their long climb or when evening fell, which Octavia took as further proof that the Ferox did, in fact, congregate around Vittoria. She had looked at Hana's old map, trying to figure out exactly how far that territory of fearsome monsters extended, but she didn't have enough information. She couldn't make sense of it, how Vittoria could have spent fifty years believing the world to be empty but for the monsters, when in fact the opposite was true. Brianne and Piper were no help in understanding it, nor was Sima. They hadn't grown up in Vittoria. They didn't know what it was to divide the whole of the world between safety inside the wall and danger outside, only to find out that the division had been a lie all along.

She was so wrapped up in her worries she didn't realize at first that Sima was caught in her own thoughts. Octavia stopped to kick ice from the claws of her snowshoe and adjust the straps. Sima walked past her without pausing or glancing her way.

"Hey, wait," Octavia said, jogging awkwardly to catch up. After the long climb yesterday, moving faster than a gentle plod was a challenge; Octavia was glad today's trek was almost entirely downhill. "We should stick together."

Sima blinked as if she had forgotten Octavia was there. "Oh. Yes. You can lead."

"I don't need to lead. The road is wide enough for both of us. We just shouldn't get separated."

Sima nodded absently. She was frowning slightly.

"What is it?" Octavia asked. "Are you okay?"

She half expected Sima to roll her eyes and brush her off, because that was the reaction she had become accustomed to, but Sima's frown only deepened.

"What if they're not there?" Sima said.

"What if who—oh." Octavia felt a clench of worry in her stomach. "Your family?"

"What if they aren't in Aeterna? What if they didn't make it?"

"Oh," Octavia said again. A feeling of helplessness flowed over her.

From the moment they had found the wrecked wagon and dead horse on East Road, she had known that the Ferox could have stalked and attacked the caravan survivors. Sima had to know it as well. But neither of them had dared voice the possibility out loud. And even if the caravan had escaped the Ferox, there were other dangers on the road. There were the clans that Octavia knew nothing about, except that even kind, helpful clanspeople marked their territory by putting skulls on spikes to ward off intruders. There were animals, like bears and wolves and wildcats. There were probably other travelers on the road, other caravans, if the smoke rising from Aeterna was any indication. There was the cold and the snow and avalanches that could race down a mountainside in an instant. There were so many things that could have gone wrong, so many ways for the people in the caravan to have been hurt, scattered, or killed.

There were the Hunters from Vittoria, too. Octavia didn't know what they would do if they came across strangers.

She wanted to reassure Sima, to tell her that her family was safe, but she didn't know that, and she was not going to lie.

She reached out to put her hand on Sima's forearm, gave a gentle squeeze.

"If they aren't in Aeterna, we'll go up East Road to look for them," she said. "We'll keep looking until we find them. No matter what."

Sima looked at her for a long moment, her dark eyes serious and thoughtful. Then she smiled slightly and took Octavia's gloved hand in her own. It was too hard to walk hand-in-hand while tromping along in snowshoes, so they let go after a couple of minutes, but Octavia's fingers felt tingly and warm for a long time after that.

They reached the flat bottom of the river valley around noon and trudged across snow-covered fields that gleamed so brightly the light stung Octavia's eyes. They had to stop to take their heavy coats off, and the cool air felt deliciously pleasant on Octavia's arms. The snow was melting in places, making every step a damp, slushy slog that only grew messier when they crossed the River Nyx and turned onto Long Road. The white stones laid by the long-ago roadbuilders were covered with a thick layer of mud and slush, scored by hoof prints and wagon tracks. Multiple groups of people had passed this way recently. Octavia hoped one of them had been Sima's caravan.

From above, the valley had seemed vast, the city distant. But once they were on Long Road, walking quickly in the sunshine, it felt like no time at all passed before they were at the gates of Aeterna.

The main entrance to the city was a tall archway in the white stone wall. The iron gates were open and so tangled up with trees and vines it looked like they hadn't been closed since the war. Three people sat in the sunshine outside the gate; they too had shed their coats and hats. One of them seemed to be napping on a bench, with his face turned toward the sun and his arm thrown over his eyes. The other two were talking until they saw Octavia and Sima approaching. They ambled into the road. One was armed with a bow and quiver of arrows on her back; the other one had no weapons, but there was a long spear leaning against the gate nearby.

The woman with the bow spoke first. She was about forty, with gray in her dark hair and skin that had been wrinkled and browned by years of sun and wind. She wore simple clothes, with boots laced up to her knees and a leather vest lined with fur.

"Greetings, travelers," she said cheerfully. "Welcome to the City of Healing."

Octavia had never heard Aeterna called that before, but she supposed it made as much sense as anything, if this was where a powerful healer lived.

"What brings you here on this fine day?" the woman asked. Her tone was friendly, but her eyes were sharp and curious. She wasn't asking just to be polite.

Sima wrung her hands and tugged at the ends of her scarf. She looked more nervous than Octavia had ever seen her, her usual confidence replaced by a fragile, trembling hope. She said, "I am looking for my family. We were traveling with a caravan on the road, but we were separated. They were coming here."

The woman pursed her lips. "We've had a few groups arrive in the last several days. Your accent—you are one of the lowlanders from the coast?"

Sima's expression brightened. "Yes. Are they here? Did the caravan make it?"

"A caravan of lowlanders did arrive a few days ago."

Sima stepped forward excitedly, looking past the woman as though she expected to find answer just beyond the gate. "They're here? Is there a sick boy with them? Are the others well?"

The woman put up a hand. "Why don't I show you where they are, and they can tell you themselves?" To her fellow guards, she said, "I'm going to take this kid to the camp." She kicked at the foot of the napping man. "Try not to sleep all day, if you can help it."

He waved at her without opening his eyes. "But it's so nice right now."

The other guard, a younger woman, shook her head. "Bring

back something to eat. This lazy lump already ate the steamed buns."

The older woman muttered, "Yeah, yeah," with a shake of her head. As she led Sima and Octavia through the gateway, she said, "There's supposed to be another storm coming, but you would never guess from how nice it is today. They say weather in the mountains can change in an instant."

"You're not from the mountains?" Sima asked. She walked right beside the woman, pulling ahead every few steps in her eagerness.

"Me? No, I've only been here since summer. I come from the east, in the hills around the River Baria. You know it?" When neither Octavia nor Sima said anything, she shrugged. "Nobody knows it, because there's nothing there to know."

Sima asked, "Did you come here to find the healer too?"

"Not at first. I was just traveling because I got tired of looking at the same neighbors and the same farms every day." The woman looked up at the city around them, taking in the broad avenue with white stone buildings on either side. "The mountain clans started talking about people gathering here, so I decided to see what the fuss was all about. But it's a good place Mother Dulcia is building here. They've only been at it for about a year, but already they've made so much progress making this place livable again. I might stay a while."

"Mother Dulcia?"

"She's the healer you're looking for," the woman said.

Mother Dulcia. Having a name to attach to the healer made her that much more real. Octavia saw Sima repeating the name to herself as they walked, her lips moving silently.

The narrow streets and tall stone buildings of Aeterna reminded Octavia uncannily of Vittoria; she kept feeling like she should catch a whiff of her family's bakery around the next bend, or hear the sound of butchers arguing in the market and cart-wheels rattling on cobblestones. But for all that the buildings and streets looked the same, the city was eerily empty. Every window was dark. Every chimney was cold. Many of the doors were broken from their hinges or removed, and nearly every window was shattered, leaving dark holes that gaped onto the street with cold, shadowy menace. Here and there they passed a building that had completely collapsed, often with scorch marks still marring the white stone rubble.

Octavia started in alarm when a flock of birds burst from a shattered chimney above the street.

But there were signs of change. In some places along the broad main road, debris and materials had been piled in the streets. A few of the buildings, those that looked studier and intact, echoed with the sound of voices and tools. In other places there were gardens with autumn's last plants still clinging to stakes or curling along the ground. Octavia didn't know if it was good progress for nearly a year's worth of work, as the woman said, but it was obvious there was work being done.

The farther into the city they walked, the more people they saw. They passed a sunny plaza where a group of young men and women were hanging laundry to dry. A bickering older couple led a mule and cart in the opposite direction. A small pack of laughing children yelped and raced out of one alley, across the avenue, and into another, and a moment later a teenage girl came barreling after them, shouting for them to stop or else she would tell their parents.

When the sound of her voice faded, Octavia could hear the low rumble of a crowd. The source revealed itself when they turned a corner and entered a large, open square.

The square was filled with people, far more than they had seen in Ira. There were so many tents and wagons laid out in chaotic lines and clusters that she couldn't begin to count them. She could see dozens of circles of benches and chairs around fires, and even a few makeshift chimney ovens built from the same white stone as the city. A pen of goats bleated in annoyance nearby, and a couple of small children led a few shaggy, stout cattle past. To the right, stretched along the eastern side of the city square, were two long rows of stalls and tables with food and goods spread out for sale. Octavia's stomach grumbled when she caught a whiff of spicy roasted meat. The buildings around the square had laundry hanging from their windows, smoke rising from their chimneys, and people hurrying in and out of the doorways. Chickens pecked and clucked underfoot, and everywhere people were talking, laughing, and bartering.

"They come from all over," said the guard. Her voice as she looked into the square was warm and fond. "It's growing crowded, but we're fixing up the buildings as fast as we can. We've made a lot of progress since spring."

Octavia could not stop staring. Ever since she had seen the smoke rising from Aeterna that morning, she had known there were people here. But she hadn't quite realized how many people—or how many different kinds of people. There were a few hundred individuals, she guessed, and many of them seemed to have brought a lot of stuff with them. She heard several accents and languages. The city square smelled of food and animals and tea and people. After so long in the quiet of the mountains and the hush of the forest, it was overwhelming.

Sima didn't seem perturbed at all, and Octavia remembered that Sima claimed Iberne was ten times the size of Vittoria. This was probably nothing to her.

Sima stood on her toes to look around quickly. "Where are

they? Where are the Ibernese? They will be in bright tents. My mother is a weaver and a dyer. You must have seen the colorful tents?"

The woman lifted her chin and pointed. "I think they grabbed a bit of space for themselves over by the fountain. That way, to the west, do you see that headless stone woman sticking up?"

Sima was already headed in that direction before Octavia spotted the statue. She ran to catch up, while the guard followed more slowly behind them. They wound through the crowded square for a few minutes before Sima stopped suddenly, then broke into a run. She was headed straight for a cluster of four or five colorful tents surrounded by painted carts, stacks of hay and firewood and supplies, and makeshift pens holding a few glossy horses. The encampment was right beside a dry fountain, as the guard had said, beneath a tall, headless statue. There were a couple of people sitting on bales of hay, and a woman crouched beside one of the wagons with tools in hand.

"Orlena? Malik?"

At the sound of Sima's voice, the people outside the tents looked up. The woman by the wagon dropped her tools with a clatter and jumped to her feet. For a second, she only stared. Then she opened her mouth and shouted, "Leila! Leila, come out here!"

Before she had even finished, she was racing toward Sima to draw her into a tight embrace. The other few people did the same, all of them gathering around her and hugging her, speaking rapidly in a combination of languages. Octavia only caught a few of the words, but it was enough to know that they were telling Sima they had thought she was dead, carried away by the monsters, gone forever.

A flap on one of the tents opened, and a woman with long black hair stepped out. Sima spotted her and wrested herself away from the others. She ran for the woman, with her arms wide. "Mama!"

"Sima! Oh, Sima!"

Sima's mother caught her in her arms and held her tight. Other people came out of the tents, including a few kids and a very old woman, and everybody was talking and exclaiming, everybody was laughing and crying, and Octavia felt awkward and out of place watching it all from the outside. She couldn't help but think how very different a reunion this was than the one that had greeted her after she had stayed outside the walls that first night, when she had met Sima. She told herself not to be jealous. It wasn't the same thing at all. But she couldn't forget that her mother had been too angry to hug her.

The guard from the gate caught up to Octavia and said, "Huh. Guess she found them after all."

"Mama, where's Pavi?" Sima was asking. "Is he okay? Is everybody okay?"

"We're all fine," said her mother. She hugged Sima again; there were tears on her cheeks. "Pavi is in the care of Mother Dulcia. He is doing well. You're the only one we've been worried about." She kissed both of Sima's cheeks, then her forehead. "We have been looking along the road, but we didn't see you. Where have you come from?"

Sima tucked herself in happily at her mother's side. "I came a different way. My friend Octavia helped me, and so did some people from a mountain clan. Octavia is from Vittoria. Octavia, this is my mother."

For the first time, the Ibernese group noticed Octavia standing to the side. She smiled shakily and said, "Hi," and tried to pretend it wasn't unnerving to have so many strangers staring at her.

"Octavia, is it?" Sima's mother said. "Thank you for helping my daughter."

The guard beside her spoke. "Did she say . . . Vittoria?"

Octavia felt a shiver of unease. "Yes?"

The guard looked at her curiously. "You didn't say."

"You didn't ask," Octavia retorted.

Sima's mother stepped forward. Her smile was gone now, replaced by a worried expression. "Thank you so much for helping Sima. Will you come and eat with us?"

"She can't do that right now," the guard said. She put her hand on Octavia's shoulder, and it wasn't a light touch. "She'll have to go talk to Mother Dulcia first."

"What?" Octavia said, surprised. "Why? I don't need a healer. I'm not sick."

"What is the problem?" Sima asked.

"No problem," said the guard. "It's what Mother Dulcia wants. She'll be back in time for dinner. Come on."

She steered Octavia away from the colorful tents.

"I don't understand," Octavia said, her voice shaking. "What's going on? Why does she want to talk to me?"

"She wants to meet everybody who comes here from Vittoria," the guard said. "Don't look so scared. She only wants to talk."

Octavia swallowed nervously as the guard guided her through the city square. Nobody had been threatening or aggressive so far. Maybe Mother Dulcia did only want to talk. Maybe there was nothing to worry about.

Octavia stopped suddenly. The guard bumped into her.

"What do you mean?" Octavia said, twisting around to look at her. "Everybody from Vittoria? Does that mean there are other people from Vittoria here?"

The guard shoved her forward. "Ask her when you meet her. Let's go."

16

The Healer

———»»———

The guard took Octavia to a large building that stretched along one side of the city square. It had once been grand, with broad stone steps leading up to tall doors and an endless expanse of windows looking over the city. But like everything else in Aeterna, it was damaged now; most of the windows were broken, the white stone was marred and cracked, and planks of wood patched the roof where slate tiles had broken away. People bustled in and out of the main entrance, taking no notice of Octavia and the guard.

The doors opened to a broad hall, which in turn led to a large courtyard.

"Through here," said the guard. "The garden is where she rests at this time of day."

Entering the courtyard was like stepping out of winter and into a warmer, gentler season. Three stories of covered walkways and white stone pillars surrounded a lush, elegant garden; there had once been a glass roof overhead, but all that remained were jagged shards around the edges. The garden itself was still green, with scattered flowers in bloom. The leaves were turning to red and gold on a few of the trees, as though the garden was slow to catch up to the changing seasons outside. There was no snow or ice, not even in the shadows. Soft green moss blanketed roots and hung from branches. In the center of the garden was a long, rectangular pool made of vibrant blue and green and yellow tiles. Many of the tiles were cracked or damaged, but they were all very clean. Waterlilies dotted the water. The cheeping of frogs echoed through the atrium, and little songbirds darted from tree to tree overhead in puffy little flashes of red and brown.

As pleasant as it was, the humid warmth that surrounded Octavia made her wary. It was neither glass nor walls keeping that garden warm and green. It was magic, quite powerful magic. The kind of magic nobody was supposed to know how to do anymore. There were stories from before the war of sorcerers who could alter the weather for their own purposes, to calm or call up storms whenever they wanted. Those stories had never ended well.

At the far end of the pool, sitting on a bench in the last patch of sunlight, was a woman. She was very old, at least eighty or ninety by Octavia's guess, with slightly stooped shoulders and thin hands. She had a book open on her lap, but her eyes were closed and her face turned toward the sun.

"Mother Dulcia," said the guard, "I've brought somebody to meet you. A traveler."

The old woman smiled. "Oh! How lovely."

"She's from Vittoria," said the guard. "She arrived with the missing Ibernese girl. The one they thought was dead."

"The girl is alive? Leila must be so relieved to have her daughter back. I know she feared the worst."

The old woman finally turned away from the sunbeam to open her eyes. Her right eye was green, but the left was completely white and surrounding by a faint starburst of scars.

Mother Dulcia said, "Come closer, child, and sit with me."

Octavia didn't realize she had stopped to stare until the guard nudged her back. Her heart was thumping and she felt a sudden chill sneak through the warmth of the garden. She dropped her pack to the ground and sat at the end of the bench, as far from the old woman as she could. Mother Dulcia had snow-white hair and wrinkled skin; her one good eye was clear and bright. She wore a simple brown dress cinched at the waist with a rope belt and boots that looked much too big for her small stature. She was smiling faintly, as though she found Octavia's scrutiny amusing. The green of her eye, the shape of her cheekbones, the tilt of her jaw, the way she held her shoulders straight, even the way she smiled, it all reminded Octavia uncannily of Master Flavia, with the same innate self-assurance and gentle strength. The familiarity was not soothing. It only made Octavia more nervous.

"Will you send in some tea when you leave?" Mother Dulcia said to the guard. The guard didn't move right away, not until Mother Dulcia turned to look at her. "Go on. There's nothing to worry about."

It took Octavia a second to realize that the guard was hesitating because of her. Because she thought that a tired, hungry twelve-year-old girl with dirty clothes and messy hair could be a danger to Mother Dulcia. It was so ridiculous Octavia wanted to laugh, but her growing unease kept her reaction locked inside. The guard gave her a stern look—maybe it was supposed to be a warning—before turning sharply and striding back across the garden.

Octavia waited, and stared, and waited, but the old woman didn't say anything. She just kept looking at Octavia, with one good eye and one blind eye, smiling. Octavia was going to have to speak first.

So she asked, "Are you the healer?"

"I am, yes. You may call me Mother Dulcia, as the others do. What is your name?"

"Octavia. Can you really—"

Octavia paused when a young woman hurried into the atrium; she was carrying a tray with a teapot and two cups, both of far finer porcelain than Octavia had ever used. The woman stared at Octavia, then nodded quickly to Mother Dulcia before retreating. Something about the way she darted in and out reminded Octavia uncomfortably of the servants at the councilors' houses in Vittoria, the ones who told her to use the side door for her bread deliveries and tutted in annoyance when she tracked slush into their kitchens. For her to have arrived so quickly, they must keep water hot all day, to be ready whenever Mother Dulcia requested tea. Octavia wondered if all the people outside, the ones sleeping in tents and wagons alongside chickens and goats in the crowded city square, knew that Mother Dulcia had a warm green garden inside this old sorcerers' palace.

"You want to ask me something?" Mother Dulcia said.

"Can you really cure any sickness?" Octavia asked. She tore her gaze away from the woman's face, trying to act casual, when in truth her heart was thumping and her throat was dry. She wished she could have learned more about the people in Aeterna before meeting Mother Dulcia.

"I'm afraid not," said Mother Dulcia, chuckling. "Is that what they say about me? I don't know if anybody in the world can cure *every* sickness. But I can cure many. I try to cure as many as I can."

"How?"

The chuckled turned into a full laugh. "Oh, now, it would take a lifetime to explain that, because it has taken me a lifetime to learn all that I know. For some I use magic. For others I use different methods. I am nothing special as a healer."

Octavia narrowed her eyes. In her experience, people who claimed to be nothing special were actually trying to say the exact opposite.

Mother Dulcia said, "I only want to help people, and I have spent my life striving to do just that."

"What about Sima's brother? Um, Leila's son? Can you help him?"

Mother Dulcia lifted the lid of the teapot to peer inside. "Not quite ready yet. Pavi is a very sick little boy, but I think I can help him, yes. Why don't you ask me what it is you truly want to ask, Octavia? Don't be afraid. I will answer as best I can."

Octavia's shoulders crept up toward her ears as she tensed. She wasn't *afraid*. There were suspicions scratching at the back of her mind, like small Ferox in the orchard just out of sight, and so many things she wanted to ask. When Sima had first told her people were gathering in Aeterna with a healer, she had imagined a small group, maybe one or two dozen who would stop for a while before heading back to their homes. She had not once thought it might mean they were coming here to stay, to clean and repair buildings destroyed in the war, to replant gardens and move piles of debris and welcome strangers at open gates.

Octavia wanted to know the truth about the world outside the walls, but she didn't know how this gathering in Aeterna fit into everything else she had learned since meeting Sima. To her Aeterna had only ever been a city of war: ruined, lost, empty. The green garden around her, with its waterlilies and songbirds, felt out of place and uncomfortable, like an ill-fitting boot.

She asked, "What are you doing here? I mean, in Aeterna? The guard said you've been here a year?"

"Not quite that long. The first of us arrived toward the end of last winter. As for the reason . . ." Mother Dulcia looked out over the pond, her expression thoughtful. "This used to be such a beautiful city. I know, yes, it was also quite terrible. There were so many people here who wielded great power in truly awful ways, and so many died as a result. But over the years I met people from the mountains in my travels, from the clans that still live here as well as others, and they made me want to remember the beauty as well. I began to wonder if we could rebuild Aeterna, not as a city of unchecked power and violence, but as a city of healing. Wouldn't that be lovely?"

Octavia didn't think that sounded lovely. She thought it sounded like a lie.

"You haven't told me why you want to talk to me," Octavia said.

Mother Dulcia inclined her head thoughtfully. "What do you mean?"

"The guard said you want to talk to everyone from Vittoria."

"Ah. Yes." Mother Dulcia lifted the lid of the teapot again and nodded in satisfaction before pouring the tea into both cups. She handed one to Octavia and took the second for herself. "You want to know if there are others from Vittoria here. Others who have slipped free of the cage."

Octavia didn't like the word *cage*, didn't like the way Mother Dulcia smiled when she said it. She lifted the teacup to take a sip. It was too hot for her to taste anything.

"Vittoria has been isolated for fifty years," Mother Dulcia went on. "But the world outside its high wall is very large, and not so far away, if one ventures outward. Surely you don't believe that nobody else has dared look beyond your great wall in all that time? Turned their back on being locked away in apparent safety?"

Until a few days ago, that was exactly what Octavia had believed. There was nothing else in the world, so there was no reason to leave. Anybody who tried would die. That was what she had learned for as long as she could remember. The wall was high, the gates solid, the Crafters powerful, and Vittoria was the only safe place left in the world. She knew now it wasn't true; very little of what she had been taught was true.

Even so, Mother Dulcia's question bothered her. Wouldn't she *know* if people were leaving Vittoria? Everybody knew when somebody didn't come back for even one night. They would surely know if somebody left for longer and never returned.

Some people did leave and never return, Octavia thought.

She took another sip of tea.

People were caught outside the walls and dragged away by the Ferox. People died in the woods. Drowned in the river or the mountain lakes. Froze to death in sudden winter storms and were never found in spring. Not often, and every one was mourned, but people *did* vanish from Vittoria. It was just that everybody assumed they died outside the walls. How many of them had truly died? How many had walked away to become the travelers Mother Dulcia had met over the years? What had they told her about Vittoria?

Her mind was racing. She took another drink. The tea was hot and bitter and the steam that rose from the cup smelled of freshly turned earth in a spring garden. It was not altogether unpleasant, though, and something about it was familiar.

Octavia's heart skipped. She lowered the teacup. She looked at Mother Dulcia, looked away quickly. Her small stature, her white hair. Her single green eye, and the other, the left, white and blind and marred by scars.

"This is, um, this is good. What kind of tea is it?" Octavia's voice trembled as she asked.

Mother Dulcia inhaled the steam from her own cup. "It's a summer bellflower blend. My daughter was a very peculiar little girl who couldn't abide anything sweet, so I had quite the challenge coming up with something she liked."

It's meant to be pleasantly bitter, Master Flavia had said, that morning in her workshop. A bellflower blend she remembered from her childhood.

It wasn't possible. Octavia set the cup on the tray with shaking hands. The entire world shrunk to the size of that green courtyard garden, with the stone bench solid beneath her and the old woman so calm beside her. Nothing else. There was a hum in her ears. The tea tasted like dirt, and her stomach felt tight and queasy.

Everybody believed that Master Flavia's mother, the infamous sorcerer Agrippina, had died at the end of the war. Camilla had killed her own sister to stop her from creating a magical weapon even worse than the plague. She was dead. Everybody knew that.

They knew it because it was what Camilla had told them.

But Camilla lied. She lied about Sima. She lied about Willa. She lied about everything.

She could have lied about killing her sister as well.

Octavia could be wrong. She wanted to be wrong about this woman with an eye missing where Camilla claimed to have struck the killing blow, and the remaining eye the same moss-green as Flavia's, and a smile that curved as Flavia's did. A very skilled healer, just as Flavia has said her mother used to be. The old woman before Octavia hadn't even claimed Mother Dulcia as her name when she introduced herself; she had only said it was what the others called her.

Mother Dulcia was Agrippina.

Octavia remembered, suddenly, what she had glimpsed on Camilla's face the first time they had met in the archway outside Flavia's shop. Camilla had said that Flavia was not like her mother, and for a fleeting moment there had been something strange in her expression. Something that had looked, to Octavia, like fear.

The hush of the atrium was broken by the slap of footsteps near the entrance. Somebody said, "No, wait, she's—"

A woman, breathless and insistent, her voice echoing from the tiles of the courtyard walkways, argued, "I have to see! They said she looks like—I have to see, I have to—"

Octavia's mouth fell open. Mother Dulcia—Agrippina—whoever she was, said something, but it sounded like the words were spoken underwater, and Octavia understood none of them. All of her attention was on the voice across the garden, on the figure emerging from the shadows. Hair the color of ripe apricots. Freckles like stars across her nose.

People vanished from Vittoria, and everybody assumed they died.

"Octavia!"

It was Hana.

17

Secrets beneath Secrets

⎯⎯⎯»»⎯⎯⎯

O ctavia was on her feet. She didn't remember standing.

It was Hana. She blinked to be certain. She wasn't imagining things. It was Hana, alive and well, running now around the side of the pond, running toward her with wide eyes, her mouth open in surprise as she cried, "Octavia! What are you doing here?"

Octavia stumbled forward, her vision blurring, and fell into Hana's arms. Hana wrapped her in a tight embrace and held her close.

"They said there was a girl with orange hair from Vittoria," Hana said, her voice shaky and damp as she laughed on the verge of tears. "I didn't think—I had to be sure—what are you doing here? How did you get here?"

Octavia leaned back to get a look at her sister's face, although she didn't dare let go. She was afraid that if she did Hana would vanish, or she would awake to find she was still asleep in the hut atop the pass—or, worse, in her attic bedroom at home, and Hana was still gone, and nothing had changed. She had so many things she wanted to say, answers to Hana's questions and a million questions of her own, and all of them were crowded in her throat like brambles choking a ditch. Her eyes filled with tears and she wiped them away quickly.

"We thought you were dead!" she burst out. "The Hunters found your knife! Everybody thinks you're dead!"

Hana's expression changed, shifting through a complicated series of emotions that Octavia didn't quite recognize—and that was all wrong, not being able to read Hana's face, even though it was the same face she remembered, the same straight nose and freckles and blue eyes, the same scar above her upper lip from where she had accidentally caught herself with a hook while casting a fishing line when she was young, before Octavia was born.

"I know," Hana said quietly. "I know, and I'm so sorry. I can explain, but you have every reason to be mad at me. A lot has happened."

"Indeed it has," said Mother Dulcia. "We've accomplished a great deal, and Hana has been a great help."

Octavia had almost forgotten about the old woman, so overwhelmed was she by Hana's appearance. She started and turned, still not letting go of her sister, to see Mother Dulcia standing by the bench with her teacup in hand. She was smiling, nothing but warmth and fondness on her face.

Hana returned the smile and said, "We all work together in the City of Healing." She squeezed Octavia around the shoulders. "I can't wait to tell you all about it. But you must be starving! And Mother Dulcia has things she needs to be doing. She's always working so hard for us. We won't bother her anymore."

The last time Octavia had heard that voice from Hana—so sweet and mild and completely unlike her normal voice—they had been returning to Vittoria on a summer evening, after a day spent tracking and hunting in the woods south of town. The guards on duty at the southern gate had questioned them sternly, but Hana had only smiled and nodded and agreed with everything they said, while at the same time telling them nothing about where they had been. Once they were through, she had burst into giggles, and Octavia had laughed with her.

She didn't feel like laughing now. She didn't know why Hana was using that voice on Mother Dulcia; she only knew that it made her uncomfortable. And everything she had been thinking right before Hana showed up and scattered her thoughts returned in a rush: Agrippina, the bitter bellflower tea. The scope of Master Camilla's lies, all of it too big inside the stormy upset of her own mind. Tears filled her eyes again. She sniffled and ducked her head and took in big, gasping breaths, but it was no use. She couldn't stop crying.

"Oh, Octavia, you're exhausted," Hana said. She let go of Octavia's shoulders just long enough to pick up her pack. "This is yours, right? I'm going to take her to get some food and rest."

"Of course," said Mother Dulcia. "We'll have plenty of time to talk later. It was lovely to meet you, Octavia."

Octavia managed a nod and a creaky, "Thank you . . . Mother Dulcia." She stumbled over the name and hoped the old woman didn't notice.

She let Hana steer her out of the courtyard garden, through the building's entrance hall, and into the golden afternoon. The sun was sinking down to the western mountains, where a line of storm clouds gathered over the peaks, and the day's warmth had given way to a brisk chill. The city square was filling with smoke as people gathered around campfires for the evening.

"Where is your Ibernese friend staying? I'll take you to them," Hana said.

"What? No! I want to stay with you," Octavia said. She couldn't bear to let Hana out of her sight, not when she had just found her again. "What are you doing here? Have you been here all along? What happened? Why didn't you come home?"

Hana pulled her close as they descended the stairs. "There's a lot to explain."

"So start explaining!" Octavia cried. "We thought you were dead!"

Hana stopped to give Octavia another hug. "I know. I know, and I will explain. But I have guard duty tonight, and I don't want you stuck alone with strangers in a drafty bunk room. It's better for you to go back to your friend for now."

"But what are you—"

"I promise I'll come find you first thing in the morning," Hana said. "I know you have a lot of questions, and I'll answer them tomorrow."

Octavia bit her lower lip. She couldn't wait until morning. There were some things too important to put off.

"Answer one now," she said. "Why didn't you come home? We thought you were dead. Mom got hurt looking for you. Badly hurt. And everybody's been . . . why didn't you come home?"

Hana closed her eyes briefly, as though the question caused her pain. "I don't know if I have a good enough reason. I have to tell you everything else to explain that, and that will take some time. Can you wait one night? Please?"

Octavia didn't want to wait even one minute, much less an entire night. As happy as she was that Hana was alive and unhurt and right beside her, all of those unanswered questions were like the storm clouds over the mountains, gathering and growing and promising trouble.

But it was unusual for Hana to plead for anything—or it had been, before, but so much had changed. Maybe Hana had changed too.

"I guess I can. Sima's family is over there." Octavia pointed across the square to the fountain statue with the colorful tents and wagons at its base. With her other hand she clung a bit tighter to Hana's arm. "Do you have to go right now?"

"I'm already a little bit late for guard duty," Hana admitted. She walked with Octavia toward the fountain, weaving easily through the activity and chaos in the square. "And Mother Dulcia doesn't like that."

Octavia shivered slightly at the mention of the old woman. "Mother Dulcia . . ." She hesitated. She didn't know how much she wanted to say or ask. She didn't know if her suspicions would sound outrageous to Hana. "Is she . . . do you know a lot about her?"

Hana stopped suddenly. She pressed a finger lightly to Octavia's lips, leaned close, and murmured, "Not here."

She dropped her hand and smiled, but her gaze darted to the left and right, taking in the people around them. Nobody seemed to be paying them any attention, but still the hair on Octavia's neck prickled.

When Hana spoke again, her voice was much louder. "She's a great woman, I agree. We're so lucky to be here with her."

"Yeah," Octavia said faintly.

Hana hugged her again, squeezing her tight. "I'm excited to tell you everything tomorrow. But I've got to get to my guard duty now."

She left Octavia there in the city square, not far from the Ibernese camp by the fountain. She turned and waved twice as she walked away, and Octavia knew she meant it as reassurance, but it was impossible to be reassured when everything was so strange.

Octavia walked the rest of the way to Sima's camp slowly, her thoughts jumbled and racing. Hana was alive. She was *alive*, and here, and she was doing guard duty for the sorcerer Agrippina, who was claiming to be a great healer, in the magical city everybody had thought was lost forever to the war. Nothing made sense.

She wanted to chase after Hana and demand answers *now*, but she knew better. Hana hadn't said Octavia didn't need to know or didn't need to worry. She had promised to explain. Maybe it had been the better part of a year since Octavia had seen her sister, but she didn't think Hana could have changed that much. Hana was still the one who had always treated Octavia not like a little kid but like a friend, like a peer, like somebody who deserved to know all the things the adults didn't think kids should know. She could trust that Hana would keep her promise to tell her more in the morning.

At the camp, a group of travelers from Iberne were gathered around a cooking fire. One of the women saw her first and said something to the others, then Sima spun around and ran over to her. Octavia thought for a second she was going to get caught up in another hug, but Sima stopped short and dropped her arms awkwardly to her side.

"Where did they take you? What did they want?" she demanded.

"Only to see . . . The healer is . . ." Octavia gestured vaguely back across the square. "Just to see . . . I guess."

She had no idea what to say. It all felt so impossible to explain.

"See what?" Sima asked, her eyes narrowing. "What are you talking about?"

"My sister's here," Octavia blurted out.

"What?"

"My sister Hana. She's not dead. She's here. She's—I don't—she didn't—"

"Wait," Sima said. "Come here."

Sima grabbed Octavia's arm and dragged her to the center of the encampment. There, she picked up two empty crates and set them a little bit away from the others, who were watching with curiosity and amusement. Sima pushed Octavia to sit on one of the crates, then stomped back to the fire. She returned a few moments later with a meal of spiced meat and vegetables wrapped in a soft flatbread, all of it so warm and fragrant it made Octavia drool.

"Now. Eat," said Sima, "and tell me."

Octavia did exactly that as the sun set and evening fell over Aeterna. She told Sima about Mother Dulcia and her strange garden, and about Hana's surprise appearance and promise to explain more in the morning. Then she realized she had never told Sima the full story of Hana's apparent death and Mom's injuries, so she backtracked to fill her in on all of that too. Sima let her talk without asking many questions, even when Octavia knew she was looping back and forth over her own story, making little sense. Her dinner was gone before she knew it—she had been very hungry— but almost as soon as she finished, Sima's mother appeared beside them with two cups of tea and some seed cakes wrapped in cloth.

"I want to thank you again for helping Sima," Leila said. Her smile was warm, her voice soft. She looked very much like Sima, with the same brown skin and eyes, the same thick black hair, the same patched but colorful kind of clothing. In the firelight, threads in her long scarf gleamed gold. "It was very brave of you to help her even when your city didn't want to."

Octavia's face warmed. "She helped me first, on the road."

Leila's smile faded. She smoothed a hand over Sima's hair. "We were so worried about her. Both of you were very brave. Did you meet the healer this afternoon?"

"Um. Yes." Octavia glanced at Sima, then looked again at her mother. Leila's expression was calm but assessing.

"What do you think of her?" Leila asked.

Octavia hesitated. She had a feeling Leila was testing her some- how, but she didn't know what kind of test it was, or what the right answer would be. She didn't even know if she knew what she thought about Mother Dulcia, who was probably Agrippina, and was certainly not a simple healer like she was claiming to be. But if she was truly helping Sima's brother, Octavia didn't want to say anything to jeopardize that.

"I think," she said carefully, "she used to be a sorcerer."

Leila nodded. "I think so too, as do a lot of others, although people only speak of it in whispers. From what Sima has told me, we don't distrust healing magic as much as your people, but there are many who feel as Vittoria does."

"But she . . . she is helping people, isn't she? Like your son?"

"She is," Leila said. "There are a great number of people here who came to her with illnesses or diseases that no other healer could cure, and most of them are well now. That Mother Dulcia is a great healer is not in question."

"What *is* in question, Mama? You always talk in riddles," Sima grumbled.

Leila smiled and tugged Sima's braid. "I like to annoy you with my riddles. But I'm afraid I don't have a very good riddle this time, or at least not one with a good answer. I only wonder why those people who have been healed are still here, rather than returning to their homes. Mother Dulcia and her closest helpers have been in this city for almost a year, and it's winter now. Anybody who wished to leave should be on the road now, yet . . ." Leila turned to look across the city square. "Here they remain. They clear the buildings Mother Dulcia tells them to clear. They dig and they repair and they rebuild and they never speak of leaving." She smiled down at them again. "Finish your tea and cake, then go into the tent. Everybody is saying it's going to snow tonight, so I don't want you sitting out in the cold too long."

After she had walked back to the fire, Octavia said, "What does she mean? Are people not allowed to leave?"

Sima shook her head. "No, it's not that. I know they've been going out and hunting and searching the road. And some caravan drivers and guides from other groups have left, because Orlena was talking about sending letters along with them. Maybe people don't want to leave."

"But your mom is right. The winter is going to get a lot worse. Maybe if everybody was in houses, but sleeping in tents through an Aeterna winter . . ." Octavia shivered. "I don't think your fellow lowlanders know what they're getting into."

"I don't either," Sima said. "But I want to."

"Hana will know," Octavia said. "She'll tell me. She has to. And what she doesn't know, we'll find out for ourselves."

Sima glanced at her sideways, but instead of arguing or answering, she just bumped Octavia's shoulder with her own. They sat there for a little while longer, drinking tea and eating sweet, crumbly cake, as the oncoming storm clouds slowly covered all the stars in the sky.

18
To Mend What Is Broken

———»»———

Clouds gathered during the night, and when morning came the first frozen, biting snowflakes began to whirl down from a low gray sky, tossed about by cold wind that whistled and twisted through Aeterna. All across the city square tents flapped noisily, smoke from the fires whipped this way and that, and people ducked their heads beneath hoods as they hurried about. It was the sort of day when Octavia would welcome a chance to help in the bakery, surrounded by the comforting heat of the ovens, pitying the customers who had to go back into the cold with their breakfasts in hand. The lowlanders in Aeterna seemed more excited than worried, however, chattering eagerly about how much snow might fall as they tightened guylines and maneuvered carts and barrels to form protective walls.

In Aeterna, the only bakery was one run out of the back of a wagon parked near the center of the city square marketplace. Two bearded men and their children sold crunchy bread and salted rolls through a window to a line of customers that wound through the market. The bakers greeted Hana by name and smiled when she told them Octavia was her sister.

"It's not as good as Dad's bread," Hana confided, when they were beyond the hearing of the bakers. She took a bite of her roll and chewed it as she walked along. "They use a different kind of wheat and sweeten it with some kind of flower nectar instead of honey. And everything lowlanders make is so salty, because they never worry about running out and everything spoils in their hot weather. But it's still pretty good."

The bread *was* too salty, and Octavia wasn't hungry anyway, having already eaten with Sima and her mother. She felt a jab of homesickness to hear Hana talk about Dad's baking. She wanted to ask if Hana felt it too, if she was wondering what their parents were doing right now, if they now believed two of their daughters were dead, if Albus had told them anything about confronting Octavia at Oldgate, if Augustus and Lavinia were crying or fighting or trying to pretend things would be okay. Octavia worried, too, about Rufus, and whether he had met the Hunters and made it safely home.

Octavia had not slept well the night before; she had lain awake for hours thinking about Hana and Mother Dulcia and Aeterna, about everything she had learned and everything she still did not know. Her mind was a muddle of tiredness and confusion. Every time she took a breath to speak she remembered Hana putting a finger to her lips and whispering, "Not here."

Not here, in the city square, surrounded by people.

Not here, where somebody might be listening.

So she held her tongue, and she let Hana talk about weather and bread and inconsequential things as they made their way to the northern edge of the square. Hana pointed out people and groups and encampments as they passed; she knew where almost everybody was from and why they had come to Aeterna. Most of them greeted her by name with waves and smiles. More than one person stopped to ask her about how to prepare for the coming storm. Hana answered their questions every time. It seemed like she was just as good at explaining things to lowlanders as she had been when she taught Octavia to hunt and track in the woods.

Finally, after so many interruptions and detours that Octavia lost count, they reached the far side of the city square. The broad avenue from the south continued there, a wide expanse of paving stones marching through the center of Aeterna. The road led straight to the broken dome of the forum, which glittered even though there was no sunlight. It was by far the largest building in Aeterna, even with half of its enclosure broken away, but there were towers around it that stood taller.

"I never really imagined it being so big," Hana said. "When people told stories about it, I pictured it a lot smaller."

Octavia was thinking the exact opposite. "I always imagined it a lot bigger. I thought it would be big enough to cover all of Vittoria."

"Huh. It's funny, I guess, that we got such different ideas from hearing the same stories." Hana walked a few steps in silence, then turned to look over her shoulder. They were well away from the city square now; there was nobody nearby. "We can talk now. Nobody ever comes up this way. People are suspicious about the forum." A pause, then Hana said, "You must be so angry with me."

Octavia didn't know what to say to that. She thought she might be angry, but more than anything she was tired of feeling so many things she didn't know how to describe. "Everyone thinks you're dead," she said.

"I was always going to go back," Hana said. "I *am* going to go back. I never meant to leave forever. I didn't even mean to leave for as long as I did. It was just . . . things got complicated."

"How?" Octavia asked. "Vittoria isn't that far. You know the way."

"I know. It's just that . . ." Hana tugged her scarf tighter as the wind picked up, whistling down the broad avenue with force. "Let me start at the beginning, okay? You can be angry and yell at me all you want, but let me at least tell you everything."

Octavia shrugged. "Okay."

"I was on patrol around Gray Bear Mountain, up on the eastern ridge. It was midday and clear, so I had a good view of the entire Nyx Valley. And I saw smoke from the north."

They were approaching the forum now, where the broad road ended and wide, stone steps rose to enter the building. There had once been a full five sets of double doors across the front, each twice as tall as a person or more, but the doors had long ago fallen away. The five doorways now looked like eyes, empty and unblinking, looking down at the city. The broken shards of the great dome were scattered all over the stairs and the road. Even those pieces, broken and dirty and slowly grinding away to dust in the elements, gleamed with more colors than Octavia's eyes knew how to recognize. She took care as they climbed the steps, not wanting to crush any more of it beneath her boots.

"I thought at first it was the watchtower north of the river bend," Hana went on, "even though nobody was supposed to be there. But it was farther north than that. So I left the trail and went around the northern side of the mountain to get a better look. I was still thinking it wasn't going to be anything important, you know? I thought maybe there had been a freak winter lightning strike or hot springs like the ones up the River Iracundia."

"That's not all hot springs," Octavia told her. "There are people there. The steam hides their smoke."

Hana shook her head. "I know that now. I guess there's a clan living there, the ruins of Ira? So close to Vittoria, and we never had any idea."

"The Clan of the Furious Dead. They helped me and Sima."

"Ah. That explains why you came over the western pass. I'm

glad they helped you."

"What did you see? When you went looking for the smoke?"

"People," Hana answered simply. "A caravan on Long Road, five or six wagons coming down out of the mountains in the east. I didn't believe what I was seeing, so I went north, up the river, to get a closer look." Hana's voice echoed as she stepped through a doorway and into the forum. "It was unfamiliar territory, and it was late in the day, but I thought I had enough time to look before returning to the watchtower. But I was so distracted that I wasn't careful. I didn't notice I was being tracked."

"You always told me it was just as important to look behind you as it was to look forward," Octavia said.

"Oh, I know," Hana said, laughing. "I didn't follow my own rule. That's why the Ferox surprised me right at sunset."

They passed through the forum's dim entrance and into the heart of the dome. Without the wind buffeting them, the morning was suddenly quiet, and the snow fell in lazy whirls. Octavia craned her neck to follow the curve of the dome to where it was broken. Birds burst from a hole high above, darting about as little black specks against the gray sky.

"I don't actually remember too much about what happened after I was attacked," Hana admitted. "They told me later I managed to crawl to the road, and one of the caravan's dogs found me, but what I remember is waking up here in Aeterna. I was surrounded by strangers. One of them was Mother Dulcia. I learned later that she and a small group had arrived in Aeterna a couple of months before, and the people who found me were some of the first to follow her here."

"Were you badly hurt?" Octavia asked.

"I was. When Mother Dulcia told me my wounds would heal in a few days, I didn't believe her. I didn't believe any healer could do that. But she did. I was on my feet a couple of days later."

Octavia frowned. Something bothered her about Hana's story.

"The Hunters said they found your knife and blood on Gray Bear Mountain," she said.

Hana looked at her. "They did? That's not right. The Ferox got me near where East Road comes down into the valley. But that would mean . . . they would have seen the tracks on the road, even if they didn't see the caravan itself. They didn't say anything about that, did they?"

Octavia understood what it meant. "No. And after Mom got hurt looking for you, the council decided the Hunters couldn't go into new territory anymore. They've stayed close to Vittoria ever since. They don't even go as far as the northern watchtower."

"But that's . . ." Hana rubbed her hand over her face. "They had to have seen something."

"Master Camilla must had made them lie," Octavia said. The words came out in a rush, but once they were spoken, she felt a jittery, light sort of relief. "They told her they saw the tracks and she made them lie about it. They've known there were people here for months. Mom must know too!"

Hana didn't look convinced. "Maybe."

Octavia was thrown by her doubt. "What else could have happened?"

"Maybe they didn't see the tracks," Hana said. "And they didn't lie. Because maybe they did find my things on Gray Bear Mountain."

"But how—" Octavia frowned, finally catching up to what Hana was saying. "Somebody moved it to set a false trail?"

"Everybody here is warned to stay away from Vittoria," Hana said.

"Same as everybody else," Octavia said. "But why . . . oh. You mean Mother Dulcia warns them. And she sent somebody out to move your knife and give the Hunters a false trail."

"She could have," Hana said. "She would even have a good reason for it."

The lowlanders had good reason to avoid Vittoria, as Sima's experience had proved. The mountain clans had good reason to avoid Vittoria, as their own tragic history had proved.

Mother Dulcia's reasons were personal.

"You . . . you know who she is, don't you?" Octavia asked. "Her eye . . ."

"Yes!" Hana said, loud enough to startle another group of birds from their nesting spot high above. Then, to Octavia's surprise, Hana laughed a little and pulled Octavia into a sudden hug. "I should have known you would know what it meant the moment you saw it. Nobody else does. At first I thought I must have misremembered or gotten confused, when I tried to ask other people about it. They just looked at me like I'd lost my mind. Then I realized they don't know, because they never heard Camilla's story about their last fight."

"And she's a healer, like Agrippina was," Octavia added. "And she looks like Master Flavia."

"Exactly. You have no idea how relieved I am to know you see it too," Hana said.

"You've never asked her about it?"

"I did, after a while. She said I was right, but it was better that people not know. They wouldn't accept help from her if they knew—and she is helping people. Mother Dulcia is Agrippina, but that means she's also a healer. She's been alive all this time. Camilla never killed her. That was a lie."

"Everything Camilla says is a lie," Octavia said bitterly.

Hana kicked absently at shards of the dome, sending them

skating across the forum's broad tile floor. "All that time we spent in the mountains around Vittoria because Camilla told us we would die if we went farther . . ." Hana looked up at the broken roof again. The snow was coming down faster, and the cold was seeping through Octavia's clothes. "All we needed to do was go just a little bit more. But we never did, because Camilla told us there was nothing but death out here. As soon as I met Mother Dulcia and the others, I wondered if somebody in Vittoria knew the truth. It's been fifty years. Somebody must have seen *something* in all that time. People have left Vittoria. Mother Dulcia has met some."

"But they never came back. *You* never came back."

Hana drew her gaze away from the dome to meet Octavia's eyes. "I think some of them may have tried to return. The Ferox are as good at keeping other people away as they are at keeping us inside Vittoria."

Octavia hadn't considered that there might be danger in going back, and now that Hana had brought up the possibility it swept a fresh flurry of worries into her mind. Rufus had gone back. The Hunters wouldn't hurt him. Master Cicerus wouldn't let the council hurt him. She had to believe that. He had to be safe. She couldn't worry about him right now.

Not when there was more she needed Hana to tell her.

"Did you even try to come back?" Octavia asked. "You could have made it. You could have come back."

"I was always going to," Hana said. "Always."

"But you didn't."

Hana sighed. "It's no small thing to tell everybody everything they know about the world is a lie. I wanted to know I was telling the truth instead of adding to the lies." She leaned over to pick up a broken piece of the dome. It glinted faintly in the winter light, casting colors from its strange, oily surface. She flung the shard across the forum as though she was skipping a stone on a pond. "When I confronted her about who she really is, Mother Dulcia told me she had come to the mountains because she wanted to help. She said she met somebody who left Vittoria a few years ago—do you remember Lefi?"

Octavia shook her head.

"I didn't think so," Hana said, with a slight nod. "He was gone when you were a baby. He was a woodsman, and one day he walked into the forest with his axe and never came back. Everybody thought the Ferox got him, but I guess he's still alive and well and living in the lowlands. Or he was when he met Mother Dulcia. He told her what it was like in Vittoria. He told her about the Ferox and the hard winters and the guards and the council, all of it. That's when she decided to come back to Aeterna, even though it took her a few years to plan to do it right."

"Why? What does she want to do?" Octavia asked.

"She told me that it isn't right that the people of Vittoria are kept in the dark about the rest of the world. She wants to help. She says she'll help me return to Vittoria when the time is right. But more people keep coming to join us here, and Mother Dulcia wants to help them too. She really does. That's not a lie. So I stayed to help her. It felt good to help her do that, rather than spend all day every day fighting monsters we could never really defeat."

"I thought you loved being a Hunter," Octavia said quietly.

"I did. But I think . . . I think I loved it because it was a way to be outside of Vittoria but also helping people. I never liked being stuck inside. I know you've always hated it too." Hana walked a few steps, her boots crunching over broken glass from the dome. The snow was collecting on the ground now, a fine layer like dust, and growing heavier. "But once I realized that the whole world is different from what we were told, I realized that maybe I didn't really know what I liked, because I'd never had the chance to learn what else is possible."

Octavia thought about how amazed Rufus had been by Marta's magical healing. The way Sima's eyes lit up when she looked out over the snow-covered mountains for the first time. Her own excitement upon learning that the roads around Vittoria still went all the way down to the sea. The world was so much bigger than she had ever thought. She wanted to learn the truth for herself and make sure everybody else learned it as well. But she hadn't before realized how the truth could grow and change with every day, how it could look so very different to so many people.

"How is she going to help?" Octavia asked.

"I don't know exactly. She has us looking for something in the ruins, the old sorcerers' towers and homes. I know there's a lot of magic here, and she uses it for her healing, but this . . . I think this is something else."

Octavia remembered what Sima had said about people coming to Aeterna to work on clearing the old city. There were signs of it everywhere, in the emptied buildings and piles of debris, but Octavia had assumed they were only trying to make the city livable again.

Hana went on. "And I don't know what it is. Most of us who have to help excavate don't know. Every time I ask she says it is all to help Vittoria. I used to think I understood what she meant by that. But I don't know anymore." Hana sighed and looked up at the sky. "We should get back. The snow is getting heavier, and somebody will notice if I'm gone too long."

Hana reached out to take Octavia's hand. The snow fell around them, cold and whirling and quiet, as they left the broken dome and walked back to the city center.

19

What the Ruins Hide

→»—

The snow continued through the entire day but tapered off during the night. When Octavia stepped out of the tent in the morning, the wind had died down and the clouds were breaking apart. The encampments in Aeterna's city square were beginning the work of digging out from under the fresh white blanket of snow.

"I believe you now." Sima scowled as she followed Octavia out of the tent. "I believe you about how much it can snow."

Octavia kicked through the knee-high snow and laughed when Sima squealed and dodged away. "This? This is nothing. If you don't have to climb out of the roof, it doesn't count."

"I wasn't as cold last night," Sima said. "Why is there more snow when it's not as cold?"

"I don't know. That's just the way it is. The snow keeps the warmth inside."

Sima picked up a clump of snow and threw it at the side of the wagon. "Ha! Having a clingy, overheated barnacle using my blanket is what keeps it warm."

"An overheated *what*?" Octavia said.

"You know. Barnacle." Sima gestured vaguely and not at all helpfully. "The little sea creatures that stick their shells to ships and rocks on the shore."

"I have no idea what that is," Octavia admitted. "But I think you're making fun of me."

"You can't pry them off no matter what you do," Sima said, her lips twitching.

Octavia looked away quickly, her face warm. She had awoken that morning feeling warm and cozy and a bit surprised she had managed to sleep at all. She had gone to bed curled up beside Sima beneath shared blankets, but her mind was so full she had jerked awake every time her arm brushed against Sima's, every time Sima's hair tickled her skin. Everything in Aeterna was strange and bewildering, but in Sima's tent, with its bright colors softened by the last light of the fire, and Sima sleeping quietly beside her, all of that had felt very far away.

It was back now, every worry and question she had. Octavia was glad for the distraction of helping the Ibernese fix up their camp as best they could: brushing snow off the tents, shoveling slush out of the animal pens, hanging blankets and clothing by warm fires to chase the damp away.

About halfway through the morning, Leila returned from visiting Pavi at the infirmary.

"He's feeling a lot better today," she said, when Sima asked how he was. "He would love to see you too. He's well enough now that he's getting a bit bored, to be honest."

"Can I go now?" Sima asked, bouncing eagerly.

Leila smiled and tugged Sima's braid, a fond and familiar gesture that Sima endured with a roll of her eyes. "Of course. You've done enough for this morning."

Sima grabbed Octavia's hand. "Let's go see Pavi."

"You want me to go with you?" Octavia asked.

"Well, yes," Sima said, like it was obvious. "If he's bored, he's going to want to meet somebody new. Come on."

The infirmary was in the same building as Mother Dulcia's garden, on the second floor overlooking the city square. It was a busy, bustling place, with people carrying trays of food and baskets of laundry in and out, and family members and friends stopping by to greet their ailing loved ones. All of the sick were kept in the same massive room at the end of the building, a bright, airy chamber with windows on three walls. There were two long rows of beds, about twenty on each side, and most of them were filled. Some of the patients were sitting upright with colorful quilts over their laps, laughing and talking and eating; others lay prone and quiet, asleep or in obvious pain. Some were coughing, some were wrapped in bandages, some were mottled with bruises or rashes, and some showed no signs of illness at all except pale skin and tired eyes. If Rufus were there, he might have known what ailed each patient, but Octavia couldn't even begin to guess.

Sima's brother Pavi was a boy of eight, and in spite of what Sima had said, he was far more interested in peppering Sima with questions than he was in anything Octavia had to say. New people weren't remotely unusual for Pavi, but his sister fighting monsters was. So Octavia was left to sit quietly at his bedside while he and Sima chatted, but she didn't mind because it gave her a chance to watch what was going on in the infirmary.

Specifically, it gave her a chance to watch Mother Dulcia.

There was a small commotion at the entrance when the healer arrived. People called out to her with greetings and questions, and she smiled and replied to everyone by name. Octavia watched as she made her way down the rows of patients, stopping to see each one, speaking to them for a while. She didn't seem to be doing any healing, not that morning, but everybody was obviously glad to see her.

Octavia watched. She watched, she listened, she paid attention to every word she could hear, every gesture she could see. Hana didn't think anybody else knew that Mother Dulcia was Agrippina, and Octavia was inclined to agree. She saw no sign that anybody was wary of Mother Dulcia.

Having that knowledge when nobody else suspected made Octavia uneasy. Mother Dulcia was obviously helping these people. One older man leapt out of bed to show off a leg that no longer hurt him; a young couple cooed and sang to a baby that was no longer feverish; a pair of sisters hugged Mother Dulcia and cried with thanks because their mother was finally resting without pain. Octavia could see plainly that the stories that brought people to Aeterna were not lies.

A small part of Octavia wanted to stand and shout, *She's the sorcerer who created the plague. She waged war against the whole world!* She felt like it was a huge, black shadow of a secret that had nowhere to go, nothing to do but to sit inside of her and roil around with sickly uncertainty. The sorcerers of Aeterna had done so much harm, caused so much death, and Agrippina had been among the worst. To see Agrippina now helping people, accepting their thanks and praise as though she deserved it, made Octavia feel off-balance, like she was crossing a raging river on a log that wobbled and tilted. She didn't know if Hana felt the same, if she still felt a shiver of fear in the woman's presence, or if over the past months she had found some way to see only the healer and not the sorcerer who lurked behind her kindly smiles. The plague had been a long time ago, and Mother Dulcia was helping these people here, now, as their families worried at their bedsides. Sima and her brother could laugh and tell stories together because of Mother Dulcia.

Octavia didn't think the passage of time was enough to forgive something as horrific as the plague. She didn't think saving people now could ever make up for killing during the war.

But she also didn't think people would listen, if she stood up to shout the truth. She was starting to understand, a little bit, how Hana could have stayed here for months, indecisive and uncertain. Octavia wanted to do the right thing, but she didn't know what it was. She didn't know what would help the most people.

Mother Dulcia stopped at a bed a few away from Pavi's to sit with an old woman for a while. Pavi was asking Sima to tell her for the third time about the clan weapons that could make monsters fall apart with a single blow, so Octavia didn't feel bad about ignoring them to eavesdrop on Mother Dulcia.

"I so want to see it," said the old woman, with a faint, thready voice.

Mother Dulcia was holding her hand. "You will. You're doing better every day."

"I'm so tired, but it keeps me going," the old woman said. "I want to send for my children and grandchildren. I want to tell them that we can all live together without being hungry or sick or scared."

"And you will," Mother Dulcia said again. "We will forge a new way by healing the wounds of the old. Do you doubt my promise to you?"

"Never," said the woman. She smiled and closed her eyes. "I never doubt you."

Mother Dulcia patted her hand. "Rest now, my dear."

The old woman drifted to sleep. As Mother Dulcia rose to move to the next patient, there was a flurry of activity at the entrance to the infirmary. Hana came in, looked around quickly, and made her way along the row of beds to whisper something to Mother Dulcia. Her boots were muddy, her clothes caked with clinging red dirt, and there was a pair of thick leather gloves tucked into her belt; she had been helping with the digging in the city, looking for whatever it was Mother Dulcia sought. Octavia's skin prickled.

Mother Dulcia's eyes narrowed as Hana spoke, then widened as she finished.

"Where?" she asked in a low voice.

"Beneath the red stone tower, west of the forum," Hana answered.

Mother Dulcia nodded. "Ah, I should have known. Take me there."

She gathered her shawl around her shoulders and went to speak to the infirmary attendants. Hana trailed after her, but not before giving Octavia a quick look. She tilted her head slightly and twitched her hand at her side. Octavia knew what that meant: *follow, but quietly*.

It seemed Mother Dulcia's people had found what they were looking for.

"Hey," Octavia said, interrupting Sima mid-sentence. "I have to go."

"What? Where?" Sima asked.

Mother Dulcia and Hana were already heading for the door. Octavia stood up. "I'll tell you later. It was nice to meet you, Pavi."

Octavia hurried out of the infirmary to the city square, where Hana and Mother Dulcia were following a slushy path toward a street on the northwestern side of the square. They were easier to follow once they left the square behind, because there was only a single line of tracks in the fresh snow; the trail wound through a maze of city streets to the base of a red stone tower.

Octavia approached carefully, keeping to the shadows. The wall of the tower was caved in at street level, and there was a massive pile of dirt and rubble just outside the gaping hole. Mother

Dulcia and Hana had joined a group of about eight others, a few of whom were leaning on shovels or perched on wheelbarrows; all of them were filthy with the same reddish dust that covered Hana's clothes. They were speaking amongst themselves, their voices echoing oddly off the broken tower, but Octavia couldn't hear what they were saying.

She needed to get closer. She found the entrance to a building across the street that faced the tower, and she crept through the ground floor to a window directly behind Mother Dulcia.

"Go on," said Mother Dulcia, nodding to the others. "I am eager to see what you've found."

"Right. Let's do this carefully," said another woman. She seemed to be in charge of the workers. "Four down, five above. Let's go."

A group of four, including Hana, descended into the excavated base of the tower, unspooling coils of rope as they disappeared into the darkness. Their voices rang out from inside, accompanied by sounds of scraping and clanking.

Finally somebody called up, "Ready!"

The leader replied, "Here we go!"

The workers who remained on the street took up the ropes. With noisy grunts and quite a lot of cussing, they pulled and pulled and pulled, until finally they heaved a large object out from underneath the tower and into the daylight. Hana and the other three inside came up behind it, pushing it from behind. They moved onto the flat street outside the tower and stepped back.

It was about eight feet tall, made entirely of wood, and consisted of a large polished base, a pillar like a tree trunk, and a ring on the top. Something about the shape was familiar, but Octavia had no idea what it was. None of the wood looked cracked or rotted away; in fact, it still had a deep, polished gleam when it caught a glint of sunlight through the parting clouds. In that light, Octavia could see the lines of metal inlaid in the wood and the deep markings charred alongside them.

"Mother Dulcia?" said one of the workers, a bit nervously. "This is it, isn't it?"

Mother Dulcia walked a slow circle around the object, examining it from its wooden base to the ring at the top. Octavia watched her with a growing feeling of dread. She had seen the device's odd shape only a few days before. She wanted to be wrong.

"It is," Mother Dulcia said.

The shoulders of the workers slumped with relief. They smiled and nodded and patted one another's backs in congratulations.

"Will it still work?" one of them asked.

"Oh, I don't think that will be a problem," said Mother Dulcia. "But we'll test it nonetheless. Load it on a cart. We'll go to the far side of the city. Make sure everybody knows to stay a safe distance away."

It was Hana who asked, "What will you use it for?"

Mother Dulcia looked up at the object's ring again. Her single agate-green eye glittered in the sunlight.

She said, "I will break Vittoria open and free the people caged within."

At her words, Octavia realized why the device looked familiar: it was the same shape as the forest of skull-topped trees on the fields outside of Ira. The shape that, according to Brianne, represented the weapon the sorcerers had used to topple their walls and overrun their city.

The walls of Ira had already fallen. So too had the dome and towers of Aeterna.

There was only one place in the mountains that had never fallen.

The people of Vittoria had no idea there was a weapon that could bring their wall down.

Octavia had seen enough. She knew now what Mother Dulcia planned to do.

She turned to crawl away from the window, but she didn't make it far. A hand grabbed the back of her coat and wrested her to her feet.

20

Mother Dulcia's Tomorrow

I t's quite all right," Mother Dulcia called from outside. "Come on out. You can have a closer look."

The man holding Octavia's coat steered her out of the building and into the open. Octavia struggled, trying to wrest herself free, but it was pointless because the man let her go as soon as they reached the group anyway. She stumbled a little, and Hana darted to her side to help her up.

Mother Dulcia smiled. "Ah! I should have known it would be you, Octavia."

"She shouldn't be here," said the head worker. "It's dangerous."

"She's doing no harm," said Mother Dulcia. "It's natural to be curious. I can hardly blame Octavia for wanting to know what we've been looking for in this city of wonders. Do you know what this is?"

Octavia knew exactly what it was, but she wanted to hear what Mother Dulcia was going to say first.

She crossed her arms over her chest. "Some kind of magic thing?"

"Some kind of magic thing, indeed." Mother Dulcia laughed. She extended one hand to touch the wooden pole gently with her fingertips. "This is a very clever invention. The magic is in the ring at the top, you see. When the device is properly prepared, you can pass something through that ring to give it different properties. It can be a very useful tool."

Octavia glared at her. "You mean a weapon."

Hana squeezed her shoulder in warning, but Mother Dulcia's expression didn't change. "A hammer can be a weapon if wielded a certain way, by a certain type of person, but that does not make it any less useful for repairing a leaky roof."

"Maybe, but you're not going to repair a leaky roof, are you?" Octavia said.

A few of the workers exchanged uneasy glances, and Hana's grip on Octavia's shoulder tightened. Mother Dulcia blinked twice. She had not moved, and she was still smiling that pleasant, unchanging smile, but Octavia felt a change in the air, a chill that came from no breeze. For several seconds, nobody spoke.

The momentary silence was broken by the rattle of clopping hooves and cartwheels on cobbles. A cart rounded the street corner. The driver tugged the horses to a stop in front of the tower.

"Good!" Mother Dulcia clasped her hands together. "Let's get it loaded up so we can take it for testing right away. No, they don't need your help," she said, as Hana let go of Octavia to join the other workers. "I'd like a word with you and your sister. Let's step over here where we won't be in the way."

Mother Dulcia led them across the street, just far enough from the tower that the others could not overhear.

"You seem a very forthright girl, Octavia," Mother Dulcia said. "So I shall be forthright with you. It is difficult to see the restrictions of a cage when one has only ever seen the protection it provides."

"Vittoria isn't a cage," Octavia said.

"Isn't it?" Mother Dulcia asked.

Octavia looked away to watch the diggers heaving the device

onto the cart. From the way they were struggling and straining, it seemed to be much heavier than it looked.

"People will get hurt if you use it," Octavia said.

Hana looked between them, confused. "I don't understand. Octavia, do you *know* what it is?"

"It's what the sorcerers used to break down the walls of the cities they attacked," Octavia said.

Hana stared at her. "How do you know that?"

"I should like to know that as well," Mother Dulcia said. "No device like this was ever used on Vittoria, and your sister's surprise tells me it is not part of the history your children are taught."

It wouldn't be, Octavia thought, suddenly angry. Camilla would never let anybody teach the people born after the war about how vulnerable walls like Vittoria's could be.

"Vittoria may not remember," Octavia said, "but Ira does. They told me about it. What's left of their wall is still standing. You can see where the weapon punched through."

"Mother Dulcia, you don't . . . you're not going to use it on Vittoria, are you?" Hana asked, her voice wavering. "Whatever it does— Octavia's right. People will be hurt. There are houses built right up against the wall all around the town."

Mother Dulcia laughed suddenly. "Oh, my dear, I have no intention of *using* it. Not like that. I cannot abide such wanton destruction."

Hana looked as skeptical as Octavia felt. "Then why do you need it?

"From the moment I heard the truth of what life was like inside Vittoria, I wanted to help. But I knew I could not merely walk up to the gate and expect to be let inside. I would not, after all, be greeted warmly." Mother Dulcia had a distant look in her eyes, as though she was seeing something very far away—or from very long ago. She didn't look so much like Master Flavia when she wore that expression, nor did she look much like Camilla. That vague look was all her own. "And so I resolved I would return only when I had the ability to remind Camilla that her power is not absolute. That she cannot keep the keys of the cage locked forever. That those she has deceived deserve a chance to look outward. It was one of her apprentices who created this device, you know. They were always building clever little contraptions."

"I still don't understand, Mother Dulcia," Hana pleaded. "What are you going to do?"

"I am going to persuade her to open the gates," said Mother Dulcia. "A horse that knows the truth of the whip's sting does not need to be struck every time. It need only glimpse the whip to act. Camilla knows how this device might sting. She will open the gates, and when she does, we will not be ignored. The people of Vittoria will learn the truth."

"Because you're going to ... what? Just tell them?" Octavia said.

Speaking the truth was, in fact, the entirety of her own plan for bringing change to Vittoria. But she wasn't an infamous sorcerer in possession of a powerfully destructive weapon. The people of Vittoria might see Octavia as a child who had been tricked by Ferox, but what they would see when Agrippina revealed herself was much worse. They had spent fifty years believing her to be their greatest enemy, the cause of the world's greatest tragedies, the reason for their isolation and struggle. They would never trust words from her mouth.

"It worked to convince you, didn't it?" Mother Dulcia said. "For both of you. As soon as you saw the truth outside of Vittoria, your perspective changed. You became able to discern truth from lies. The same will happen with the others. I will liberate Vittoria." Mother Dulcia's lips thinned to a line, and the distant look faded from her eyes, replaced by something much sharper and darker. When she spoke again, the calm was gone from her voice. In its place was a tight, angry tremble. "For a long time my sister and I believed ourselves to be on the same side, but as the war went on I realized that I had to do what I could to stop it, and that was why I did what I did. I was ultimately successful. But Camilla only wanted to prolong the war, because she could never be satisfied. She was addicted to the fear and chaos the war created. She loved that power. That was why I had to stand against her. But I did not go far enough. She should never have been allowed to hide away like an animal in a burrow, safe in a domain of her own making. For so long I believed she had simply faded away, pathetic and forgotten."

The meaning of Agrippina's words rang through Octavia's mind like bells on a clear morning. She was saying she had created the plague to stop the war, to sicken and kill so many people in so many cities across the land that they could no longer fight back, and she still believed it to have been a righteous action.

Hana reached for Octavia's hand and held it tight; her eyes were wide, her mouth open slightly. She understood as well. They were both silent with shock, and Mother Dulcia was not yet finished.

"Fifty years is not enough time to scrub the world of the harm she's done, to make amends for the harm she forced others to do," said Mother Dulcia, her voice trembling with anger. "Five hundred years would not be enough. I should have rooted her out long ago."

Octavia remembered what Master Flavia had said about her aunt and mother: *Magic can only be created by sacrificing something else, something important and valuable.* Camilla had stopped playing music as she grew more powerful. The sisters had turned against each other at the height of the war. Agrippina had sent her own daughter away right before she created the plague.

Octavia didn't know how the creation of magic worked. She didn't know how a person could cut out their love for somebody else and exchange it for power. But she did know that Agrippina was not speaking of her sister with regret, or grief, or a longing for reconciliation. She had only anger.

And, as quickly as it had showed itself, that anger tucked itself away. Placid calm took over Mother Dulcia's expression, smoothing the lines and softening her eyes, as effective as donning a mask. It was a transformation so complete Octavia had to suppress a shudder.

She wanted, quite suddenly, to be very far away.

"Ah, they're ready now," Mother Dulcia said, with a smile. The workers had loaded the device onto the wagon and tied it down with ropes, and they were now discussing where they were going to take it for the test. "I will join them, but you will head back to the square. I have another task for you."

It was only because Octavia was watching Hana carefully that she saw how Hana hid her wariness. "What do you need?" Hana asked.

"You know the road to Vittoria better than anyone here, and we need that road to be passable for wagons for the entire distance," Mother Dulcia said. "First thing tomorrow, I want you to take a group to assess the conditions, clear any obstacles, and report back. Take drivers and people capable of hard work. I imagine it will take a few days."

"Tomorrow?" Hana said, surprised.

"There is no reason to wait," Mother Dulcia said. "We have what we need."

"But I thought . . ." Hana looked over her shoulder at the device, then at Octavia. "Is there a hurry? The weather isn't going to get any better. Traveling during the winter isn't—"

"Hana." Mother Dulcia's voice was sharp. "I learned the moods of these mountains many decades ago. I am well aware of the weather."

Hana closed her mouth tightly.

"I am surprised at you," Mother Dulcia went on. "I would have thought you would be eager to help free Vittoria from its cage as soon as possible. I thought that was what you wanted. You know you cannot truly break the chains in your own mind as long as others remain ignorant."

"I am," Hana said quietly. She was holding so tight to Octava's hand that it was starting to hurt. "I do. I do want that."

"You have the afternoon to prepare. You'll leave in the morning." Mother Dulcia's expression softened, and she was smiling once again. "Yours is a very important task, Hana. If our path is not clear, then nothing else is possible. I know you understand."

Mother Dulcia left them to join the others. The wagon lurched into motion, the device swaying, and began to rattle deeper into the streets of Aeterna. Hana watched them go, then held out her hand to Octavia.

Octavia waited until they had walked a few blocks back toward the city square, putting several streets between them and Mother Dulcia, before she spoke.

"Do you believe her?" she asked.

Hana sighed. "About what part? I believe that she wants to help the people of Vittoria."

To Octavia it had sounded like Mother Dulcia's desire to help Vittoria was twisted up with her desire to take away Camilla's power. The two urges were so intertwined that Mother Dulcia probably didn't even realize they weren't the same thing. Octavia didn't know if Hana realized it either, because Hana had spent so many months away from Vittoria. She hadn't been beneath its high wall since last winter. She didn't know how scared everybody had become after her apparent death.

Octavia hadn't even recognized Camilla's tightening grip for what it was, because there had been too much else occupying her mind. Hana's supposed death, Mom's injury, the council keeping the Hunters close, Bram befriending ghosts in the mist, Willa's anger in the archway on River Street and bloody death in her own home, Camilla smiling as she spoke about what they could learn from a creature like Sima, it was all part of the same long thread. Hana's disappearance had made Camilla wary, for she had known all along that not everybody who vanished from Vittoria died in the wilderness. She had responded by holding the Hunters closer to Vittoria, where the Ferox kept strangers away. She had strengthened Vittoria's isolation even as Aeterna filled with people from afar, until Willa told her about Bram's friend in the forest. Until Sima was separated from her caravan on the road. Until Octavia had stood before the council and told the truth as she knew it.

Camilla wanted to keep Vittoria alone. She wanted the gates guarded, the wilderness of Ferox impenetrable, the walls solid and high.

Octavia wanted people in Vittoria to learn the truth about the world outside their town, but to do that they also needed to learn the truth about what was inside. She wanted, she realized, the same thing as Mother Dulcia.

What she didn't know was if she wanted it in the same way, for the same reasons.

She didn't like that the only person inside Vittoria that Mother Dulcia seemed to think about was her own sister.

"I mean about that device," Octavia said, after she and Hana had walked another couple of minutes in silence. "Do you believe that she doesn't intend to use it?"

"I don't think she wants to hurt people," Hana said.

"There are other ways. She could have gone to Vittoria months ago. Or sent you or somebody else."

"I know," Hana said, miserably. "I know all of that. But she does help people. You've seen it. I think she does want to help. She just wants to make them listen."

Octavia stopped walking. She tugged on Hana's hand to make her stop as well.

"That's what they said to the people of Ira," she said. She thought about Brianne's pale face, her quiet voice, so at home on the mountainside, talking about the history of her people and the fifty-year-old wounds that had never quite healed. "The sorcerers told them they wanted to talk, to negotiate how Ira could support Aeterna during the war. When the people of Ira said they didn't want to be part of the war, the sorcerers used that device to smash through their walls and send Ferox into their city." Octavia squeezed Hana's hand a little tighter, trying to make her understand. "They said they only wanted to talk, but as soon as talking didn't get them what they wanted they destroyed the city. And . . . I don't know, maybe it's different, maybe Mother Dulcia really doesn't want to hurt anybody except Camilla, but—"

"But you don't spend months searching for a weapon like that unless you plan to use it." Hana let out a long breath. "You're right. I didn't want to admit it, because she does so much good, but this . . . She's obsessed with Camilla. We have to warn people. Maybe nobody will believe us, but we still need people to know that she has that weapon. Any warning is better than nothing."

"What do we do?" Octavia asked.

Hana laughed a little. "I somehow doubt marching up to the

gate and telling the guards to look out for sorcerers on the road is going to work the way we want it to, not if Camilla has everybody convinced the Ferox can look and act like humans now. I was hoping you had an idea. You're the one who's spent the last several days sneaking around and breaking prisoners out of jail and fighting monsters and hanging out with strange clans."

She let go of Octavia's hand to wrap her arms around her in a big hug. Octavia leaned into it gratefully, eyes closed.

Then her eyes popped open and she leaned back.

"You're right," she said.

"Of course I'm right, I'm the oldest," Hana said. "Right about what?"

"I *did* do all that."

Hana patted Octavia's head right at the point of her knitted cap. "Yes, and you were very brave and very foolish."

Octavia ducked and swatted her hand away. "No, listen to me. I have an idea. You have to take me with you."

21

Monsters Gather

After spending a day lying completely still beneath a wooden bench in the back of a cart, hidden by scratchy sacks, with various tools and weapons poking her from every angle, Octavia was having second thoughts about her plan.

"Every one of my new bruises is your fault," Sima muttered as the cart hit another bump, jostling them together.

"You didn't have to come with me," Octavia countered quietly. She hadn't even asked. It was too dangerous for Sima to return to Vittoria, but Sima had refused to listen to Octavia's objections.

Sima huffed. "I could be sitting by a fire on a pile of blankets right now."

But she shifted slightly to grab Octavia's hand and squeeze it. Octavia's face warmed as she smiled, both disappointed that she couldn't see the look on Sima's face and relieved that Sima couldn't see her own.

Octavia considered a bunch of things to say, each one more embarrassing than the last, before finally settling on, "I wonder how far—"

One of the workers in Hana's group shouted something from up ahead and the cart lurched to a stop. Hana shouted orders to the group; the murmuring voices faded as they moved away. Another tree in the road. Octavia hadn't been able to do more than peek outside for a glimpse of the blue sky dotted with clouds, but she guessed they had been south of the open fields around Aeterna for some time, and well into the forest if the number of fallen trees was any indication.

From up the road came the distinctive sound of axes chopping wood, and a couple of minutes later footsteps approached the cart. The steps came around the side, then stopped at the back. Octavia held her breath.

"They're all busy right now," Hana said quietly. "I'm going to set your packs and snowshoes out. After I leave, count to thirty so I have time to get back to the group and distract them. Then get your stuff and head uphill and into the woods."

Keeping her voice low so it wouldn't carry, Octavia asked, "Where are we?"

There was a rustling and scraping as Hana lifted their supplies out of the cart. "About two miles south of the northern watchtower. The road is in better shape than I expected." She sounded worried; a passable road meant Mother Dulcia would be able to set out as soon as Hana returned to Aeterna. "You'll be able to make it to the watchtower at the river bend before dark, but you'll have to be careful. The Hunters might be there too."

"I know. We will be," Octavia said.

"I'll slow her down as much as I can," Hana said. "But you should expect strangers at the gate in a matter of days. She has sleighs and strong horses. Once she sets out, it won't take her more than two days to reach Vittoria."

"I know." Octavia wished she could see Hana, give her a hug and hold tight for a while. There was no time for that. "You be careful too."

"We'll be back in Aeterna tonight. Don't worry about me. I'm heading back up the road now. I'll keep everybody looking in the other direction while you get into the woods."

Hana's footsteps moved away from the cart. Octavia started counting, as Hana had told her to, and when she reached thirty Sima let go of her hand. It was time to leave.

They wriggled out of the back of the cart and crouched to grab their packs and snowshoes. It was mid-afternoon, later than Octavia had realized while hidden beneath the cart's bench; they had maybe two hours until sunset. A sharp breeze sliced down the valley, promising a cold night ahead. Hana and the others were about a hundred feet away, chopping branches from a large tree that had toppled into the road. None of them were paying any attention to the carts and supplies. Octavia and Sima darted from the road into the dense forest, where they climbed the hill a ways before stopping to put on their packs.

They crept along on the slope for a good distance, only descending to the road when they were so far past the fallen tree that they could not see it anymore.

Once they were on Long Road again, they strapped on their snowshoes and raced south as evening approached. There were almost no obstacles on the road; their progress was swift. But that meant Mother Dulcia's progress would be swift too. And she might set out as soon as tomorrow or the next day. Octavia felt the need to hurry grow stronger with every step.

It was after sunset and growing dark before they reached the watchtower. They watched for a while from the safety of the trees, but there was no sign of light or smoke. There were no Hunters here.

Octavia and Sima made a fire to warm the watchtower and ate dinner quietly, talking about their plan and everything that could go wrong. They grew more and more quiet as it got later, and they had mostly fallen silent by the time they made up their blankets to sleep. They had not heard any Ferox all evening.

"I still think you shouldn't have come with me," Octavia said, after they had extinguished the lamp and laid down to sleep. "It's too dangerous. If they catch you again—"

"Octavia." There was a shuffle in the darkness as Sima turned onto her side. Octavia turned as well, so they were lying face-to-face in the darkness, their noses only inches apart. "It's dangerous for you too."

"I know, but it's my town and—"

"This is bigger than what's dangerous for us," Sima said. "It's about more than Vittoria. It's more important."

Octavia was quiet. She waited for Sima to go on.

"All over the lowlands, all the people we met while we were traveling, for them the war is a long time ago." Sima's voice was quiet as she spoke, but earnest and serious. "Even the ones who remember it, they say it was a long time ago, it isn't like that anymore. They can say there are no sorcerers and no monsters anymore because those things are only here, in the mountains. They say, as long as those old problems stay in Vittoria, then they aren't a problem for lowlanders. But it wasn't so long ago, was it? It wasn't so far away. That's only what we told ourselves so we didn't have to worry about Vittoria or the mountains. Walls are only stone and mortar. It's what people believe that gives them power."

Before she had met Sima, Octavia had imagined Vittoria as the one bright spot in a world of danger, terror, and darkness. After she met Sima and learned more about the world beyond the walls, she had begun to see Vittoria as the lowlanders and the clans and Mother Dulcia saw it, as a stubborn, festering wound in a world that had otherwise healed.

Now, as she lay in the darkness with Sima's soft words wrapping around her, she knew that neither view of her home was correct. Because Vittoria was, after all, just another town. Its wall was only a wall. It had always been able to open its gates, to cooperate with outsiders to defeat the Ferox, to accept travelers and let people wander. Vittoria had not made that choice yet. But it could. It could leave the Sorcerers' War in the past, where it belonged.

This was at once a very small truth and a very large one. She fervently hoped she would be able to make people understand.

The next morning, they rose before dawn to set out. Octavia was aware, as she was hefting her pack and tightening the straps on her snowshoes, that Mother Dulcia might be setting out from Aeterna that very morning. The watchtower at the broad bend of the River Nyx was only about four miles from the one that stood at the junction with the River Iracundia, where Ursa's scouts had spotted Hunters a few days ago. Try as she might, Octavia could not see any sign of the clan scouts. She told herself she could feel them watching, but it might have been wishful thinking.

From there, it was a straight route south to Vittoria, along a road that was maintained and clear, through tamed and protected fields.

Anybody who so much as glanced to the north would see them coming down the open road, so they crossed a bridge just south of the River Iracundia to reach the eastern side of the Nyx. A Hunters' trail wound through the forest there, just above the terraced fields. It had not been used since the last snowfall, perhaps even longer, and breaking trail through the snow was slow and tiring. Octavia was so focused on following the trail it was midday before she noticed how very empty the land around them was.

That there was nobody on the trail was to be expected, but there was also nobody in the fields or pastures. She didn't hear a single herder calling to their animals, nor the ring of cow or sheep bells. There were no guards or Hunters patrolling the road. There were no Crafters inspecting or repairing the protective walls and fences. There was no one fishing on the river, not even the small group of older women and men who normally cast their lines every day, in any weather and all seasons.

They were completely alone, except for the Ferox.

She heard the first just after their brief noon rest. The out-of-season birdsong startled Octavia, and as soon as she heard it, she was on guard for more. She began to see tracks in the snow and mud, and before long both she and Sima were catching glimpses of Ferox the size of rabbits and squirrels darting through the underbrush.

"There are a lot of them," Sima said, after they had spent a few minutes listening warily to a strange chirp on the hillside above them. "Are there normally this many?"

The chirping slowly moved away. Octavia shook her head. "No. It's definitely not normal."

She had spent so many afternoons in the woods around Vittoria, both with Hana and without her, and she had never seen or heard so many Ferox in one day. It was a distinct contrast to the day before, when she hadn't seen a single one. The Ferox didn't tend to gather so close to Vittoria, where there were always people and protective charms.

Something had changed to draw them closer to the town. Octavia didn't know what it was, but it couldn't be good. Whether the Ferox were keeping people inside Vittoria or keeping others out, it was unusual and worrying to have so many darting about in daytime, even if they were the small ones that did little harm. That only meant the large ones were lurking nearby, waiting for darkness. She still had the short spear Ursa had given her, and Sima still had her arrows, but a handful of arrows and an unfamiliar weapon were never going to keep them as safe as avoiding the monsters entirely.

Adding to Octavia's worry was her aching awareness of the sun creeping across the sky. She imagined Mother Dulcia on the road already, with the device mounted on a sleigh and an eager group of followers trailing her. They would move swiftly. They could reach Vittoria tomorrow. As much as Octavia could hope for something to delay them, she couldn't count on it. She had to assume they were on their way.

Vittoria's high wall came into view late in the afternoon. It had been a clear, sunny day, but as the sun set a brisk wind picked up, rattling and groaning through the trees, making it hard for Octavia to listen properly. As she and Sima reached the fields across from Oldgate, near where they had followed the Hunters' trail on their escape from Vittoria, they hid in the woods and waited. She didn't want to reach Vittoria much before dusk, when there was a risk of being seen by the guards atop the wall, but neither did she want to be out after dark with so many Ferox around.

"I don't like this," Octavia said. She whispered even though there was nobody around. "Where is everybody?"

"You said nobody stays out after dark," Sima said.

"Yeah, but people go out before that."

"Maybe the Ferox have frightened them?"

"Maybe." It didn't sit right with Octavia. "I just wish I knew what was going on inside."

Sima shifted her position slightly. Her voice very even, she asked, "Do you think they aren't allowed to leave at all now?"

It was exactly what Octavia was afraid of, and having Sima put it into words made it all too real. If Camilla couldn't control what people believed about the outside world, she might try to remove them from it entirely. If they couldn't step outside the wall, they couldn't look for strangers on the road. If they couldn't pass through the gates, they couldn't wonder if each person coming in was one they had seen before. It was what Vittoria had done in the earliest days after the war.

It was how Camilla had convinced them they were alone in the first place.

When the evening bells began to toll, Octavia picked up her pack and hefted her spear. She checked that Master Flavia's charmed metal key was in her jacket pocket, easy to access with no searching or fumbling. The evening bells sounded different tonight: deeper, slower, with a tone that seemed to vibrate through the forest. Octavia pressed her fist to the center of her chest; she could feel it there as well.

Sima drew her bow and fixed an arrow to it. They looked at each other, nodded, and left the protective shadows of the forest to cross the fields.

They were halfway across when Octavia heard a noise from behind. It was something between a crow's cackle and a cough. She turned, spear raised, searching the shadows for the Ferox. Even as she did so, she heard a scrape of metal on stone from the other direction. Her heart was thumping.

"Help me." The voice was small and faint. "I'm so cold. Help me."

Sima pointed with her arrow, and Octavia saw a Ferox slinking along a stone wall on the northern side of the field. It was little more than a dark smudge against the pale snow, but the sound of its metal spines dragging on stone made her skin crawl. It wasn't a huge Ferox, but it was big enough to be dangerous.

The crow's cackle came again, now from the south. Octavia whipped around just in time to spot another dark shape jumping over another stone wall. There were two of them, one on each side.

The second was much larger, like a deer or an elk, with jagged, crooked spikes for antlers.

"Keep going," Sima whispered, with a nudge at Octavia's shoulder. "I'll watch them. You get ready to open the gate."

Octavia nodded. As much as she hated it, she had to turn her back on the monsters and keep going. She could trust that Sima would keep her safe.

But as soon as she took another step, she heard the Ferox again. "Help me," it said.

Then, echoing it a second later, another voice from the north: "Help me."

And from behind them, in the forest: "I'm so cold."

And from the south, farther than the crow's call: "Please help me."

There were more than two. There were four, five, six or more shadows leaving the forest and moving across the fields, slinking and creeping and scuttling toward Vittoria across the burning ground.

As the seventh and final evening bell tolled its last, Octavia broke into a run.

They could not fight so many Ferox. Their only hope was getting through Oldgate. She heard Sima's footsteps behind her, and the rattling spines of the nearest Ferox as well, but she didn't look back. She dug the key from her pocket and held it tight in one hand. Just as she reached the gate and skidded to a stop before it, she heard the *twang* of Sima's bow. The Ferox let out a yelp, and Octavia's hands shook as she fit the key into the lock. Sima loosed another arrow, and there was a crashing sound as the deer-sized Ferox stumbled to the hard, icy ground. Octavia turned the key, forcing it through its stubborn stiffness, and looked over her shoulder. The small spiky Ferox had fallen apart completely, like the ones Brianne and Piper had hit with their spears. The larger one had not, although there was something wrong with the way it was moving, as though it no longer had control of its limbs. The lock clicked, and Octavia pulled the gate open. When she looked again the deer-like Ferox was trying to tug itself along with just its front legs, as its hind legs had crumpled beneath it. One of its forelimbs fell off and it lost its balance. It howled, and another Ferox appeared in the darkness behind it, leaping over a field wall and charging toward them.

Sima raised her bow again, but there was no time for that. Octavia grabbed her arm and hauled her through the gateway. She shoved the gate shut and locked it, and a second later the Ferox slammed into the iron bars with a deafening roar. Octavia and Sima stumbled away from the gate. It shook as the Ferox rammed it again, but Master Flavia's charms were working. The gate didn't so much as tremble under the monster's onslaught.

Somewhere far above, at the top of the wall, a guard shouted.

"Come on," Octavia whispered. Her heart was racing, her breath short, but they had no time to linger. "We have to go before they spot us."

That was, it turned out, much harder than Octavia had anticipated. It was barely an hour after sunset, and Vittoria was eerily quiet. Every shop was closed, every street stall shuttered. Lamplight shone in the windows, but there were none of the usual sounds of the evening. No music, no laughter, no people shouting across alleys to catch up with neighbors. No herders calling to their sheep and goats as they led them into their pens. It was as though all of the day's business had ended the moment the evening bells sounded, and everybody had scurried into their homes and locked the doors before the chimes were even finished.

Everybody except the guards.

There were guards everywhere. They patrolled in groups of two or three, bundled up against the cold for the long night ahead, speaking in murmurs when they met and casting their eyes about suspiciously. The commotion at Oldgate had drawn several of them to the western side of town. Octavia and Sima had to duck into alleys, sheds, barns, and empty doorways as they made their way across town, sometimes hiding for several minutes until the guards moved away.

A few times she overheard them talking, and from those bits of conversation she was able to piece together that this wasn't the first night so many Ferox had gathered in the burning ground. Guards positioned atop the wall swore they had seen a Ferox the size of a bear on Long Road in broad daylight. The council had ordered all the town's gates closed during the day. Already people were wondering if they would ever be able to leave Vittoria again.

"It just makes me wonder who's next," said one guard, walking slowly past a garden where Octavia and Sima were hiding in a shed. "People say they're seeing monsters everywhere, but Willa's been the only one to die."

"Almost like the creatures were hunting her," said the other guard. "If there are creatures inside at all. We've only got the council's word for that."

"I don't like it," said the first. "It makes me wonder what they're not telling us."

They moved away, so Octavia couldn't hear what they said next, but that brief exchange made her heart skip. If the guards were talking about the strangeness of Willa's death and the obvious absence of Ferox within Vittoria, that meant they were questioning Camilla's lies. She may have shut the gates during the day and shuttered the town after dark, but she could not stop people from listening and watching and wondering.

It meant they might be ready to hear the truth.

Clinging to shadows and dodging guards the whole way, Octavia and Sima crossed the Nyx and scurried up River Street to the archway beneath Master Flavia's workshop. Octavia knocked on the door, softly at first, then more forcefully. She was beginning to worry that Master Flavia might not be home when she heard footsteps on the stairs and the rattle of a lock. The door opened.

"What is the—" Master Flavia broke off with a gasp.

"We have to tell you something," Octavia said. "Can we come in?"

Master Flavia touched her fingers to her lips, then stepped back. "Yes, yes, come in! Before they see you. Go on upstairs."

She locked the door behind them before following. The workshop was quite dark, with only the fire on the hearth giving off a soft orange glow, but there was light coming from the doorway that led to Master Flavia's private chambers. She ushered them into a cozy library, where there was another fire burning merrily with a plush chair before it.

"You must be Sima," Master Flavia said. "I'm glad to see you are well, but why have you come back here? Did you not find your family?"

"We found them," Sima said. "They are unharmed."

"Oh, that's good. When Rufus returned without you, we were worried about what could happen." Master Flavia gestured at a wooden bench. "Sit, sit. Tell me everything."

"Sima's family aren't the only people we found," Octavia said. "There is a whole big group of people in Aeterna. They've been gathering for months, and now they're coming here. A sorcerer is leading them. They're going to attack Vittoria."

"A sorcerer?" Flavia said.

Octavia swallowed. Her throat was so dry it hurt.

"Agrippina," she said. "Your mother."

Master Flavia went still. The only sound in the room was the crackling of the fire. Octavia felt Sima shift beside her, a gentle bump against her shoulder, but neither spoke. In the firelight, Master Flavia's expression was impossible to read. Her lips moved silently. Guilt blossomed in Octavia's chest. She should not have said it like that, without warning or explanation. She had been thinking only of giving the warning, not of how the truth would affect Flavia, for whom Agrippina had been more than a long-dead enemy spoken about in stories and warnings.

"I think . . ." Flavia reached backward, feeling for her chair before she sat down. "I think you need to tell me everything."

It took a very long time to do exactly that. Master Flavia had endless questions, many of which neither Octavia nor Sima could answer. But she believed them: about the people in Aeterna, about Mother Dulcia's true identity, about the wall-smashing device even now trundling down the road toward Vittoria.

After they were finished, Master Flavia stood up and said, "I have to go speak to Cicerus and a few others."

"What are you going to do?" Octavia asked.

"We will arrange to warn the people who live closest to the walls, so they might evacuate quickly if it becomes necessary. We have also been speaking to some Hunters and guards who are not happy with the council's decisions. They can help more once they know what to look for." Flavia wrapped a cloak about herself. "You will stay here for the night. It's too risky for either of you to be spotted in town, and you need the rest after your journey. There is food in the kitchen and blankets in that chest over there." She gave them a quick flicker of a smile. "Stay inside, stay quiet, and get some rest. I suspect tomorrow will be a challenge for all of us."

Then she was gone, and Octavia and Sima were left alone in the warm library.

Sima tugged off her boots. "What's she going to do? Will it be enough?"

Octavia wanted to say yes. She wanted to say that everything would be okay, now that the problem was in the hands of Masters Flavia and Cicerus and other adults. She wanted to go to sleep trusting that whatever happened tomorrow would be peaceful.

"No," Octavia said. "I don't. I think we're missing something."

Sima tilted her head curiously. "What do you mean?"

"I'm not sure." Octavia began to unlace her boots. "I don't like that there were so many Ferox outside the wall. Why were they there? They don't run at Vittoria in groups like that. Mostly they don't come that close to town at all. I know we talk about them like they're wild animals, but they're really just magical weapons that do what they were created to do. They shouldn't have changed their behavior, unless . . ."

"Unless something made them change," Sima said.

Octavia nodded. "That's what I'm afraid we're missing."

A log settled in the fire, sending up a bright spray of sparks.

Sima stood abruptly. "We should eat and rest." She held out her hand. "Tomorrow is going to come no matter what we do."

Octavia took Sima's hand gratefully and let herself be pulled to her feet. "I wonder what kind of food a master Crafter keeps in her kitchen?"

Dinner was a problem they could solve right now. Everything else would have to wait.

22

The Unfinished War

M aster Flavia returned during the night while Octavia and Sima were asleep and left again for a couple of hours in the morning. Upon her second return, she gave Octavia and Sima a late breakfast as well as news from around Vittoria.

"Unfortunately, the council has placed only their most trusted guards atop the wall," Flavia said, sipping her bitter bellflower tea. She had not sat down; she paced anxiously beside the table. "We hope our allies will hear news of any movement on the road immediately, but we can't count on it. It is very frustrating not knowing what's happening outside. We might have very little warning before we have to act."

Octavia tore off a piece of bread. It was from her family's bakery—she would recognize the scoring on her father's loaves anywhere—but she could not let herself think about that. There were more important things to deal with than her own homesickness and worry.

"What about me and Sima?" she asked.

"I think it's best if you go over to Cicerus's infirmary. There are people out and about now, so if we wrap you up in hats and scarves nobody will notice."

"What will we do there?" Octavia asked.

Master Flavia smiled down at her. "Stay safe, I hope."

Octavia glanced at Sima, then looked back at Flavia. "I mean to *help*."

"Your warning is help—"

Flavia was interrupted by a thunderous knocking at the downstairs door. Octavia startled so badly she spilled her tea. Sima's eyes widened in alarm. The knocking continued, and with it came muffled shouts.

Master Flavia set her teacup down calmly. "I better go see who that is. Stay here, with the door closed, and keep quiet."

She swept out of her personal chambers and into the workshop, shutting the door firmly behind her. Her footsteps creaked on the stairs, and the rumble of voices carried through the floor, too low for Octavia to understand what they were saying.

"Do you think they've spotted people on the road?" Sima whispered.

"They could only get here so fast if they traveled through the night," Octavia replied. "And that's not . . ."

Not something people from Vittoria would do, but Agrippina was not from Vittoria and did not share its fears.

"I don't know," Octavia admitted.

Heavy footsteps thumped on the stairs, and Master Flavia's voice called out, "This is very unusual. Just what do you hope to find?"

"Whatever it is you're hiding," a man said.

Octavia felt a chill. She recognized that voice. And from the way Sima's hands closed into fists, it was clear she recognized it as well. It was Master Etius.

"Search everywhere," he said. Footsteps thumped across the floor; there were three or four people with him. "Be thorough."

"I'm not hiding anything," Master Flavia said. "Honestly, why are you wasting your time here?"

"You told your apprentice not to come by today. You are clearly hiding something."

Master Flavia's voice drew nearer to the closed workshop door. "Really, now, I told Penelope to stay home because I thought her parents could use the help, with how strange everything has been lately."

Sima met Octavia's eyes and stood slowly, careful not to scrape her chair on the floor. Octavia did the same. She grabbed Sima's pack and boots, and she pointed silently toward a large wooden storage chest.

"*Hide,*" she mouthed.

Sima nodded, then pointed at Octavia in question.

Octavia shoved Sima's things at her and shook her head. She helped Sima into the chest and shut the lid, just in time to hear Master Etius asked, "What's back there?"

"My home," said Master Flavia. "Are you interested in my kitchen, Etius?"

Octavia looked around wildly, searching for another hiding spot. Under a table or chair. Between bookshelves. Below the kitchen basin. Nothing would fit her and her things. She looked hopefully at the windows, but they were locked shut.

"Step out of the way, Flavia," Master Etius said.

Another voice said, "Nothing out here."

"You checked the storage places?"

"Even the cupboards."

That meant they would look in the chest too, when they got into this room. Octavia turned one way, then another. She couldn't let them find Sima. She didn't want to think about what Master Etius would do if he caught her again.

"Do the same in all the rooms," Etius said.

Octavia had to stop them.

She pulled open the door.

"Are you looking for me?" she said.

Master Etius blinked in surprise, his mouth slightly open. Octavia wondered if he really hadn't expected to find anybody or anything, if he was only here to pester Master Flavia. He recovered quickly, however, and snapped at the guards, "That's the Silvia girl. Seize her. Take her things as well."

"She's only a child!" Master Flavia cried. "Surely there's no reason—"

"We won't harm her," Etius said coldly. "As for you, harboring a fugitive in the middle of town . . . Camilla will deal with you later."

Ignoring Master Flavia's protests, the guards grabbed Octavia by her arms and led her out of the workshop. She put up a bit of a struggle, just to make it look like she meant it, but she didn't want to give them any reason to keep searching Flavia's home. She didn't dare meet Flavia's eyes, lest she give something away, but she hoped Flavia and Sima understood. It was better this way. She had to keep Sima safe.

With Master Etius leading the way, the guards hustled Octavia through town to the Council Hall. People stopped and stared and muttered on every street, and a few who recognized her called out questions, but nobody did anything to stop or challenge the guards. It was a bright, clear day, without a trace of clouds in the sky. The guards would be able to see a great distance up Long Road. She hoped they were watching.

When they reached the Council Hall, Etius said, "Take her upstairs. I'll alert Camilla."

He swept away, his impractical white coat billowing around him. One of the guards, the one carrying Octavia's pack and spear, went with him. The other two steered Octavia up the stairs.

"Where are you taking me?" she asked. She hoped that with

Etius gone the guards might be more willing to answer. "What's going on?"

"Shut up," said one guard.

So much for answers.

Octavia wanted to ask them what Master Camilla wanted or whether anybody had been spotted on the road, but what came out, to her surprise, was "I want my parents."

The first guard snorted, and the second one rolled her eyes and said, "You're worried about your parents now, after all the trouble you've caused them?"

"I want to talk to them. Are they okay?"

"Everybody's okay except you," said the first guard. They reached the top of the stairs, and the guards nudged Octavia through an open doorway and into a wide, bright room. It was some kind of sitting room, with padded chairs and sofas arranged around delicate tables. The guards in their black uniforms and heavy coats looked out of place, but not nearly as out of place as Octavia felt in her dirty traveling clothes.

"Why is the whole town locked down?" Octavia asked. "Is nobody allowed out at all?"

"To keep the peace," said one guard, while at the same moment the other said, "Because it's safer this way."

The guards exchanged a glance.

"Those are Master Camilla's orders," the first guard said firmly. "We are only following her orders. She tells us what we need to know."

There was a shout from downstairs in the Council Hall. The second guard stepped into the hallway to look down the stairs. When she came back, she said, "I'll see what they want. Keep an eye on her. You." She jabbed her finger toward Octavia. "Sit down and stop talking."

"I know the real reason she doesn't want anybody out," Octavia said. "I'm surprised you haven't figured it out yet."

"Shut up," the guard said again.

"Don't you wonder why the gates are locked?"

The guard took a menacing step toward Octavia. "*Shut up*."

Octavia took a breath. She had come back to Vittoria to tell the truth. She might as well start now. "She doesn't want you to know—"

The guard whirled around and stomped out of the room, slamming the door shut behind him. The click of the lock followed immediately.

That was not exactly how Octavia had imagined her truth telling would go. She sunk into one of the soft chairs, feeling a vicious bit of pride knowing that she was probably making it very dirty. But almost at once she jumped to her feet again and ran to the windows. The room had a fine view of Center Square and much of River Street. She hadn't had much chance to notice when the guards were bringing her here, but although there were a lot of people out and about, it didn't look like a normal day in Vittoria. There were no market stalls set up, nobody shopping or selling or arguing over prices. Most people were gathered in groups of four or five, casting uneasy looks over their shoulders as guards hurried past. A group of Hunters left the Council Hall and strode quickly north on River Street, toward Wyvern Gate. A few Crafters emerged from the narrow streets of their quarter to point and talk and frown. She didn't see Masters Flavia or Cicerus.

Octavia watched for some time, insulated from the noise by the windows and walls of the Council Hall, her nervousness growing with every minute. There was definitely something going on. Octavia needed to know.

She ran over to the door to pound on it. "Hey! Hey, I know

you're still out there!"

There was no reply from the guard outside.

"Hey! You need to listen to me! There are people outside Vittoria. That's what Camilla doesn't want you to know! They've been there all along. The war didn't kill everybody. And Camilla didn't kill Agrippina."

The locked clicked again. Octavia stepped back but didn't stop talking.

"That's what she's so afraid of. She's afraid that people will figure it out," she said.

"Do not mistake my love of Vittoria for something as childish as fear."

The door swung open, and Camilla stood before Octavia. In one hand she held the spear Ursa had given to Octavia. The familiar guards were behind her, watching Octavia warily.

"Hello again, Octavia," said Camilla. "I confess I did not expect you to survive long enough to return."

"I survived because the people outside helped me," Octavia said. "Including Agrippina. You never killed her. You lied to us."

"Master Camilla," one of the guards said nervously, "what is she talking about?"

Camilla was smiling, but it was a tight, thin smile. She stared hard at Octavia.

"Bring her," she said. She turned on her heel, not sparing so much as a glance for the guards, and strode down the hallway.

"But she's saying—"

"Bring her!" Camilla snapped.

The guards didn't have to drag Octavia this time; she was following Camilla before they even moved. They didn't go far, only to the next room, but this one had doors opening to a large balcony overlooking Center Square. Camilla opened the doors; a rush of noise flowed into the room from outside.

"Come here, Octavia," Camilla said, stepping onto the balcony. "You want to know what's happening to Vittoria? Come and look." To the guards she said, "You may leave. Report to Master Etius to help with our defenses."

On the balcony already were other members of the council— but not Masters Etius or Cicerus.

The commotion in Center Square was growing frenetic. Guards shouted at people to move out of the way, to go home, to bar their doors. People shouted at guards demanding to know what was going on, where was the danger, were the Ferox attacking. Toward the south, people were gathering on the balconies and rooftops of the Crafters' Quarter. Right below, on the steps of the Council Hall, Master Etius was bellowing orders and pointing with his long, thin arm toward the north.

"Are they here already?" Octavia asked, her heart thumping.

Camilla narrowed her eyes. "A short while ago our guards atop the northern wall spotted something unusual. They claim it looks like travelers on Long Road, or monsters disguised to look like travelers. Of course, it might be an illusion."

"And it might not be," another council member said quietly. Those near her shifted awkwardly, but Octavia couldn't tell if it was because they wanted to silence her or because they agreed.

"It's not an illusion," Octavia said. "It's not the Ferox either."

"You would say that, to deflect us from your guilt in this matter," Camilla said. "It is no coincidence that this threat has arrived right after your return. It followed you here."

Octavia stared at her. "Followed me? They didn't need to follow me! There's a great big road right there! It's impossible to miss!"

One of the councilors cleared his throat. "Perhaps the girl can tell us who she believes—"

"It's Agrippina. It's her sister," Octavia said. "And she's—"

Camilla interrupted with a loud laugh. "Ha! The child is raving."

"I'm not! She's been in Aeterna. She has a bunch of—"

"This is growing tiresome," Camilla said, as though Octavia weren't speaking at all. "We must—"

"She has a bunch of people with her and a weapon for attacking the walls! The one the sorcerers used on Ira and all the lowland cities! *There are people coming to Vittoria!*"

"What are you talking about?" a councilor said.

"Aeterna?" said another.

"Do not listen to this girl." Camilla's voice was growing shrill.

But her protest came too late. The councilors were talking rapidly to one another, and Octavia's shouting had carried to the square below.

"What's going on?" one woman shouted.

And another answered, "There are people outside?"

"What people?" somebody else asked.

"There is no reason to be frightened!" Camilla called out. She set Octavia's spear against the railing to raise both of her hands. "The walls will protect us from whatever approaches outside! We will not be tricked or cowed!"

"It's not a trick!" Octavia said. She was shouting on purpose now, hoping her voice would reach as far as Camilla's. "The sorcerer Agrippina is alive, and she's coming down from Aeterna with a sorcerers' weapon! Camilla lied about Vittoria being alone in the world, and she lied about killing her sister, and now she's lying to you about what's outside!"

As soon as they heard *sorcerer* and *weapon*, panic spread through everybody who could hear. The councilors argued loudly, the guards and people below shouted questions and demands at each other, and Master Etius waved his arms frantically as he bellowed, "To the gate! We will defend Vittoria! Secure Wyvern Gate!"

"No, wait!" Octavia shouted. "They have a weapon to smash through stone! Stay away from the walls!"

Nobody was listening. Octavia watched in horror as throngs of people headed right where she didn't want them to go, right to the gate where Mother Dulcia and her people were approaching. Octavia turned desperately to Camilla, trying to think of something, *anything*, that would make the woman listen.

Camilla was not looking at her. She was looking out over Vittoria, but her gaze was distant, as though focused on what waited beyond the wall. There was a slight smile on her lips. The anger that had twisted her expression before was gone, replaced by a calm serenity that sent chills down Octavia's spine.

"I had wondered how she would come for me, when she came," Camilla said.

The councilors on the balcony fell silent. Octavia recalled the brief flash of fear she had seen on Camilla's face the first time they met, when Camilla had mentioned her sister. It hadn't meant anything at the time.

Octavia had not known then how much of her world was shaped by Camilla's fear of Agrippina, knowing she still outside Vittoria, knowing she would want revenge.

"I expected something more insidious," Camilla went on. "A plague in the river. A blight on the crops. My sister was always proud of her subtlety."

"Master Camilla," a councilor said, "what are you saying? Agrippina is alive?"

"You defeated her in battle," said another.

"Didn't you?" asked a third, quietly.

Camilla did not appear to be listening. "But she was never as clever as she believed herself to be. Fifty years to stew and scheme and plot, and she's forgotten that everything she will imagine, I have already considered. Etius!" Her voice rose sharply. She looked down toward the steps.

"Yes, Master Camilla?"

"Signal the guards atop the walls. They must be ready."

"Ready for what?" a councilor asked shakily. "Camilla, what's going on?"

Camilla finally remembered the people gathered around her. "It's quite simple. My sister has come to finish the war."

"She only wants you," Octavia said. Her voice was small and tremulous. She couldn't seem to catch enough breath. The councilors were listening now. "Just go out there. Open the gates. There won't have to be any fighting if you go out to meet her. Nobody else will get hurt if you go to her."

Camilla laughed. "I have been waiting fifty years for her to come to me. I'm certainly not going to—"

Whatever it was Camilla was not going to do was lost beneath a rumble of thunder.

But it wasn't thunder, because the sky was clear and cloudless. The noise made the entire city tremble, rattling windows and walls in every building. Birds burst into flight from rooftops, and the councilors grabbed for the balcony railing. Octavia could feel the sound as much as she heard it; it made her teeth ache and her neck tense. When it ended a peculiar hush fell over Vittoria.

A hush that was broken, seconds later, by the loud crack of breaking stone. A cloud of dust rose from the north end of town, right where Wyvern Gate stood. People began to scream.

And over it all, deep and resonant and steady, came the sound of the evening bells.

23

Camilla and Agrippina

———»———

A second rumble of thunder followed the first. All of Vittoria was trembling. Dust billowed in great clouds from the direction of Wyvern Gate, obscuring what was happening at the base of the wall. The councilors on the balcony were in a panic, babbling out questions and demands, not listening to one another. In the square below, Master Etius shouted commands at the guards, but they didn't seem to hear him.

Octavia's ears were ringing. She had to do something. She couldn't make her feet move.

The wall still stood over the growing cloud of dust, but Octavia couldn't see more than that. The northern side of Vittoria was filled with shouts and cries and the horrible, cracking sound of breaking stone.

And over it all, the evening bells rang.

There was no reason for them to be ringing in the middle of the day. And they didn't sound quite right. It was hard to tell, with so much other noise filling the town, but the chimes were faster than usual and slightly discordant. Only six of the seven bells were tolling; the bell tower over Wyvern Gate remained silent.

"Etius!" Camilla shouted.

Master Etius looked up at her, his expression stunned and overwhelmed. "Camilla? What ... what's happened? What is this?"

"Why is Wyvern Tower ignoring my command?"

Etius's eyes widened. "But Camilla, the gate, don't you see, the gate—"

"Go up there and ring the bells yourself, if you can't make your pathetic guards do it!" Camilla shouted. "Do you think Agrippina will wait for you to gather your wits? We must be ready to meet her *now*! The bells must ring!"

"Camilla, what are you doing?" one of the councilors said.

Another said, "Forget the bells! What do we do?"

Nobody was paying any attention to Octavia. She had to do something, but fear was like a living thing in her throat, clawing at her insides and swiping at every thought as soon as it formed. She was distracted, momentarily, by the gentle tinkle of Master Camilla's charms as she gestured broadly and shouted another command to Master Etius. She used to make magical instruments, Flavia had said.

Instruments and clever magical devices.

Octavia's heart thumped. It was suddenly hard to breathe.

The bells had been tolling when Octavia and Sima saw dozens of Ferox surrounding Vittoria.

There was a tiny bell-like chime of magic when the weapons from the Clan of the Furious Dead struck a Ferox.

And there had been bells at night when Willa was killed. Her neighbors had heard them, mistook them for dawn or dusk. There had been broken things all over her home.

Nobody knew the name of the sorcerer who had created the Ferox. It had been stamped out of history, erased as effectively as a blank spot on a map, as effectively as Camilla had erased the outside world for the people of Vittoria.

Camilla, who used to create magical musical instruments, but gave it up for more power.

"It's for the Ferox," Octavia said.

Her throat was dry, her voice too quiet and quavering to carry over the voices of the councilors. They were angry and confused and scared; they had no idea what was going on. They had trusted Camilla for so long they had never even questioned the rules and habits she put into place. They believed her when she said nobody in Vittoria would use magic for anything but protection.

"It's for the Ferox!" Octavia shouted. She grabbed the nearest councilor by the sleeve. "She's ringing the bells to draw the Ferox! She's controlling them! They're *her* monsters!"

There was a brief, stunned silence. The four councilors on the balcony and Master Etius below all stared at Octavia with their mouths open, their eyes wide.

"What," said Master Etius. "Camilla—this girl—what?"

"Oh, come now, Etius," Camilla said, with a jingling sweep of her arm. "You know we must take drastic measures to protect Vittoria. I thought you agreed with me."

"But not—"

Master Etius's protest was interrupted by a scream rising from the cacophony to the north, a man's voice made piercing by shrill, wild terror.

"Ferox! Ferox in the town! They're here!"

Other screams rose to join him, and one voice became many, all of them shouting the same warning.

"The Ferox are here! The Ferox are in Vittoria!"

"Well," said Camilla, gazing out across Vittoria. "I suppose six bells will do for now. The results might even be interesting."

She was still smiling.

"Camilla, is this girl speaking the truth?" Etius said. "Are the bells bringing the Ferox into Vittoria?"

Camilla scoffed. "Are you deaf as well as stupid? Can't you recognize a change in the rhythm of the bells? I have no need to bring in creatures from the wilderness when there is so much material to work with here."

The terror holding Octavia in place broke, like a cage of glass shattering all around her. She shoved past Camilla to grab her spear from where it rested against the balcony railing. Camilla was so surprised she stumbled backward; she caught her balance and reached for Octavia, but Octavia was already out of reach.

"She's been using them to control us all along!" Octavia shouted at the councilors. "Stop *listening* to her and do something!"

Octavia didn't wait to see their reactions. She ran down through the Council Hall and out the front doors, barreled past Master Etius and the guards. Nobody tried to stop her.

She considered running back to the Crafters' Quarter for Sima and Master Flavia, but she decided against it at once. The noise had probably already drawn them out; she might never find them in the chaos. Instead Octavia ran north as fast as she could, weaving around frantic adults and crying children in Center Square to reach River Street. As she ducked and dodged her way up the road, she heard cries all around about Ferox, about invaders, about sorcerers, calling for help, calling for weapons, calling for each other. Nobody knew what was going on. Everybody was terrified. The dust from the attack, as white as the stones of the wall, hung in the air thick and low to the ground, making Octavia's throat scratchy and her eyes watery. Octavia looked for familiar faces, for her family or neighbors, for Master Cicerus or Rufus, but she didn't see any of them. The dust clung to faces and clothes, making everybody around her look like pale white ghosts with mouths open in fear and wide, wide eyes.

Octavia was only halfway to Wyvern Gate when she saw the first injured people staggering along the street, clinging to the buildings, filthy and dazed, with blood dripping over their faces. Others were being carried on blankets and coats fashioned into makeshift stretchers, with broken and bloodied limbs dangling as their helpers jostled through the crowd. Just a bit farther, she began to see houses and buildings that had been struck by chunks of white stone from the wall. Some of the pieces were large enough to have smashed completely through walls and roofs. Everywhere people were trying to dig into the wrecked buildings, shouting at those who were hurt or stuck inside.

As Octavia neared Juniper Street, she saw a butcher shop that had been struck by a piece of white stone as big as a cart. The stone had destroyed the front window and part of the wall. The butcher stood just outside his own door, staring at the damage. He didn't move as people rushed and bumped all around him. His gray hair was white with dust; there was a trickle of blood at his left temple. He was holding his left arm out from his side, his sleeve and fingers bloody, as though he didn't know what to do with it. Octavia knew the man. She knew his entire family. He sold pork and goat to the bakery twice a week, and every time he came by he would sit with Dad and drink a cup of tea and share the gossip from the herders and butcher shops and smokehouses. Octavia didn't see any of his grown children who worked in the shop with him.

They might be trapped. Nobody was helping. The butcher could barely stay upright. Octavia turned sharply to run over toward him.

The debris in the front of the butcher shop shifted. Stone and wood and glass crunched and tumbled, and Octavia felt a wild stab of both hope and fear, that the butcher's family might be trying to crawl out from under the pile. But no hands or limbs emerged, and the debris continued to move.

Wooden planks with splintered ends twisted and twitched into stiff, awkward legs. Chunks of broken stone rolled about and toppled into the lone long line of a spine. Shards of glass crackled and turned, glinting in the sunshine as they formed a sharp, bristling pelt. With every sweep of the newly formed limbs, bones from the butcher shop joined together to make long, uneven claws with meat and sinew still clinging to them. There was no head, barely any body at all, and every proportion was wrong, every motion unsteady, but it was growing and moving and changing.

They weren't coming from outside. That's what Camilla had meant when she spoke of having material to work with in town. The spell cast by the bells was creating Ferox inside Vittoria.

Octavia lunged forward and jabbed her spear at the Ferox. There wasn't really anything for her to stab into, because it didn't have much of a body, but as soon as the tip glanced over the stony spine and struck a wooden limb, the spear sang in her hand, a single chiming note so clear and so loud she nearly dropped the weapon. But she held on, and the Ferox began to fall apart as it took its first wobbling steps. She stabbed at it again, to be sure, and a shower of wooden splinters and glass shards fell to the ground.

Octavia turned to the butcher, who was staring at the collapsed Ferox.

"How?" he said. "What?"

"Come on." Octavia tugged him away from the building. She looked around until she spotted another neighbor, the candlemaker whose shop was next door. She shoved the butcher toward the woman. "Help him!"

Octavia didn't stick around to offer explanations. There was no time for that. The bells were still ringing—still ringing, ringing, *ringing*, the sound was going to drive her mad—and everywhere the wreckage from Agrippina's assault was forming itself into hideous, trembling, malformed Ferox. They were slow and clumsy when they first came together, and utterly silent. Townspeople were fighting the monsters with hammers and axes, jabbing into their wobbly joints with brooms and knives, using anything they had on hand. It was working better than it would have on the Ferox outside the wall. These were young, hastily born of incomplete magic. Maybe the townspeople could beat them.

They had to beat them. There was so much wreckage, and so many monsters rising from it.

With her spear, Octavia destroyed every Ferox that she could, but it seemed like as soon as she broke one apart another formed to take its place. More than once she looked around, hoping to hear the zing of an arrow and spot Sima's red scarf in the crowd, but there was no sign of her. Octavia's spear wasn't going to be enough. No matter how many monsters she destroyed, more would come.

She had to stop them from forming in the first place.

"Octavia?"

She whirled around at the sound of her name. There was a scuffle and a shout, and a familiar figure stumbled into the street in front of her.

It was Albus, and right behind him were Lavinia and Augustus. Albus had a bruise forming on his face, and Lavinia's hand was bleeding. They were all dirty and rumpled.

"Octavia?" Albus said again. "What are—where have you—you're back?"

Before Octavia could answer, Lavinia shouted and shoved Albus to the side as a long, thin Ferox with far too many limbs staggered out of an alley toward them. Its legs cracked and rasped as it lurched forward—on three limbs, with two more outstretched and feeling about for prey. Octavia hefted her spear, but before she could close the distance an arrow struck the Ferox right in its neck. It crumpled into a heap at Albus's and Lavinia's feet.

Octavia whirled around. That was one of Sima's arrows. She had to be close, but Octavia couldn't find her, there were too many people in the street, everybody fighting and running in different directions—then a spot of red above the street caught her eye.

There, on a rooftop two stories above River Street, Sima raised her arm to wave, then turned sharply to fire again.

Lavinia pulled the arrow from the rubble of the Ferox. "What is this? How did it do that?"

"Magic," Octavia said shortly. "It can destroy the Ferox, but we don't have enough, we need—"

She stopped. Seeing the arrow in Lavinia's hand gave her an idea.

"The bells," she said.

"What?" Lavinia said.

"We need the bells?" Albus said doubtfully.

"No, no, we need to *stop* the bells. You have to get up to the bell towers. Make them stop ringing." Octavia pushed Lavinia's hand, the one gripping the arrow, back toward her. "Use that for any Ferox you can't get past. They're really weak right now because the seventh bell isn't ringing."

"How do you—"

"Listen to me!" Octavia shouted, interrupting Augustus's question. "Didn't you notice that the Ferox started forming as soon as they started? That's Camilla's sorcery. You have to stop them!" Her voice grew shaky and tears sprung into her eyes. "Please. I promise I'm not lying, I haven't been—"

"We know," Lavinia said. "Albus told us about your friend from outside. About what the council tried to do. We talked to Rufus."

"He's over that way, by the way, with the healer," Albus said, jerking a thumb over his shoulder. "Mom is up by the gate with the Hunters. They've been waiting for something to happen."

"We believe you," Lavinia said. "We can help."

Albus said a word that would have definitely earned him a scolding from their parents, had they been there. "There will be guards below each bell tower."

"So we figure out a way past them," Augustus said. He was holding a broken rolling pin in one hand and still wearing his baker's apron, and every part of him from head to toe was covered with both flour and dust. He looked utterly ridiculous. They all did, and Octavia wanted to hug them so hard and never let go, and she wanted to ask about Mom and Dad, and she wanted to apologize and explain and tell them everything, but there was no time.

"We'll start at Orchard Gate," Lavinia said. "It's the closest."

"Go," Octavia said. "Go as fast as you can!"

"You're not coming with us?" Albus asked.

Octavia shook her head. "The people outside—I have to tell them, I have to stop them—just go!"

"But what are you going to . . ." Albus's question trailed off as he stared at something behind Octavia.

She turned. Sima was pushing her way through the crowd. She called out, "Octavia! She's coming this way!"

"Who's coming?" Lavinia said.

"The sorcerer," Sima said.

Octavia gripped her spear tighter. "Camilla."

The noise from farther south on River Street was changing. Although they were still surrounded by people shouting and fleeing and fighting the Ferox, a peculiar calm crept up the street, dampening the sound of the battle, even as the tolling bells seemed to grow louder. The crowd shifted, with people pushing to the sides and scrambling into buildings and alleys, shoving and jostling to hurry out of the way.

Camilla was walking up River Street. She did not move quickly;

her pace was measured and deliberate. In each hand she carried a handbell, which she rung with each step, so that the bells and all of the charms on her bracelets and necklaces were chiming together.

And with every step, the road itself quivered and coiled and rose beneath her feet, curling into humps and stretching into limbs, drawing in scattered wood and tools and broken glass, all of it churning into half-formed Ferox in her wake. Few of the monsters endured; most fell apart almost immediately. Camilla didn't seem to mind. She walked along with her gaze fixed straight ahead, letting the incomplete Ferox writhe and collapse around her, not paying the least bit of attention to the people who cried out in panic and tumbled out of her way.

"You have to go." Octavia grabbed Lavinia and pushed her away from the road; Albus and Augustus followed. "You have to stop the bells. We can't wait any longer!"

"We will," Lavinia said. "We'll stop them."

"Whatever you're going to do," said Albus, "don't be stupid."

Octavia made a face. "*You* don't be stupid."

They pushed through the crowd and were soon out of sight. Nobody noticed. Everybody was watching Camilla.

"What are we going to do?" Sima asked.

"Something stupid," Octavia replied.

Sima raised her eyebrows.

"We're going to run for the gate and put ourselves right between two powerful and angry sorcerers," Octavia said. "I haven't figured out the rest yet."

"Oh," said Sima. She shrugged. "That is pretty stupid. Let's go."

Octavia gave her a wild grin and held out her hand. Sima grabbed it, and they ran.

People were clearing off the road ahead of Camilla, so once Octavia and Sima broke free of the crowd it was a lot easier to move. Before long Octavia was able to see through the dust and finally get a good look at the wall.

There was a gaping hole where Wyvern Gate had once been. The gate and all the stone around it had been smashed away completely, leaving a massive, jagged archway over a road strewn with rubble. The force of the blast had toppled three of the five monuments commemorating the explorers lost after the war.

There were fewer people close to the gate, and those who remained were largely guards and Hunters, who were fighting the Ferox that rose from the debris. Octavia finally spotted Rufus and Master Cicerus on the other side of River Street, tending to an injured guard on the front steps of a building.

She was about to call out to Rufus when a flash of orange hair caught Octavia's eye through the whirling dust and commotion. She spun around to find Hana—but it wasn't Hana.

It was Mom. She was with the other Hunters, fighting a large Ferox near the fallen explorers' monuments. Her cane was nowhere to be seen; she was using a long spear instead, striking at the monster so swiftly and deftly it was as though she had forgotten about her injured leg.

Octavia gaped in wonder. She knew Mom had been the leader of the Hunters because she was the best of them, but she had never seen her in action before. Mom dodged a Ferox's swiping claws and jabbed her spear into its shoulder. With a smooth, fast twist, she dislocated the joint and detached the forelimb. The Ferox stumbled, and Mom lunged again to spear its other shoulder.

Even as that Ferox toppled, another was forming behind her, as stone and wood and twisted pieces of iron gate wound and curled into a massive snake. It grew taller and taller, until it was twice as tall as a grown person and loomed ominously over Mom.

She hadn't noticed it yet. It was close enough to attack.

Octavia shouted a warning, but everybody was shouting; her voice was swallowed by the cacophony. She lifted her spear and ran instead. An arrow flew over her head, but the snake bent to the side and Sima's arrow glanced off its flank, taking only a clattering handful of road cobbles with it. The monster's great head split open—a yawning mouth full of black iron teeth—and it bent to close its jaws over Octavia's mother.

"No!" Octavia screamed. She scrambled forward, flinging herself over broken pieces of stone, and threw her spear as hard as she could.

Her aim was true. The spear buried itself in the Ferox's body right below its head. The jaws snapped shut as the creature faltered, and Mom stumbled to the side right beneath them—but it wasn't a stumble. Somebody pulled Mom to safety as the Ferox fell to pieces where she had been standing.

"Hana," Mom said.

"Hi, Mom," Hana said. Still holding on to Mom's wrist with one hand, she yanked the spear from the Ferox and tossed it back to Octavia. "Are you hurt?"

"Hana," Mom said again. "But you—"

"I know. I have a lot to tell you, but first—"

She broke off and tugged Mom to the side again, this time to make way for ten horses and riders thundering into Vittoria through the shattered gateway.

One of Vittoria's guards bellowed, *"They're coming in!"* His voice carried, echoing from the wall and the buildings around the square, loud enough to catch the attention of people nearby.

But instead of attacking when they came inside, the riders pulled their horses to a sudden halt and looked around in bewilderment. Octavia recognized a few of the riders as guards and workers from Aeterna; they looked shocked, afraid, even horrified at the chaotic scene they had ridden into. The horses whinnied fearfully and shied away from the Ferox, while the Hunters wove around them and shouted for them to get out of the way. A cat-like Ferox sprung onto the back of one horse and tugged the rider to the ground. Both horse and human screamed. As the Ferox began to drag the rider away, Mom and Hana rushed the creature together to stop it.

Behind the riders on horseback came people on foot, and among them was Agrippina. She walked slowly, using a long spear for support as she stepped into the square. There she stopped, heedless of the battle all around her.

Her expression was placid. Her followers might have been shocked by the destruction the sorcerers' weapon had inflicted upon Vittoria, but Agrippina was not. She did not even seem to notice the fighting. She leaned on the spear casually. The gaze of her single green eye was fix steadily ahead to where River Street met the square between the remains of two fallen memorials.

Camilla had arrived. She stood between the broken stone monuments with her bells in hand. She rang them once, and the sound was barely loud enough to be heard over the chaos. Only the closest few Ferox reacted, turning toward her sharply, like dogs responding to their master's call. She rang the bells again, drawing the attention of those people nearest to her, who gasped and pointed and tugged one another away from her.

The third ring of her handbells, struck in time with a chime from the bells on the wall, reverberated so loudly that Octavia could feel it in her bones. The sound swept over the Hunters and guards and healers, over Agrippina's followers still struggling with their horses, over everybody nearby, startling them into a brief silence. The noises from farther down River Street and elsewhere in town continued, as did the tolling of the evening bells, but for a stunned moment, the square before Wyvern Gate was quiet but for the fading echo of Camilla's bells.

"Very nice," said Agrippina. She tapped the end of her spear twice on the ground. "Your control has improved quite a lot, I think."

"Of course it has," said Camilla. She stepped around the smashed remains of a vegetable cart, her nose wrinkling in distaste. The street cobbles trembled and twitched around her, but they didn't form anything more than gentle waves, like ripples on a pond. "I've been perfecting my craft for years. I'm afraid I can't say the same for this . . . little mess you've caused. Have you abandoned your more insidious methods in favor of simply smashing every obstacle?"

Behind Camilla, across the street, Rufus helped Master Cicerus to his feet, and Cicerus took a few steps into the square. Nobody else dared move, not even the Ferox.

"Camilla," he said. "Agrippina. Why are you doing this?"

His voice was loud enough to carry, but neither woman appeared to hear him.

"Would you prefer I trap an entire town of people within walls of ignorance and fear?" Agrippina asked. "I have no use for deceptions such as that."

Camilla laughed. "You loved the deception during the war, when you told the frightened mobs you meant to help them while spreading a plague instead."

"I did mean to help them," Agrippina said. "I wanted them to stop fighting."

"It worked, I suppose. The dead do not fight."

"Neither do prisoners who don't know they are prisoners." Agrippina lifted her spear to point around her, sweeping it to encompass what she could see of Vittoria in the bright afternoon sunlight. "Whatever their cage may look like. However kindly their captor pretends to be. This is what you have always wanted, isn't it? To be thanked for your cruelty so that you might tell yourself it is kindness."

"Camilla, Agrippina, the people of Vittoria are not yours to use for your unfinished battles," said Master Cicerus, taking another step forward. "There is no need for more violence."

"Your opinion is *not* noted," Camilla said, without looking at him. "My sister has attacked our home. I will not let her get away with it."

Although Camilla was tall while Agrippina was diminutive, it was hard to ignore the resemblance as the two sisters faced each other across the small square. Right between them was the place where Willa had wept over Bram's body on the day before the first snow.

Another voice spoke from the crowd behind Camilla. "He's right, Aunt Camilla, Mother. You must stop this."

People shuffled aside to let Master Flavia through. She was panting heavily, as though she had run all the way up River Street. Her skirts were torn, her face streaked with sweat and dust.

"Flavia!" Agrippina exclaimed. "My dear, it has been so—"

"You must stop this," Flavia said sharply. "Look around you. Look at the damage you've done."

"I do what is necessary," Agrippina said.

"This is not your fight," Camilla said. "Step out of the way."

"There is no need for a fight at all," Flavia countered. "Nobody here wants to fight except the two of you, and your reasons belong in the past, with a war that's been over for fifty years."

"She's right," said Cicerus. "Listen to her. You can stop this."

"Mother," Flavia said. "Please."

Octavia took a step forward. She stopped. She didn't know what to do. Agrippina and Camilla were looking only at each other, as though they had forgotten there was anybody else in the world. Flavia and Cicerus standing to the side, the fallen monuments, the evening bells still ringing, all of Vittoria, all of the damage and confusion and fear, it all faded from their notice. There was nothing left but two old women with the same agate-green eyes and mirrored wounds to mar them, and stretched between them was an invisible thread of family and magic and hatred and fear that had first been spun in the war more than fifty years ago.

The moment ended when Camilla looked up suddenly and said, "Why are they stopping?"

Only then did Octavia notice that the noise around them had changed. The sounds of people fighting and calling for help still carried from down River Street, but the town was growing quieter.

Octavia turned in a circle, tilting her head to listen in every direction.

There were fewer bells ringing now. The bell tower over Orchard Gate was silent, and those that remained were discordant, falling out of rhythm.

"Oh dear," said Agrippina, with a teasing lilt in her voice. "How easily your clever scheme falls apart. What can you do if your bells cease to ring?

"Why are they stopping?" Camilla demanded again, her voice rising in anger. "Who's doing that?"

She raised one of her bells and snapped it toward the waiting Ferox. The bell clanged loudly, and three of the creatures lifted their head in response. Camilla rang her bell again, and the Ferox began to move, not to attack the surrounding crowd but to shove through it. People shouted and cried out and tried to get out of the way of the swiping claws. She was sending them to the bell towers. She was sending them after Octavia's siblings.

"No! You can't!" Octavia shouted.

She lifted her spear and charged into the square, jumping over a piece of toppled monument with the names of dead explorers carved into its side. She ran for the nearest Ferox and thrust her spear at the creature, but she was only close enough to hit one hind limb. The leg fell apart, and the Ferox stumbled, which gave Octavia a chance to get closer and aim for its middle. She heard the twang of Sima's bow and the *whoosh* of an arrow flying overhead. She drove her spear into the Ferox and watched it crumple in time to see first one arrow, then another, strike the second creature in the throat. It disintegrated into a heap, allowing Octavia to climb over the crumbling remains on her way to the third Ferox.

But before she could reach it, Camilla stepped into her path. "*You*. What are you doing?"

"She is beating you," Agrippina offered. "You're being foiled by a child."

Camilla wasn't listening to her. She was focused on Octavia now, her face twisted with rage. "Don't you understand that we are under attack? You are *aiding the enemy*!"

Another of Sima's arrows flew overhead to strike the third Ferox in the thorax. It too began to fall apart.

Flavia said, "I think Octavia knows who the true enemy is. You must stop this, Camilla."

Camilla turns to face Flavia with narrowed her eyes. "You would tell *me* what to do?"

She raised her arms and brought her bells together with a mighty crash, so loud that stone crumbled from the shattered gateway and damaged buildings all around. The street at her feet erupted into a fountain of cobbles and dirt. The debris formed itself into a Ferox as big as a bear, maybe bigger, with claws of twisted iron and teeth of splintered wood. It reared back and lunged for Flavia.

Several things happened all at once.

The Ferox swiped one of its massive forelimbs at Flavia. Master Cicerus pushed Flavia out of the way. She stumbled and fell, toppling out of reach of the creature. Agrippina let out an angry shout and swung her spear toward Camilla. Octavia jumped forward, flinging her spear, and there was a twang and a whisper as one of Sima's arrows flew. Both spear and arrow struck the monster, but not before its claws caught Master Cicerus across his stomach and chest.

Red blossomed from the wounds. Flavia cried out, and Rufus rushed forward to catch the old man as he fell.

The Ferox began to fall apart, disintegrating around Octavia's spear and Sima's arrow. Even as it did so, it raised its other forelimb to strike again, but that limb fell apart before it could complete the blow. The creature's debris rained down, pelting Flavia on the ground, Rufus where he knelt over Master Cicerus, and Agrippina, who stood before them with her spear thrust forward into the very center of Camilla's chest.

Camilla gasped, a small and strangled sound, and clutched at the weapon. Agrippina drew the spear back with a jerk, and Camilla fell forward onto the remains of her Ferox. She swayed on her knees for a moment as blood spread across her chest.

"What?" she said, her voice little more than a wheeze. "What?"

Slowly, slowly, she slumped over and fell onto her side and was still.

Agrippina turned her spear to lean on it again.

"There," she said. "There. You don't have to be afraid anymore."

Rufus was kneeling beside Master Cicerus; already his trembling hands were red with blood and his face streaked with tears. Cicerus was not moving. There was no fluttering of his eyes, no gasping for breath, no rise and fall of his ravaged chest. His blood had stopped flowing. Flavia crawled over to Rufus's side and touched Cicerus's face gently, fingers fluttering over his eyes. He was dead. Octavia knew from the stricken look on her face, from the way Rufus's breath caught. Master Cicerus was dead.

Silence fell over the square. For a moment, it was so quiet Octavia could hear the people around her breathing, waiting, afraid, watching and waiting. There were no more bells. The last had fallen silent. There were no more Ferox.

Flavia looked from Camilla to her mother, her eyes wide.

"Mother," Flavia said, "what have you done?"

24

The Quiet After

——≫——

Agrippina stepped toward Flavia with both hands extended. "My dear, it has been so long. But it's over now. She can't keep you trapped with her lies anymore."

Flavia looked up from where she knelt at Master Cicerus's side. There were tears streaking through the grime on her face. "I've been here all along. We've all been here."

"I know. That's why I've come. I waited too long to save Vittoria."

"Save?" one person said. Octavia couldn't see who it was. "You've wrecked part of our town!"

"Where did they even come from?" somebody else called out.

"Who are these people?" said another voice.

"What do they want?"

The questions grew louder and angrier as the crowd pressed closer, fists and weapons raised. A group of guards and Hunters surrounded Agrippina's people, who looked around anxiously but did not dismount their horses or drop their weapons.

"They came from outside!"

"Has she come to spread the plague?"

"There are more of them on the road!"

"There is no reason to continue fighting," Agrippina said. Her voice remained eerily calm, as though she didn't notice the fear and unease all around her. "We are here to help you."

Flavia shook her head. "No. No, Mother. This isn't help. This is harm. People have been killed."

"A necessary sacrifice for the truth," Agrippina said. She looked down at Camilla. There were no more rattling breaths from Camilla's chest, no more blood flowing from her wounds. She was dead, but the look on Agrippina's face was not one of regret, or grief, or even triumph. Her expression was completely placid, as though killing her own sister had caused no more ripple in her mood than a fly swatted away.

There was a scuff and a scrape as Mom stood up, leaning heavily on Hana for support.

"How dare you?" Mom said, her voice tight with anger. "How dare you attack our town and call it help? How dare you kill our elders and call it necessity?"

Voices from the crowd called out in agreement. People began to pull Agrippina's people down from their horses and shove them to their knees, wrenching the weapons from their hands. The outsiders looked around in bewilderment, waiting for Agrippina to tell them how to respond, but she didn't even turn. It was as though she had forgotten them entirely.

Agrippina was looking at Mom and smiling. "Are you Hana's mother? You look so much alike. Hana understands why we had to return this way."

"Not like this. You didn't have to do it like this," Hana said. To the others, struggling now on the ground, she called, "Don't fight them! They won't hurt you! Mom, tell them you won't hurt them. They're not warriors. They barely even know how to fight."

Mom's eyes were narrow. "If they are not warriors, why have they come to Vittoria to help a sorcerer commit an act of war?"

"That isn't why we came here!" Hana cried.

Agrippina laughed. "Isn't it? You have known all along the people of Vittoria would never listen to reason. I believed what you told me about your home. You are the reason I chose this path."

The crowd was growing angrier and louder. Octavia could feel it as well as hear it, the murmurs and unease rippling outward, the rising tension as more fists clenched, more shoulders squared. She heard *traitor* and *liar* and *sorcerer* and *murderer*, all the accusations gathering like a thundercloud, and she knew that with one wrong move, one wrong step, the fighting would start again. She didn't know what to do.

Mom took an unsteady step forward, then another, until she was standing only a couple of feet from Agrippina.

"Do you think we're stupid?" she said. She was not quite shouting, but her voice rang with the clarity and force that had helped her lead the Hunters for so long. "Do you think we are so abominably stupid that we would believe that? That the great and fearsome Agrippina, who brought an entire land to its knees with her sorcery, could be manipulated by a girl who is barely twenty-one years old?"

"The sorcerer is a liar!" somebody shouted, to a chorus of agreement.

"I am not the one who has lied to you," Agrippina said. She was still trying to hold on to her calm, but she darted glances from side to side, watching the crowd warily. Her followers, held on the ground by the guards and townspeople, were struggling to get free, although not as much as before. Like everybody else, they looked to Agrippina and listened, but she still ignored them. She said, "Camilla lied to you. She lied to you for fifty years, and now you are like children awaking from a nightmare, unable to see what is truth and what is illusion. Awakening Vittoria to the world that lives beyond its walls is no small task, but I can lead you."

Octavia couldn't keep quiet any longer. "We don't want another sorcerer! We don't need you!"

The crowd shouted in agreement. "We don't need her!"

"She isn't welcome here!"

"Strike her down!"

"She's too dangerous!"

"Wait," Flavia said.

She had been quiet for some time, kneeling by Master Cicerus's side, but now she stood with Rufus's help. She held up one hand and looked around, waiting for the crowd to fall quiet.

"It is true that there is much we do not know about the world, and it is true that we have believed a great many lies for entirely too long. But that does not mean we will make the same mistake as before," Flavia said. She nodded solemnly at Octavia. "Octavia is right. We do not need another sorcerer. We do not need to keep fighting battles that are better left in the past. We do not want you, Mother. You are not welcome here."

There was a brief silence, then somebody said, "You can't send her away!"

And another called, "She has to answer for what she's done!"

"They all have to!"

Flavia looked toward Mom, and for a long moment they said nothing, holding a silent conversation that Octavia couldn't understand. Mom nodded slightly, and Flavia raised her hand for silence again.

"And they will," Flavia said. "The damage done to Vittoria is great, and we will not let it go unanswered. But we are not sorcerers who respond only with thoughtless violence, and certainly not when so much of our town is rubble around us."

"We will imprison the sorcerer and her followers for now," Mom said, "so that we can deal with the damage and make sure our townspeople are safe." She gestured to a group of Hunters. "Take Agrippina and those of her people who have entered Vittoria to the Council Hall. Do not harm them. They will be treated well." Then she turned to Hana and said, "We must ensure those who remain outside the wall intend us no harm, even if they have not yet participated in an attack."

"I know," Hana said quickly. "They won't cause trouble. They'll give up the sorcerers' weapon. They can't use it anyway. They aren't sorcerers. They're just people, people from all over. You can lock me up with them to be sure. We won't cause more trouble."

"How can you be certain?" Flavia asked. "They have followed my mother this far."

"Only because they believed what she told them about Vittoria," Hana said, pleading. "You can understand that, can't you? How easy it is to be led astray by a sorcerer's promises?"

Flavia looked at her steadily, then nodded. "We cannot risk more fighting today, not with our city damaged and vulnerable." She gestured to the Hunters. "Take my mother and these people to the Council Hall."

"But I saved you," Agrippina said faintly.

Flavia looked at her with pity before turning away. "We have much to do. We need healers to tend to the wounded, and we need to be sure everybody has a place to stay for the night. Augusta, will you organize a search?"

Mom nodded sharply and raised her voice to address the crowd. "If you are uninjured and able to search, start with the buildings nearest the wall, where there's the most damage. From there, work toward the center of town."

"I hear somebody!" came a shout from the outer edge of the crowd. "Somebody's trapped in this building!"

Suddenly everybody was moving again. A pair of healers came

forward to move the bodies of Cicerus and Camilla; they spoke quietly to Rufus as they did so and gently led him away. A group of Hunters took Agrippina and her followers away, and Hana went outside with several guards to gather the rest. There was jostling, murmuring, muttering, but without the Ferox, without Agrippina, without even the strangers, there was nobody left to fight, and far too many people in need of help.

Sima touched Octavia's arm. "Come on," she said quietly. "We can help too."

It was slow and difficult work, searching through the damaged buildings for survivors. Master Flavia's warnings had reached many people nearest the wall, but not everybody had been able to get out in time. Octavia worked alongside Sima through the afternoon and into the evening. Nobody was letting kids go into damaged buildings, so they helped bring the wounded to the healers and find friends and families of people who had been separated. Every time they were able to get somebody to safety, every time they reunited children with their grateful parents, every time they located another person believed lost or killed, it felt like a small victory, something to cling as the hard day wore on. Octavia barely even noticed the light fading until somebody started calling for lanterns, but the work didn't end with the daylight.

When it was fully dark, Hana and a few others began bringing food and water around.

"I thought you were going to get locked up with the others," Octavia said.

Hana's smile was a bit wobbly. "I thought I was too, but everybody has so much else to do, I think they keep forgetting that I wasn't here all along. I can help out here for now."

Octavia very much doubted anybody had forgotten about Hana, but she did think it likely that people simply didn't know what to do with her yet.

Hana offered Octavia one of the last meat pies. "Dad made them, so you know they're good."

Octavia hadn't realized how hungry she was until food was before her. "You saw Dad?"

"Yeah." Hana sighed. "He cried and told me we would talk later."

That sounded about right for their father. "What about . . ."

She looked down the street toward where their mother was still striding about, telling people what to do. She had been on her feet for hours; her leg had to be hurting badly by now. But she showed no signs of flagging. It was the most animated Octavia had seen her in months.

"It'll be okay. We'll be okay." Hana touched Octavia's shoulder. "I better go make sure everybody has something to eat. Here." She handed another pie to Octavia. "Bring this to Rufus, over there. The healers need rest too."

Octavia hadn't spoken more than a few words to Rufus in hours, as they had both been too busy. She stopped first to grab a large clay cup full of tea from one of the warming fires, then walked over to find Rufus sitting on the ground with his back against a wall. He didn't look up when she approached and dropped down next to him. The stone was cold and she was exhausted; she felt a chill seeping through her clothes and tiredness weighing her limbs as soon as she stopped moving.

"This is for you," she said. She nudged the pie into his hands. "Dad made it."

He took the pie but didn't say anything.

"There's tea too," she said.

"Thanks," Rufus said quietly.

But he didn't eat. Octavia felt a helpless pang. She sipped the tea and took a moment to look at Rufus in the patchy lantern light. His clothes were filthy and stained, his face smudged and his hair sticking up in every direction. His eyes were rimmed with red, but he had wiped his tears away. His hands were scrubbed pink and clean. Master Cicerus had always been adamant about healers having clean hands.

"Are you . . . okay?" she asked. She already knew the answer, but she didn't know what else to say.

Rufus shrugged.

"You should eat," Octavia said. "I know you must be hungry."

With a sigh, Rufus took a bite of the meat pie. He chewed slowly and swallowed. "I'm going back to the infirmary soon. It's getting too cold to treat people outside."

"Are you with . . ." Octavia stumbled over her question. "The other healers . . . are they okay? Do you have enough help?"

"We're doing what we can," Rufus said, his voice rough. "He trained almost all of them, you know. So we all know . . ." He trailed off. He looked away for a moment, sniffled, cleared his throat. "We all know what to do. What Master Cicerus would be telling us to do. So we have to do it."

"You are doing it," Octavia said quietly. "He trained you all well."

"I keep forgetting," Rufus said. "I keep looking up to ask him something and thinking he just went to help somewhere else, then I remember . . . I can't believe he's gone."

He fell quiet as he ate, and Octavia stayed beside him. She knew there was nothing she could say to make Master Cicerus's death easier for Rufus, but she wasn't going to leave him alone. She shared the tea and sat by his side and, for the first time in hours, let herself think about what was happening elsewhere in town. What people heard when they came to help, what they learned about what was going on, what they believed, what they dismissed as rumor or lies. By now, she figured everybody had to know that Camilla was dead and Agrippina was alive and locked up in the Council Hall. What they made of that was another matter entirely.

There was a scuff of footsteps on the street, and Sima sat down at Octavia's other side. She had her own pie in hand, one that was still steaming hot. She groaned tiredly as she leaned against the wall.

"That boy over there keeps asking me if Iberne floats on the ocean," she said.

Octavia and Rufus leaned out together to look.

"What boy?" Octavia said. There were people gathered to eat down the street, but none of them seemed to be paying particular attention to Sima.

Sima waved vaguely. "Some boy."

"What did you tell him?" Rufus asked. His voice was still rough, but his tone was genuinely curious.

"I told him we train sharks to pull our boats across the water." Sima took a bite of her dinner and chewed for a moment. "You don't know what sharks are, do you?"

"They're, um, big fish?" Rufus said. "I read about them once. Really big predator fish?"

Sima rolled her eyes.

"Was he bothering you? Have people been . . ." Octavia didn't quite know how to ask.

Sima understood anyway. "Not really. They're too busy right now to think about it. Your sister is helping. They know her."

Too busy, Octavia thought, or too stunned for it to sink in yet. The people of Vittoria would react to the strangers later, when they stopped asking questions about floating cities and started asking questions about what they had known of Agrippina's plan.

For now, there were murmurs of distrust, a few scuffles and arguments, but for the most part everybody was still reeling too much to think about who they were working alongside.

It wouldn't last. Fifty years of disbelief and fear didn't vanish in a single horrible afternoon.

But at least nobody was calling anybody else a monster right now.

"I don't understand why Agrippina had to come here like this," Octavia said. "Why hurt so many people just to claim you want to help them? What's the point?"

"Some people don't care if they have a point," Sima said. "They just want power. The sorcerers fought the war because they didn't want the lowland cities to slip from their control, but they didn't have to do things like create the Ferox and the plague. They did that because they could. Because they wanted to."

Rufus groaned as he stood up. "I have to get to the infirmary."

Octavia looked up at him. "Do you know how many . . . I mean, how many people are hurt? Or . . ." She swallowed thickly. "Dead?"

Rufus shook his head. "Not yet. A lot of people knew to run away from the wall as soon as something happened, but . . . Maybe we'll know by morning."

He waved tiredly as he trudged away toward River Street. It was fully dark now, but there were lanterns, lamps, and torches set up throughout the northern part of town. The streets were filled with people gathering in small and large groups, huddling around fires and sharing food and tea. Some people were crying with fear and grief. Others were laughing with relief. The dust had mostly settled, leaving a fine, pale grime over everything. Octavia didn't know if she was imagining it, but it felt like the night wind from the north was a bit sharper, a bit stronger, now that it could sweep into Vittoria through the hole in the wall.

"What do you think will happen tomorrow?" Sima asked.

Octavia looked up past the rooftops to the wall. There were lanterns glowing in the high towers, but twilight had come and gone without a single chime from the bells. It was a clear night, with stars sparkling above the lights and smoke of the town.

"I don't know," Octavia said.

It was an odd feeling. For her entire life, every morning in Vittoria had dawned the same way, with the ringing of the bells and the opening of the gates, and the townspeople emerging from their protective shell to tend and protect their lonely valley. The shell was broken now. The valley was not lonely anymore. There was new and unfamiliar work to be done, as there would be for days, weeks, even longer. She didn't know where it would lead. She didn't think anybody else knew either, and that was why they were laughing and crying in equal measure.

She drew her legs to her chest and pulled her coat tighter around her.

"Are you cold?" Sima asked.

The chill was seeping through her clothes, but Octavia didn't want to move just yet. "Not really."

Sima sat forward and tugged her scarf off. She wrapped it around Octavia's neck, knotted it loosely under her chin, and smiled.

"There," she said. "It's the most colorful thing you've ever worn."

Octavia laughed and tucked her nose into the scarf to hide her blush. It smelled like smoke and dust, and it was just as dirty as everything else she was wearing. Sima leaned in, bumping her shoulder against Octavia's before reaching down to take her hand. They could rest a little while longer.

25

The Roads of Vittoria

————»»————

The shortest day of the year was bright and clear and cold. There was a fat, fresh layer of snow over the Lonely Vale, softening every sharp edge to a rounded hump, turning the deep green pine forests and brown fields into swaths of textured white. It was morning, and the sun had not yet reached the bottom of the valley, but it shone brilliantly on the high peaks above.

In the shadows of the orchard trees, Octavia broke fresh trail through the knee-deep snow. She had Sima's scarf tugged up over her nose, but she was already growing warm beneath her coat. The snow was powdery soft, which was nice because it didn't cling in icy chunks to her snowshoes, but it also meant walking felt a bit like trying to navigate a pile of goose down.

"That's far enough!" Mom called.

Octavia turned to look down at her. Mom and Flavia were standing in the flat area beneath the orchard terraces, pointing this way and that as they conferred with each other. They were still in shadow for now, but the sun's rays were creeping across the valley and would soon reach them. Octavia's gaze lingered on the road for a moment, as it did nearly every day. Sima had returned to Aeterna weeks ago to rejoin her family. Octavia hadn't seen her since. Albus teased her for wearing the colorful scarf every day, and Hana gave her wry, knowing looks each time she returned from exchanging news with the people in Aeterna. Every day Octavia hoped to see a caravan of painted wagons headed south on Long Road.

It had been two months since Agrippina had come to Vittoria for what people were calling the Last Sorcerers' Battle. Calling it that seemed foolish to Octavia, when nobody knew what sort of trouble the future might bring, but she understood why the name stuck. Nobody wanted it to happen again.

Outside the patched wall and repaired Wyvern Gate, Long Road was now lined on both sides with chunks of stone from the wall and the explorers' monuments that had been crushed during the attack. There was one piece for every person who had died: forty-eight in all, marching up the road in twin lines, a reminder of what had happened for everybody who passed through the gate. The two stones nearest the gate, huddled side by side in the shadow of the wall, were for Willa and Bram.

There was no stone for Camilla. Some people had argued for it, others against, and in the end everybody had decided all forty-eight were monuments to her years of control over Vittoria.

Mom's voice rose again: "Go one more tree to the north and fix it there!"

Octavia waved to show that she understood and tramped through the snow to the next tree. This was an apricot orchard, dormant for the winter but still smelling faintly of sweetness and summer. Octavia dropped her pack into the snow and dug out a hammer, a few nails, and one of the carved wooden plaques she had helped Flavia fashion in her workshop. She nailed the plaque into the trunk just above the top of her head. The sound of her hammer startled a pair of robins out of a nearby tree. They twittered angrily as they flew away in a cloudburst of snowflakes.

There were still Ferox in the Lonely Vale. There probably would be a for a long time, the Crafters said, even without Camilla's bells ringing every night. Magic that had been strengthened and reinforced for fifty years could not be easily dispelled, and those Ferox that endured were among the toughest. It was still dangerous to go out after night or venture far alone. The Hunters were back to scouting through the woods, looking for any sign of danger so that they might warn herders and foragers away, as well as to protect the roads for travelers.

Because there *were* travelers on the roads now. It had started as a trickle, a few wary people making their way down Long Road after news of what happened reached Aeterna, but over the weeks visitors from afar had grown more and more common. Many came to Vittoria only because they were curious about the town that had been isolated for so long; they wanted to gape and gawk and ask questions that everybody very quickly grew tired of answering. But others came for different reasons, better reasons. Mountain clans sent representatives to talk with Vittoria's newly elected council—a council that, for the first time in fifty years, had only a single magical Crafter among its members. Lowlanders arrived with news to share and goods to trade, as well as a seemingly endless supply of letters and messages from people who hoped that, even after decades, they might find family or friends alive in the mountains. Albus's master, Aife the knifemaker, had received a letter from a brother she had believed dead since the war.

"She cried," Albus had said, in a low, awed voice, when he told Octavia about it later. "I didn't even know she *could* cry."

Vittoria was different now. Most of the differences were good, but they were also a lot to take in. Octavia was glad for how busy the bakery was, how people had stopped worrying about food stores lasting through the winter, how slowly and steadily the suspicion that had once greeted every stranger was being replaced by curiosity, anticipation, even eagerness. But it was still a lot, and she was always glad for the chance to spend a morning outside of town.

"Count down twelve trees and do the next!" Mom shouted.

"Got it!" Octavia replied. She picked up her bag to move along the orchard terrace.

Some days Octavia went out with Hana and the other Hunters; other days she learned from Flavia in her workshop; yet other days she helped Mom and Flavia with the protection charms outside the wall. It was a compromise, of sorts, and also an apology, even though Mom had never said as much. It wasn't Mom's way to say something like that outright. She spoke with her actions instead, and that meant she dragged Octavia out of bed three or four days a week to head out into the cold without ever admitting she had changed her mind about Octavia's training.

Octavia's thirteenth birthday was in just over a fortnight, and she was still waiting for Mom and Dad to talk to her about what sort of apprentice she would become. She wanted to ask them if it even had to be the same anymore, if everybody had to decide at thirteen how to spend the rest of their lives now that nobody was trapped in Vittoria forever. She would ask them. She planned to. She just hadn't found the right time yet.

By the time Octavia had finished placing charms along the fourth and final terrace, the sun had reached the valley floor and Octavia had shed her coat and hat. She hammered the last nail into place, then gathered up her things to rejoin Mom and Flavia. As soon as she drew close, she could see that Mom's leg was bothering her; there was a sheen of sweat on her face and a tightness in her jaw. The new head healer, a jolly woman who teased all of her patients as though they were scampering children, kept telling Mom not to push herself too hard, now that she was walking more and more, but Mom never seemed to listen.

"Where next?" Octavia asked. She knew better than to say anything about Mom's leg. It was smarter to pretend not to notice until Mom said something herself.

"I think we've done enough here for now," Flavia said. "Come by tomorrow morning, Octavia."

"Not this afternoon?" Octavia asked.

"I'm afraid not. There is going to be another meeting on the ongoing matter of my mother."

Mom made a noise in her throat. "Another one?"

"Another one," said Flavia.

Nobody could decide what to do about Agrippina. The new town council argued about it constantly. Some people said she ought to be locked up forever because of all the people who had died in her attack. Others pointed out that Vittoria didn't have any real way to lock somebody up forever; all they had were a couple of cells in the Council Hall that had only ever been meant to house people for a night or two. Some wanted to banish her; others wanted to never let her out of their sight. Agrippina offered her advice and expertise to the healers, but she never voiced opinions or suggestions regarding her own fate.

Some people thought that meant the fight had gone out of her, but Octavia wasn't so sure. She thought it more likely that Agrippina had simply never thought about what would happen if she triumphed over Camilla but Vittoria didn't want her as a savior. She had never considered it. She didn't know what to do with a town that didn't want her to lead them.

Flavia held out her arm to Mom. "Help an old woman back to town, Augusta. I'll need a pot of tea before I'm ready."

Mom gave her a look that said she knew Flavia was only pretending to need help in order to subtly offer it, but she extended her arm anyway. Indeed, since the battle Flavia had seemed younger than her sixty-odd years, as though the defeat of her aunt and cowing of her mother had removed the weight of their lifelong burdens from her shoulders.

Octavia followed along behind them as they headed back toward town. The snow was beginning to slump with the sun on it. That might mean avalanches if it snowed again. She looked to the slopes of Gray Bear Mountain, where once or twice every winter a great cascade of snow swept down to cover Long Road. She hoped travelers on the road knew what to look out for.

There, to the north, thin lines of smoke rose against the blue sky. A small encampment had already grown up at the junction of the Rivers Nyx and Iracundia. People were calling it River Camp; the elders in town said there had once been a village there and hoped there would be again, because it was such a convenient stopping place. Octavia thought maybe they ought to ask Ursa and the Clan of the Furious Dead first if they wanted a village right at the edge of their territory.

There was somebody on the road now. Octavia squinted and shaded her eyes; the sun was so bright it stung. It still gave her a thrill to see a group of people and animals on the road, even after it had become commonplace during the past two months. She didn't know if she would ever get used to it. She didn't know if she wanted to, because it was a good kind of excitement and she very much preferred that to the bad kind. There was too much snow for wagons, so she guessed the brightly painted shapes gliding along behind their horses had been converted to sleighs.

She stopped in her tracks.

The bold colors stood out against the white road. There was blue and green and red and yellow, a patchwork of painted boards and designs. She recognized those colors. She had been watching for them for two months.

"It's the caravan from Iberne!" she shouted.

Mom and Flavia looked at her in surprise, then turned to where she was pointing.

"Goodness, my eyes aren't what they used to be," Flavia said, squinting. "How can you tell?"

"They have painted wagons," Octavia said. "It's them. I know it's them. Mom, can I—?"

Mom watched the caravan for a moment. "Go ahead," she said. "Say hello to your friend."

Octavia broke into an awkward, stumbling run. There was no way to run gracefully in snowshoes.

"Octavia!" Mom called after her.

She turned. "What?"

"You can bring her over later," Mom said. There was an odd waver in her voice. "If they would like. We'd love to meet her family."

Octavia opened her mouth. Closed it. Opened it again. It took her a second to realize this was Mom's way of apologizing for what she had done when Octavia first brought Sima to Vittoria.

"I, uh. Okay," Octavia said. "Okay!"

She started running again. She ran out of breath long before she met the caravan, so she slowed to a walk when she reached the road and trudged north. A piercing worry broke through her excitement: she didn't know if Sima and her family were with the Ibernese caravan now. They might have stayed in Aeterna. Or they might have left weeks ago by East Road and were in the lowlands already. As the caravan drew close enough for her to hear the rattle of the harnesses and the calls of the drivers, she felt nervous and jittery. She moved to the side of the road so she wasn't standing right in their path.

Then what she had assumed was a bundle atop one of the sleighs suddenly started waving and shouting, "Hi! There she is! Hi!"

It was Pavi, wrapped up in so many clothes and blankets he was shaped like a potato. As soon as he started shouting, Sima jumped down from the back of the sleigh, stumbled, righted herself and ran for Octavia. She was a blur of black hair and bright clothes, then she was tackling Octavia from the side, grabbing her into a hug and knocking her into the snow.

"How did you know we were coming?" Sima demanded.

Octavia laughed and tried halfheartedly to shove Sima away. "I didn't. I just saw you on the road."

Sima grabbed a handful of snow and tossed it at her. "Is that what you do now? Watch the road for travelers?"

"No. Just for you."

Sima blinked. "Oh."

Octavia looked away, her face burning. She swiped a scoop of snow at Sima and tried to get to her feet. It was no easy task with her long snowshoes on, so Sima stood to pull her up with both hands.

"Hello, Octavia!" Leila called out as the caravan passed by. "It's good to see you!"

There were greetings from others as well, and Octavia returned them all with a smile. She couldn't wave, however, because Sima had not let go of her hands.

"I, uh, I thought you were staying in Aeterna," Octavia said.

"We talked about it," Sima said. "But nobody wants to stay in tents for the whole winter."

A knot formed in Octavia's stomach. "So you're going back to Iberne?"

Sima tilted her head to one side. "Didn't Hana tell you?"

"Tell me what?"

"She said that several of Vittoria's weavers were killed, and the town would probably need more." Sima furrowed her brow. "She really didn't tell you?"

"I knew about the weavers," Octavia said. Their shops had been clustered together on a street close to Wyvern Gate. "But Hana didn't say anything. Do you mean your mom wants to stay here?"

"For a while, anyway," Sima said. "Pavi is doing better, but we want him to have a warm home for the winter, not long days in wagons and tents." She shrugged and looked down the road after the caravan. "We gave up everything to bring him here. We'd have to start over in Iberne too, if we went back."

"Everybody is starting over, in a way," Octavia said.

"And besides," Sima said with a sly smile, "somebody has to give Vittoria more colorful things to wear. Don't you ever get tired of so much brown and gray?"

"Very," Octavia said with a laugh. "I'm not giving your scarf back."

"I don't want it back," Sima said. She bit her lip and looked down. "I mean . . . you can . . . it looks nice on you."

Octavia's face was so warm she marveled that steam wasn't rising from her cheeks. They ought to hurry after the caravan. They couldn't stand there in the snow all afternoon. But she didn't want to let go of Sima's hands. She didn't want to disturb the glorious winter day that surrounded them.

"Do you think . . ." Sima glanced away. "Will it be okay in Vittoria? Will people mind that we stay?"

Octavia stopped herself from offering immediate reassurances. Even though she hated the worry creeping across Sima's face, she was not going to say something that was untrue or uncertain, not even to make her feel better. There were so many answers to Sima's questions that Octavia barely knew where to begin. Some people would be suspicious about the strangers and angry that outsiders wanted to stay; they wouldn't like that new-comers wanted to move into homes and jobs left empty by the dead. Others would be excited and curious and nosy. Others still would only care that they could sell their wool and buy new cloth. Most people, probably, wouldn't quite know how to feel or what to think. It was all so new, so strange and so unfamiliar, that Sima's family would no doubt face all of that and more at the same time.

But the people of Vittoria had to start somewhere. Their world was expanding around them. With every new group that ventured out or arrived, with every trade of goods or exchange of news, with every meeting of strangers on the road, with every argument about newcomers that echoed through the Council Hall, with every new accent heard in the narrow streets and alleys, the world was growing larger every day. Nothing would stop it now.

"My mom wants your family to come over later," Octavia said. "My parents want to meet you all properly."

"My mom will love that," Sima said.

"Good," said Octavia. She swung their hands between them. "Let's go."

But neither of them moved. They stood together, hand in hand, the sun warming their shoulders, as a soft breeze carried shouted greetings from down the road, with the glittering snow and blue sky, the mountains tall and pointed and gleaming all around, all of it so beautiful Octavia felt like only her snowshoes and Sima's touch were keeping her anchored to the ground.

The End

Acknowledgments

I want to thank my editors, Alex Arnold and Jessica Yang, for all of their help in making this novel better. It's a special kind of joy and privilege to work with editors who put so much into a book, and I have appreciated every minute of it. I also want to thank the rest of the team at Quirk for their enthusiasm and support through the entire process.

Thank you as well to my agent, Adriann Ranta Zurhellen, for everything; to my sister Sarah Genna for valiantly helping me (and two cats) move to another state in the middle of this book's deadline; to my friends Audrey Coulthurst, Casi Clarkson, Leah Thomas, Lynnea Fleming, Shannon Parker, and Lauren Dixon for all their support and sympathy and commiseration.

Finally, endless thanks and appreciation to all the teachers, librarians, and booksellers who worked so hard through virtual schooling and lockdowns to keep getting books into the hands of the kids who needed them.